For Alana and Melissa: you're the reason I write

GRAY
RETRIBUTION

ALAN McDERMOTT
GRAY RETRIBUTION

THOMAS & MERCER

Published by Thomas & Mercer, Seattle

www.apub.com

Amazon, the Amazon logo, and Thomas & Mercer are trademarks of Amazon.com, Inc., or its affiliates.

ISBN-13: 9781477823866
ISBN-10: 1477823867

Cover design by The Book Designers

Library of Congress Control Number: 2014903903

Printed in the United States of America

Chapter One

Monday 30 September 2013

'Heads up. We've got movement to the north.'

Simon 'Sonny' Baines lay on the roof of the farm building and listened as the approaching band of guerrillas made a beeline for the building. Below, Len Smart, Carl Levine and Jeff Campbell took up defensive positions against the low wall that ran around the perimeter of the house. Their movement was silent in comparison to that of the attacking force, which announced its presence by crashing through the undergrowth like a herd of elephants headed for a watering hole.

The three men on the ground trained their sights on the treeline that bordered the eastern edge of the smallholding, remaining silent as they waited for the assault force to make an appearance. The noise grew louder as the attackers approached, then suddenly stopped dead.

Silence covered the area as the nocturnal orchestra took a time out. It seemed as if even the animals and insects wanted to watch the action unfold.

Len Smart slowly wiped a bead of sweat from his brow, careful not to make too quick a movement in case it was seen by the enemy. Mosquitoes danced around his head, kept at bay by the insect repellent, but their incessant buzzing told him that he wasn't in Kansas anymore.

As if the oppressive humidity weren't reminder enough.

Without warning, muzzle flashes lit up the edge of the forest. None of the defensive team returned fire, preferring to lull the enemy into advancing out of the trees and into the kill zone. The small-arms fire continued for a few seconds before petering out, allowing silence to return.

All remained still for over a minute, then Sonny's voice came over the comms. 'Got people in the grass at your ten and two. Looks like they're trying to flank us.'

Len Smart was on the right of the trio and he saw his target a hundred yards away. Rather, he saw the top of the three-foot-tall grass sway gently as the unseen assailant crawled slowly through it. Night-vision goggles would have come in handy, but he would have to make do with the sliver of moonlight that cast a dull shine over the African plantation. Besides, there were four of them and an estimated enemy strength of around fifty, so in Smart's mind they easily had the locals outnumbered.

'Got him,' he said, and Levine on the other end of the line confirmed that he also had a bead on his man.

The AK-47s opened up once more, but the three men continued to save their ammunition and keep their locations hidden. They spotted a couple of armed men advancing slowly from the trees but held their fire, preferring them to get a little closer before engaging. From the rooftop, Sonny watched the scene unfolding below him, oblivious to the wraith-like figure scaling the rear wall.

Nwankwo Okeke was clad in an ancient British Army smock and trousers, the disruptive-pattern material a throwback to the late seventies. His features, like those of the four Englishmen, were obscured by the black and tan camouflage face-paint. The exception was that underneath the disguise, his skin was the colour of night, the war paint applied more for effect than concealment.

The chatter of gunfire from the trees intensified, and the occasional grenade came arcing towards the defences. They landed pitifully short, but the noise they generated helped to mask Okeke's approach. He reached the lip of the roof and peered over. Sonny lay five yards away with his back towards him. Okeke eased himself up on powerful forearms and quietly swung a leg over the edge. He waited, hand over his holster, but Sonny continued to focus on the battle beneath him.

Okeke eased forward, one hushed step at a time, silently drawing his nine-inch knife from its leather sheath.

Two yards.

One.

He fell on Sonny's back and yanked his head backwards, drawing the blade across his victim's throat. With Sonny down, Okeke made an animal call that signalled his friends below. They broke from cover at the rear of the building and raked the trio's positions with AK-47 fire.

Smart, Levine and Campbell, all facing the other way, realised too late that they'd fallen for a feint.

They never stood a chance.

Chapter Two

Monday 30 September 2013

'Jesus, Johnny! Where the hell did you come from?'

Sergeant Nwankwo 'Johnny' Okeke grinned and clapped Sonny on the back. 'When you share a bedroom with six older brothers, you learn to tread lightly if you want to pee in the night.'

'Well, I'm just glad you used the dull edge of your knife,' Sonny said, rubbing his throat.

In the yard below, the other three training instructors removed the keys from their rifle attachments and slotted them into their vest control units to silence the alarms that were screaming in their ears. The rigging they wore had numerous sensors sewn into the webbing, and when hit by a beam from an enemy rifle it registered a hit. Enough hits—or a single hit in a critical area—and the alarm sounded. The only way to turn it off was to use the key from the rifle's laser mount, and doing so rendered the gun unusable.

'Nice spotting, Sonny,' Smart grumbled from the ground below.

Okeke smiled down at him from the edge of the roof. 'Don't be so hard on him, Mister Len. You had every right to be confident, but over-confident? That is what we used against you. Perhaps next time you won't make it so easy for us.'

Smart was stung by the remark but held his tongue. The sergeant was, after all, perfectly correct.

On arrival in Malundi, a landlocked state which had gained independence a year earlier, they'd been distinctly unimpressed with the recruits they'd been asked to train. The lack of discipline had been immediately apparent, and that first impression had led to them underestimate the locals.

It wasn't a mistake they were likely to make again.

Gigs like Malundi were the staple for Minotaur Logistics, the private security firm operating out of a London office, but unless Smart and his team delivered, their reputation would be in tatters. Work soon dried up when word of shoddy performance got out.

'Tomorrow night, it'll be your turn to defend, Johnny. We'll show you how it's done.'

Okeke threw a mock salute and disappeared from view, still smiling.

'You reckon we're getting too old for this shit?' Levine asked.

Smart shook his head. Like everyone else employed by the company, his team had extensive SAS backgrounds, and what they'd shown that night had been well below standard.

'Just too complacent.'

He went into the building and pulled a bottle of water from his backpack. The liquid was warm but it still felt good as he gulped it down. The other three instructors joined him.

'These guys are a lot more switched on than we gave them credit for,' Sonny observed, and the others agreed.

They'd expected a comfortable couple of days, with live-fire exercises during the afternoon and assault training at night. The first part had gone as expected, with inaccurate shooting and poor ammunition management from almost every recruit. Expecting more of the same, they had allowed themselves to grow lax in the evening.

The resulting farce didn't sit well with them.

'I think we should introduce them to the sentinels tomorrow night,' Levine said, and the others smiled in approval.

'Let's get back to base,' Smart said. 'I've got to write a report for the boss and the colonel.'

They gathered their belongings and left the building in single file, only to find that Okeke had created an *ad hoc* honour guard, which laughed raucously as the four instructors traipsed to their ancient Land Rover.

'Never mind the sentinels,' Campbell said under his breath. 'I'm tempted to bring live ammo tomorrow.'

Smart waved Okeke over and put an arm around his shoulder. 'I'll give you that one, Johnny, but don't push your luck.' He glanced at his watch and added six hours. 'I want everyone on the range at nine o'clock, and make sure they've got their game faces on.'

Chapter Three

Monday 30 September 2013

Tom Gray stared at himself in the mirror and wondered where the years had gone.

Although his fortieth birthday was a year away, he already had a few flecks of grey peppering the light brown hair on his temples, and the plastic surgery he'd gone through hadn't done anything to make him look younger.

But then, that hadn't been the intention.

The first round had been partly reconstructive, and partly meant to hide his identity, though he hadn't had a say in it. The more recent sessions spent under the knife had sought to undo what James Farrar had done to him just after the explosion two years earlier.

At least his six-foot frame remained hard and fit, the result of his daily runs and his wife's cooking.

Gray noticed a piece of fluff on his eyebrows and swatted at it, and was shocked to see half of the hairs fall into the sink. The bald area above his eye appeared bruised, and as he touched it the skin came off, revealing the bone above his eye socket. He was staring at the lump of flesh between his fingers when the door opened and his son walked in.

'Daddy, what's this?'

Daniel held an inhaler in his hand, a cloud of gas escaping it.

'No! Put that down!'

He ran to his son, but with each step the boy seemed to get further away, and Gray's legs felt as though they were battling through treacle. He reached out a despairing hand towards the child as the skin on his fingers began to bubble and blister.

He screamed.

'Tom!'

Gray was immediately awake. His wife looked down at him, and despite the poor light he could see concern etched on her face.

'Same dream?' Vick asked, caressing his face.

Gray nodded. The same dream he'd been having for a year, ever since his friend Andrew Harvey had been good enough to disclose everything MI5 had on the virus Gray had been exposed to sixteen months earlier.

Initially, Gray had hoped the inhaler that terrorist Abdul Mansour dropped was leaking harmlessly, but on arrival at the hospital to be treated for his knife wounds, he'd been whisked into quarantine with no explanation. He and four armed police officers had been kept overnight, but despite a series of tests the doctors found no reason to keep them isolated. It was a few weeks later that intelligence operative Andrew Harvey had told him the truth, but only after swearing Gray to secrecy.

According to Harvey, MI5 had suspected Mansour of carrying a variant of the Ebola virus. Lab tests, however, had revealed its true nature. Gray's relief at the time had been genuine, but the recurring dream suggested that subconsciously he wanted another son, another Daniel, and Mansour had robbed him of that possibility.

'I wish you'd see someone,' Vick said, but Gray once again shrugged off the idea. He didn't see the point in spending hundreds of pounds—even though it was money he could easily afford—and opening up to a complete stranger. Talking it through with a shrink wasn't going to solve anything as far as he was concerned.

A tiny voice broke the silence, and Gray leaped at the chance to escape the conversation before Vick could press her point. He walked through to Melissa's room and picked up his three-month-old daughter, cradling her gently and kissing her head before laying her down on the changing mat. He was quite adept at baby ablutions, insisting on doing his fair share so that Vick could catch up on her rest. He had a new nappy on Melissa within two minutes, and after another kiss he handed her over to her mother for a feed.

The alarm clock told him it was almost five in the morning, and he had no inclination to go back to sleep.

'I'm going for a run,' he said, and slipped into a pair of shorts and T-shirt. After a few stretches outside the front door, he set his iPod to the start of an old, favourite rock album and headed down the driveway. As he approached the gates he hit the button on a key fob and they slowly swung open. Once through, he hit the button again and looked over his shoulder to make sure they closed after him. He jogged the three hundred yards to the main road and began the first of two circuits of the area, each one just over two miles in length.

After forty minutes he returned home and found the girls fast asleep, so he took a shower and prepared breakfast before settling down in front of his laptop. He checked his emails but found nothing that couldn't wait until he got to the office, so he went to the Foreign and Commonwealth Office website to see if any new travel warnings had been issued. As Managing Director of Viking Security Services, which provided bodyguards and combat training, it paid to keep an eye on the troubled regions of the world.

Two cups of coffee later, he kissed the girls as they slept and crept out just before seven in the morning, the early start designed to beat the traffic on his way into London. He reached the office within thirty minutes and made a coffee before sitting at his spartan desk: only an in-tray, phone, computer and notepad on display.

Gray was halfway through answering his emails when a new one came in. The sender was one of his biggest clients, and he immediately opened it. After reading the short message twice, he sat back in his chair and covered his face with his hands.

He'd founded his company after leaving the SAS a few years earlier, and it had been growing at a phenomenal rate when he'd sold it following the death of his first wife and son. The money had been used to fund his campaign to make the government take a tougher stance with repeat offenders, but on reflection it hadn't been the best idea he'd ever had.

For one, it led to him being severely injured, nearly fatally, and the subsequent year had seen more than one attempt on his life. His crusade had also cost the lives of four close friends, and he might have thought their deaths worthwhile if the government had listened to any of his suggestions for reforming the judicial system. Two years on from his standoff in the Sussex countryside, the only change in sentencing guidelines had been a mandatory whole-life term for child murderers. While Gray wholeheartedly agreed with that particular change, it saddened him that career criminals were still being treated with kid gloves and getting away with community sentences.

It wasn't something he liked to dwell on, though. Having taken his best shot, he'd long ago realised that nothing he did would change the government's collective mind.

What did matter was seeing one of his main sources of income walking away.

His solicitor, Ryan Amos, had warned that this might happen and had cautioned Gray against buying his old company back. Given the fact that two years earlier, Gray and his associates had kidnapped five career criminals and paraded them on the internet while holding the country to ransom, Amos had thought it unlikely that household names would want to be associated with him. Gray had been labelled a terrorist by many, which was a stain not easily removed from one's character. The fact that millions of people had supported Gray's actions meant nothing to multinationals with wholesome images to maintain.

Gray had ignored the advice, hoping that by creating a subsidiary company he could distance himself from the spotlight, but he'd underestimated the tenacity of a tabloid reporter. As far as the public had been concerned, Tom Gray had died during the terrorist attack instigated by Abdul Mansour, but after his brief appearance on the BBC News channel he had been inundated with requests for interviews, all of which he'd declined.

Donald Boyd hadn't been one to take no for an answer.

Gray had lost count of the number of times he'd been confronted by the man, be it outside his home, in the supermarket or even at the cinema. It soon became clear that doing an interview was the only way to stop the nonsense. But Gray had decided that Boyd wouldn't be the one to get the scoop.

Vick, with a background in journalism before she set out as a travel writer, knew a few friends who would spin the story sympathetically, and Gray had allowed one of them, Sheila, to tell his side of the story. She'd suggested going the whole hog and writing a biography, but Gray was content with just getting it out in the open and putting an end to the hassle. Financial gain had never been his motive, but now, with clients walking away, a lucrative book deal didn't seem such a bad idea.

After being snubbed for the story, Boyd had done some digging into Gray's affairs. A lot of the information was in the public domain, but Gray was convinced money must have swapped hands at some point, because almost every single client had been mentioned in Boyd's full-page article.

It had only been a week since the story broke, and now four blue-chip companies had terminated their contracts with Viking's subsidiary, Minotaur Logistics. The latest, an oil conglomerate, was worth over a million a year, and it wasn't going to be an easy hit for the company to take.

Personally, Gray remained financially sound, but it was his staff that he felt sorry for. He knew all of them by name, having served with a lot of them in the Regiment. The others had come highly recommended from serving officers he kept in touch with, but almost all of them were men with families to support, and doing hazardous work for a fair day's pay was all they knew. Quite a few would struggle with the transition to a traditional nine-to-five job, but with work drying up he would have no alternative but to let a lot of them go. Not even the money he was likely to make from the British Army for the rights to his 'sentinel' prototypes would be enough to keep them all on even a meagre retainer.

Gray looked through his client list and noted three more companies likely to sever ties with him. That only left roughly a dozen foreign customers that he could rely on. The new kingdom of Malundi was one such contract, with a six-month training schedule having just kicked off. According to Len Smart, while their charges weren't competent in many respects, they did possess a tactical awareness that wouldn't take long to fine-tune. This wasn't news Gray wanted to hear now, as it meant there was little likelihood of Malundi's president extending the contract or taking on additional resources.

He put in a call to Andrew Harvey. Once adversaries, they were now good friends, and Gray had picked up a few pieces of work thanks to Harvey's insider knowledge.

'Andrew, how's things?'

'Good, mate. How's the family?'

They chatted for a few moments, getting the pleasantries out of the way.

'Anything on the horizon that I should be interested in?' Gray finally asked.

'Nothing that you haven't already seen on the news,' Harvey told him. 'I'd love to help you out, but the foreign desk has been pretty quiet this week.'

'That figures. There's never a military coup when you need one.'

Harvey promised to get in touch if he knew of any situations that might prove beneficial to Gray.

'We're having a dinner party on Friday,' Gray said. 'Why don't you come along, and bring a friend this time.'

'Sounds great. I can be there by seven, if that's all right. Oh, and Tom, don't go doing anything stupid to Donald Boyd.'

'Don't worry, those days are behind me, but I've asked my solicitor to consider suing him for loss of earnings. It doesn't look promising, though.'

Gray put the phone down, and wondered if Harvey would actually bring someone this time. Vick was a lovely woman with a heart of gold, but she was always trying to set Harvey up with one of her friends, despite his insistence that he much preferred the bachelor life.

Another email interrupted his thoughts, and he slumped in his chair as another big fish escaped his net.

Chapter Four

Monday 30 September 2013

Ken Hatcher bagged up the oranges and handed them to the elderly lady. 'That'll be one pound fifty, please.'

The customer gave him the correct change and thanked him before exiting the shop, leaving Hatcher to reflect on his first eight hours in business.

Takings hadn't been as much as he'd hoped for, but he knew it would take time for word of mouth to bring patrons to his fruit and veg establishment. The location was, truth be told, his second choice, but the preferred spot on the high street was simply too expensive. Still, his was the only outlet selling fresh produce in a one-mile radius, and he was hopeful that the lack of competition would help to make his first business venture a success.

If it didn't, he knew he'd never hear the end of it.

His wife was far from happy at the amount he'd invested in the shop, and despite his projections she saw nothing in the future but failure and leaner times. The fact that he'd used all of his redundancy money and borrowed from family members to finance the project hadn't sat well with Mina. She'd begged him to look for work in the software field he'd known so well for thirty years, but Hatcher was under no illusions as to his prospects. With unemployment so high, finding another development role while in one's early fifties wasn't easy, especially when companies could take on someone fresh from college for half the salary.

He was determined to prove Mina wrong, despite the inauspicious start, and he headed for the door to take in his display so that he could close up for the evening. Through the window he saw two men approach the shop, and he held the door open for them, offering the same welcoming smile that every customer had been treated to throughout the day.

'Evening, gents. What can I get you?'

The elder of the two, in his early fifties and still sporting a full head of close-cropped, chestnut hair, returned his smile. The younger one sauntered through the shop, idly perusing the goods on sale.

'Didn't know we had a grocer's on the manor,' the man said, his accent marking him as a local.

'We opened this morning,' Hatcher told him, the smile still on his face.

'Is that right? And how was your first day?'

'Not too bad,' Hatcher lied.

'Glad to hear it.' He extended a hand. 'The name's William. William Hart.'

Hatcher shook it. 'Ken.'

Hart's grip was firm, almost painfully so, and he looked Hatcher in the eyes. 'Have you spoken to your new neighbours?'

'Not really,' Ken admitted. A few weeks earlier he'd enquired about footfall with a few of the shops on the street, but hadn't let on that he was planning to set up business.

'Then I suggest you do,' Hart said, all pretence at amiability instantly gone. 'They will clue you in to the insurance arrangements we have in place.'

Hatcher looked at the man, fear fluttering in his chest as the nature of Hart's visit became clear.

'Got any kids, Ken?'

Hatcher hesitated, then nodded. 'A son. He's about to start university.'

'Ah, just like Mr Singh down the road. He's got a boy about the same age. Tragic accident, that one.'

'Accident?'

'Yeah. Seems Mr Singh wasn't too keen on accepting our offer. Still, being confined to a wheelchair doesn't stop the kid studying, does it, Aiden?'

The other man shook his head but remained silent. The two looked similar: father and son, Hatcher guessed.

Hart was smiling, but there was no warmth to it. 'You've got a little gold mine here, Ken. No local competition and a decent location. There's a lot of money to be made.'

Again, Hatcher nodded, but was fearful of where the conversation was heading.

'The trouble is, you're close to a council estate which has a high rate of unemployment, and those kids like nothing better than to terrorise shop owners. Don't they, Aiden?'

The son gave a mischievous smile, and the family resemblance was even more obvious.

'Fortunately, they listen to me,' Hart continued, 'and I can tell them to behave themselves when they're in the area. For a small fee, naturally.'

Hatcher struggled to control his voice as he asked the question, dreading the answer.

'How much?'

'Three hundred,' the elder Hart said, and Hatcher felt like the blood had drained from the upper half of his body. The projections he'd been working with—while on the conservative side—left him little room for an extra commitment of that amount.

'There's no way I can afford three hundred a month!'

Hart laughed and gave Hatcher a mighty whack on the back. 'It's three hundred a *week*, Ken.'

While Hatcher tried to recover from the bombshell, the two men headed for the door.

'Aiden will be back next Monday for the first payment,' Hart senior said over his shoulder and picked up an apple on his way out.

Ken Hatcher walked slowly, mechanically to the stool behind the counter and collapsed onto it, his mind numb as he tried to come to terms with the last few minutes. He sat there for a quarter of an hour, picking at his lip as he fought for a solution, and it took him a while to recognise the sound as the door chime tinkled to announce another customer.

After serving the woman and adding another couple of pounds to his takings, he brought in his display and closed up for the night, all the while considering his options. As he set the alarm, he made his decision. He would speak to the surrounding shop owners in the morning, and if Hart's threat was real, he would consider going to the police.

There was one thing he wouldn't do, though, and that was to involve Mina.

Chapter Five

Tuesday 1 October 2013

Nafari Cisse sized up the small stone in the middle of the dirt road and pictured himself in the last minute of the African Cup of Nations final. His penalty could win it for Malundi, and as the crowd roared, he took a run up . . . and scuffed it, the pebble skittering feebly into the long grass off to his left.

It didn't matter.

His twelfth birthday was just a couple of weeks away and his father had promised to buy him a proper football, one made from real leather, not the cheap, hard plastic one his friends played with at school.

Nafari picked up the pace, eager to be one of the first into class. The school building was designed for roughly thirty children, but more than fifty pupils managed to cram themselves in each day, and desks were on a first-come, first-served basis. His teacher wouldn't stand for bullies turning up late demanding a seat—not that he would ever consider such a thing for fear of a beating from his father—and so he always made sure he was one of the first at the door when Miss Olemba opened up.

He heard the sound of a vehicle approaching from the rear and moved off to the side of the narrow track to let it pass, but it slowed as it neared and pulled up alongside him. The windows were wound down and he could see three male occupants. The front passenger leaned out of the window, his right arm flopping lazily against the hot, red door.

'Hey! How do I get to Milanga village?' he asked, his manner friendly.

Nafari pointed down the track. 'Go down here until you see a giant tree and turn right there, then you go past the watering hole and turn left and . . . '

'Someone else told me to turn right at the watering hole.' The man continued to smile, despite his challenge. 'How do I know you're telling the truth?'

'I *am!*' Nafari said, full of indignation. 'I go to school there every day.'

The passenger laughed. 'Okay, Simba, calm yourself. If you're going that way, why don't you come with us to make sure we don't get lost?'

The boy liked the idea of taking his first ever ride in a car, and he was still quite a long way from school, but his father's warning about not talking to strangers was at the forefront of his mind.

'It's okay,' he said, 'I'll walk.'

The man's demeanour changed instantly. He pushed the door open and for the first time, Nafari could see the machete in his left hand. He tried to run but got no more than five yards before an arm wrapped itself around his waist and he was swept off his feet. The rear door flew open and Nafari was bundled in before a rag was forced into his mouth and he was covered with a dirty blanket.

'One word and I'll kill you.' The rear passenger pressed the flat blade of his own machete against Nafari's skull.

Tears streamed down the terrified youngster's face, but he stayed as quiet as he could. In a country where life was cheap, he didn't want to anger his captors.

They drove for more than an hour, and having never been more than five miles from his home, Nafari had no idea where he was or where they were going. Despite the windows being open, he was desperate for a drink when they reached their destination two hours later.

He was ordered out of the vehicle and led to a heavily wooded area, where a haphazard collection of crude buildings had been built. Care had obviously been taken when constructing one particular hut, and in its doorway a giant of a man was overseeing unarmed combat practice. The combatants were all boys, ranging from Nafari's age to their late teens, and instructors were standing by to admonish anyone who showed their opponent mercy.

He was shown into a shack where three frightened boys were sitting huddled together. Nafari was shoved inside and the door secured from the outside.

Despite being petrified, he tried to strike up a conversation with the others. He discovered that they'd arrived the day before and had been in the hut ever since, and though they'd been fed and given water, they had no idea why they were being held captive.

One of the boys had a persistent cough and complained of stomach pains, and the others put this down to the cigarettes they'd all been forced to smoke. They, too, had abdominal cramps, and the only thing that relieved the pain was to smoke some more.

As if on cue, the door opened and a man stood in the doorway, wearing nothing more than combat trousers and a pair of boots. He lit two large roll-ups before handing one to Nafari.

'Smoke.'

It wasn't a question, and he tentatively took the cigarette, looking at the other boys for guidance. They were far more interested in the cigarette the man still held. He grinned as he tossed it in front of them, causing a scramble for the first toke.

The largest of the three came out victorious and sucked greedily, taking three long drags before eventually passing it along. Nafari got a kick in the thigh and was once more ordered to have a go. He thought briefly of disobeying, but when the man pulled his machete from his waistband, he did as ordered.

The harsh smoke burnt his throat and he coughed violently, bringing another grin from his guard.

'Again.'

Nafari took another draw, tears welling in his eyes. This time the he managed to inhale and immediately felt strange.

'That's good whoonga,' the soldier said.

The cigarette Nafari was smoking had been spiked with a psychotropic drug that made the user susceptible to suggestion. As Nafari's eyes glazed over, the guard began working on the boys.

'Who is your father?' he shouted.

The words were heavy in Nafari's head, and it took him some time to arrange them into a coherent sentence.

'My father is Hans . . . '

When the slap landed it felt like the skin had been torn from Nafari's face.

'*You have no father!*' the guard shouted. He let the news sink in for a few seconds.

'Who is your mother?'

Nafari was still reeling from the blow, and the question was repeated.

'I . . . my mother . . . '

Another blow landed. '*You have no mother!*'

Nafari dropped the cigarette and the guard retrieved it, forcing it into the boy's mouth.

'More!'

As Nafari took another drag, the guard went to work on the other three, repeating the same questions. Having been through the procedure before, their answers matched the soldier's expectations, and he knew that in a couple of days they'd be ready to join the rest of the population for the next step of their induction.

Chapter Six

Wednesday 2 October 2013

Len Smart checked his watch and let the other three training officers know that it was time to kick off the exercise.

Sonny Baines—so nicknamed by his colleagues long ago because of his youthful good looks and blonde hair—toggled the view on the handset that he was using to communicate with sentinel number one. After a few seconds of playing with the settings, he declared them good to go.

'All set for three-round bursts every four seconds, with an angle variation of six degrees.'

'Okay,' said Smart. 'Let's see how clever these guys really are.'

The sentinels were set up in the treeline, around five yards in. There were four in all, spread out a dozen yards apart. Each unit consisted of a round base containing two hundred rounds of 7.62 mm ammunition, fed through a seven-inch central tube to the electronic firing mechanism that sat atop it. The four-inch barrel meant the effective range was two hundred metres, which was more than enough for the engagements it was designed for, and the tiny video camera mounted on the barrel fed real-time pictures to the operator.

Sentinels had initially been designed to give retreating troops a little breathing space, allowing them to fall back while their enemies were pinned down by the automated fire. They had a default setting that allowed quick deployment, or if time permitted, the units could be preprogrammed, as Sonny had done. To prevent them from falling into enemy hands, a small explosive package could be detonated, which would destroy the electronics and render the device useless.

That wouldn't be necessary during this training exercise, however. The electronic laser attachments were in place to register any hits, and with all preparations complete, Smart led his team on their silent circumnavigation of the farm. It took them over an hour to make their way to the rear of the building, crawling most of the way on their bellies while remaining at least five hundred yards from the target.

Once they reached their staging position, Smart focused his binoculars on the building and saw a dozen alert Malundians training their eyes in his direction. He signalled for Sonny to kick off the attack, and as soon as the automatic fire began drifting from the other side of the compound, the guards began to drift away from their posts. He was about to give the go signal when Sergeant Okeke's head appeared over the edge of the roof.

Smart couldn't hear what was being said, but it was clear from his gestures that Okeke wanted his men to remain in place. An argument ensued, and the Malundians reluctantly did as they were told. A minute later, one of them stuck his head around the corner and obviously realised that there were four weapons firing at them. He waved a derisory arm in Smart's direction and gestured for the men guarding that side of the building to follow him.

'Clear,' Smart whispered into his throat mic, and two of his men hurried forwards at a crouch. After twenty yards they dropped to the ground and kept watch while Smart and Sonny leapfrogged them. They maintained this discipline until the first group were within forty yards of the low outer wall.

'Wait!'

Levine's hissed command made sure they all kept their heads down as Okeke's head once again appeared on the roof. The man was apoplectic, shouting commands that could be heard over the gunfire as he urged the men back to their posts. When he disappeared again, Levine ordered them to go in for the kill.

The result was a technological bloodbath.

Smart threw a flash-bang onto the roof and Sonny was up in seconds to mop up the dazed soldiers, their vests screaming with each virtual hit. Smart and Levine ran to the left while Campbell covered the right, and their guns blazed as the stunned troops tried to work out how their enemy could be in two places at once. Their rifles were quickly rendered useless as the instructors taught the Malundians a clinical lesson in how to clear a hot zone.

Once the last of the alarms was neutralised, Smart singled out the soldier who had ignored Sergeant Okeke's instructions to cover the rear.

'Hansi, you were doing fine, right up to the point where you left your post.'

The man threw his rifle to the ground and squared up to Smart.

'You cheated!' he snarled. 'We were only expecting four of you!'

Smart was unfazed, having faced down far more intimidating men in his time.

'And that was your mistake,' he said, his voice even. 'You'll never be able to accurately predict enemy numbers, so if you are told that ten men are approaching you should assume that there are others. That's rule number two in how to stay alive longer than a week.'

'So what's the first rule?'

'Rule number one is to turn around and walk away, right now.'

Hansi looked Smart in the eye but saw nothing to suggest the instructor was joking, and all of a sudden the Malundian's confidence drained. With his bald head and bushy moustache, Smart knew that he looked more like a salesman than a fighter, but his authoritative voice and hard stare made it clear that he wasn't a man to mess with. He could see that Hansi was by no means a coward and seemed grateful when Sonny trotted up and offered a distraction.

'Meet your enemy,' Sonny said, placing two of the sentinel units on the ground.

The men gathered round as he explained how they worked, and Hansi took the opportunity to ease away from Smart on the pretence of getting a better view of the devices.

Okeke took his place, putting his head close to Smart's ear.

'Don't be hard on him, Mister Len. He lost a son recently.'

'Sorry to hear that.'

Okeke nodded. 'It happens more and more these days. His son went to school in the next village and never came home. He was only twelve.'

'That's a shame,' Smart said, suddenly feeling sorry for the man. 'Shouldn't he be out looking for him?'

'They are never found. In the last six months, eight boys have vanished from his village alone. It is happening all over the region.'

'Always boys?' Smart asked, as a possible explanation popped into his head.

'A girl was taken a few months ago, but her body was found soon after. She had been raped. But mostly they are boys.'

This suggested to Smart that someone was recruiting boy soldiers. It was not a new phenomenon, especially in Africa. For years, militias and even government forces had been known to recruit children as part of their fighting force, sometimes enticing them, often through abduction. Once enlisted, the boys would frequently be treated to drugs intended to addict and enslave them. One drug that Smart had heard of was the particularly nasty whoonga: a combination of heroin and the anti-retroviral AIDS medication Efavirenz—usually cut with detergent or rat poison—that was so addictive that people sometimes infected themselves with AIDS simply to gain access to the much sought-after key ingredient. Although treaties had been signed outlawing the practice of creating child armies, Smart had recently learned that nearly a quarter of a million boy soldiers still served throughout the world.

He shared his thoughts with the sergeant.

'I thought so, too,' Okeke said, 'but there is no-one in this country that would have a need for them. The army doesn't use them, and there are no guerrillas in Malundi.'

'What about neighbouring countries?'

Okeke shook his head. 'There have been no major conflicts in the region for some time. All of the abductions have been in the south of the country, which points to Kingata, but that would make no sense. Why give us our own land and independence if they plan to do this?'

As with every assignment, Len Smart had done his homework prior to deployment, and the recent history of Kingata hadn't given too much cause for concern. The crime rate was actually lower than most African countries, but one name had cropped up again and again in news reports.

Sese Obi, a self-proclaimed warlord, was thought to be behind a string of high-profile robberies and murders. It was reported that he had a following of between thirty and seventy men, though no-one knew the exact figure. He was said to be less than pleased with the president's decision to grant the Agbi people their own land in the form of Malundi, and was suspected of being behind several subsequent attacks on government targets.

Smart asked Okeke if Obi could be behind the kidnappings but got a snort of derision in reply.

'Obi is a thug, nothing more. He would have no need for boy soldiers.'

Well, someone has. Smart made a mental note to fire off an email to Tom Gray to see if he could shed any light on the matter.

Once Sonny had finished demonstrating the new equipment, Smart told everyone to head back to the barracks in preparation for the next phase of the training.

'Tomorrow we'll show you how to set up an ambush.' He smoothed his moustache while creating a dramatic pause, then smiled. 'Then you'll see how effective the sentinels really are.'

Chapter Seven

Thursday 3 October 2013

Sese Obi drove into the camp just as the sun reached its zenith, and his men immediately dropped what they were doing and gathered near his Land Rover. One of his lieutenants, Baako, rushed to open the door and Obi climbed out of the vehicle.

'Everyone is here, sir, as you asked.'

Obi nodded and walked to the edge of the clearing, a hundred armed men trailing in his wake. He stopped under the shade of a tree and used a handkerchief to wipe the sweat from his brow as he mentally recited the speech he was about to deliver. When he turned to face them, he could see that he had their complete attention.

And so it should be, he thought. It wasn't often that he got to address them in person, one of the drawbacks of being the most wanted man in Kingata.

He got straight to the point.

'The Agbi people think they can take our land and we'll just sit back and accept it. But they are *wrong!*'

A huge roar erupted from the crowd, and he savoured the moment.

It had been a long, frustrating year, and he'd been tempted on more than one occasion to kick his plan into motion early, but he was glad he'd taken the time to build up his formidable force. Each of the men before him had been displaced as the country was divided, and all wanted to reclaim what was theirs.

For Obi, though, the land he'd lost was not the most important factor. It was worth a few thousand dollars at best, a trifling amount in the grand scheme of things. What he'd needed was a common grievance to act as the catalyst for building his army, and playing on his men's anger over their lost tribal land had proven a masterstroke.

His days of car-jacking and robbery were now a thing of the past. He'd made enough money to buy all the guns and ammunition he needed. No more hit-and-run attacks on minor government targets, or pointless assassinations, either. Those acts had served their purpose: to cement his reputation as a man fighting a worthy cause. His followers, too, had swallowed the lie, though he would not disappoint them. His men would have their land back, but he would rule it once the Malundi government fell.

'Our attacks so far have been nothing but pinpricks on an elephant's arse. They think we are ineffectual, but we will soon show them that Kanto land belongs to Kanto people, *and we will not give it up until every last Agbi has been banished!*'

Another roar came from the crowd, this time more sustained. It took a while to silence them so that he could continue.

'Tonight, *we strike!*'

As the soldiers celebrated, Obi called over his lieutenants and walked them to a quieter area.

'Are you sure none of these men have connections to the target?' he asked.

They shook their heads. 'We double-checked,' one said. 'None of them have any association with the village. They will do what is asked of them.'

'They'd better,' Obi warned them. 'This attack must go to plan.'

He looked over at the dancing crowd. Six months earlier he had commanded barely fifty people, but these hundred men now represented just ten per cent of his own private army. It was a formidable number, but he still needed more to crush the tiny Malundi forces. The next stage of his plan would see that following increase dramatically.

'Kgosi, let me see the Agbi prisoner.'

He was led to a wooden shack, and walked in through the open door. A soldier dressed in camouflaged fatigues was chained to the back wall. Congealed blood caked his mouth and nose, and his right eye was swollen.

'What is this?' Obi roared.

'Sese?' The lieutenant didn't understand his concern.

'How are we to make the world believe that he attacked the village if he looks like this? What happened to him?'

'It happened during his capture,' said Themba, the man who'd been guarding the prisoner inside the building.

Obi could see that the wounds had been inflicted more recently than that. 'Do not lie to me!' He swung a solid arm and caught the guard on the side of the head, knocking him into the corner of the small room. Obi stood above the cowering figure, his two-hundred-pound frame blotting out the sunlight streaming in through the door.

'Some of the men started the khat early, sir,' Kgosi tried to explain. 'They got a little carried away.'

Obi had arranged for a consignment of the drug to be delivered to the men. When chewed, khat imparted a feeling of euphoria and excitement. The idea was to have them in a frenzied state when they launched the attack, but some had seen fit to start early, which further enraged him.

'You will guard this man with your life,' he yelled at Themba, as he lay on the floor. 'If I see another mark on him before the end of the day, I will leave your sorry carcass in the village, too!'

He turned and stormed out of the shack, astonished at their inability to follow simple instructions. He had wanted to be a long way from the imminent massacre, but with the mission being so crucial to the overall plan, that clearly wouldn't be possible. He would have to lead it himself.

Chapter Eight

Thursday 3 October 2013

Sese Obi ordered the trucks to stop a mile from the village of Zamwetta, much to the disappointment of his men. Their grumblings were in vain, though. If he was going to make this attack look like it came from Malundi, he could hardly drive straight up to the village. Instead, he would lead his soldiers north until they reached the border, and then traverse it for a few hundred yards before advancing south to the target.

After distributing the remainder of the khat, he took point and began the trek into the darkness. Although there were no border guards anywhere near the area, he demanded silence throughout the march. The prisoner was bound and gagged, just in case he tried to raise the alarm at any point.

After forty minutes they could see the silhouettes of shanty houses on the horizon. Obi ordered them to stop, gathering the lieutenants around him.

'I want this to be quick and brutal. The people of Kingata must be outraged at the carnage and demand action against the Agbi. Spare no-one, and I mean, no-one!'

The men nodded and split up to spread the word among their respective teams.

At precisely two in the morning, he waved an arm and the group covered the last three hundred yards to the village, an almost complete circle of huts with a central communal area. The buildings were constructed of whatever material had been available at the time, and while most had mud walls over a wooden frame, a few were constructed of timber oddments, with bits of corrugated steel filling the gaps.

As Obi and his men reached the outskirts, a dog started barking at their approach, and one of his men silenced it with a burst from his AK-47. On that signal, the rest opened up, automatic fire raking the fragile buildings. Bullets shredded the walls of every dwelling as screams began to pierce the night. Obi's soldiers kicked down doors and dragged the hysterical occupants out into the darkness. Most were females and children, the majority of the men elderly, infirm, or both.

A fire was started in the centre of the community and Obi's army began lighting torches, which they used to set the roofs alight, most of which were thatched and caught quickly. One hut was spared and the Agbi prisoner dragged into it. Obi joined them inside and pushed the bound man into the corner. He staggered to his feet and tried to plead with them through his gag, but Obi wasn't in the mood for listening and unloaded half a clip into his chest.

'Remove his bindings,' he said, 'and bring me one of the male villagers.'

An old man was brought in moments later and Obi ushered him into the centre of the small room before shooting him once in the head. He placed the Kalashnikov in the old man's dead hands and walked out of the hut and into the congregational area, where the carnage continued unabated.

Bodies littered the ground and blood soaked into the dirt from a thousand wounds. His men had abandoned their rifles and were finishing the job off with machetes, hacking at the helpless victims. Several women were in the process of being raped, as was a girl who appeared to be no more than twelve years of age. It didn't seem to matter to his men that these were Kanto, the very tribe they were supposed to be fighting on behalf of.

Obi lit a cigarette and let the men have their fun for another ten minutes before ordering the last of the villagers to be dispatched. Some men wanted to take female prisoners but one look from Obi soon changed their minds, and they finished them off to bring an end to the massacre.

The night took on an eerie feel following the transition from slaughter to silence. Even the night creatures held their counsel, as if afraid to draw attention to themselves.

Less than half an hour after the attack began, Obi ordered everyone to make their way back to the trucks, and they followed the route they'd taken on the way in. He had to remind them to maintain silence on the return journey, but only until the bloodlust and effects of the khat had worn off.

Once they reached the vehicles, he ordered his men to disperse and told his driver to take him back to the training camp. It was just a few miles from Zamwetta and he wanted to make an early start on the next phase of the plan. His lieutenants already had instructions to visit the neighbouring villages to inform them of the attack and stir up as much anger and resentment as possible.

In a couple of days' time, his men would lead a march into the capital, demanding action against Malundi, though he knew his government would resist all calls for an outright war. While the politicians stalled and sought a diplomatic resolution, Obi would continue to rally the people. Several of his men had ties with Kingata's armed forces and they would intensify their lobbying to convince as many soldiers as possible to join the cause.

Three weeks, he told himself. Three short weeks, and he would take his place as the leader of a nation.

Chapter Nine

Friday 4 October 2013

Tom Gray checked the CCTV and saw Andrew Harvey's car parked outside the gate to his house. He hit a button on the panel to allow his friend access.

'Come on up, Andrew,' he said through the intercom, and the gates slowly opened. Harvey eased his Ford Saloon through and up the short drive to the front of the house, where Gray was waiting at the open door.

'No date tonight?' Gray asked.

'Sandra had to work.' Harvey shrugged and seemed to be doing his best to sound convincing. 'She was called in at the last moment. That's the trouble with dating a doctor.'

'I'm sure Vick will be disappointed,' Gray said, holding the door open for his friend.

It turned out that his wife was closer to annoyed.

'I wish you could have let me know,' she grumbled. 'I hate it when food goes to waste.'

'There's little chance of that,' Harvey said, as a wonderful aroma drifted through from the kitchen. 'Even if I'd known sooner, I wouldn't have told you. It just means more for me.'

Suitably appeased by the flattery, Vick returned to the cooking. Gray joined her and returned moments later with a couple of beers.

'So what's the real story?' Gray asked quietly, as he sat down on the sofa. 'Still single?'

Harvey glanced towards the kitchen and, satisfied that he wasn't going to be seen, he nodded.

Gray felt a little sorry for him. Harvey was still in his mid-thirties and had a face that, while not particularly striking, still caught the eye of the ladies from time to time. Having rugged, after-shave-advert looks wouldn't have done him much good in his chosen profession, as the ability to blend into a crowd was important for an MI5 operative.

Despite having no problem finding female company, Harvey simply seemed to prefer the single life. His work often kept him in the office late, and the unsociable hours had damaged more than one relationship before it had a chance to blossom. There had been a special lady in Harvey's life, but that had turned sour once she stopped believing he was at work, instead imagining him cavorting with a mistress, a tale that had brightened up one of Gray's duller evenings.

He knew that, rather than face further recriminations, Harvey preferred to keep his own company.

'How's work?' Gray asked, changing the subject.

'Much the same as always, but some news came in from the Africa desk that might concern you.'

Gray sat to attention. 'Possible work?'

'Not quite. There was an attack on a Kanto village in Kingata last night. By all accounts it looks like an Agbi incursion from Malundi, but their president is denying all knowledge.'

'I've got a team out there,' Gray said.

Harvey nodded. 'I know, that's why I'm giving you the heads-up. We think someone is trying to trigger a conflict and your guys could get caught up in it.'

'Len Smart said that in the last few months a lot of teenage boys have disappeared from villages near the Kingata border. He thinks someone might be using them as boy soldiers. Have you heard anything along those lines?'

'The desk might have something on it. I'll ask when I'm back in the office.'

'Len thought a local warlord called Sese Obi might be involved. I've done a search on the internet but he doesn't seem like a big-time player.'

'That's because he isn't,' said Harvey. 'He was on a list of people suspected of attacking the village, but way down at the bottom with a rating of highly unlikely. Mind you, none of them seemed likely candidates. I checked him out anyway, and he's been making some noises in the last twenty-four hours, but I agree with their assessment. Whoever's behind this, they appear to be the new kids on the block.'

Gray wasn't happy that his team were potentially in the middle of someone else's war. True, his job was to send his men to the world's hotspots, but they were usually briefed on current threats and knew the enemy they faced. He'd selected Len's unit for this particular mission because of the relative safety, given what they been through in the last couple of years, but it looked like they could end up back in action a lot sooner than any of them had imagined.

'What do you think? Do I need to pull my men out?'

Harvey shrugged. 'That's your call. It might have been a one-off, or it could all blow up overnight.'

Gray quickly weighed up the options. With business so scarce at the moment, this wasn't the time to overreact. Besides, they could handle themselves. Len might look more at home at a sales convention, with his receding hair, bushy moustache and a few extra pounds around the midriff, but he was a brilliant soldier. Truth be told, they all were. Sonny looked like a cheeky, twenty-something slacker, but he could hold his own with the best of them.

The ones Gray was most concerned about were Carl Levine and Jeff Campbell. The pair were nondescript and looked somewhat similar, but Campbell had six inches and forty pounds on Levine. Both were the fighting equals of Sonny and Len—that wasn't an issue. What worried Gray was that both were married, and Levine had the added duty of a teenage daughter to raise. He dreaded the thought of having to tell Anne and Sandra that their husbands would never be coming home—especially after having sent Levine on a low-risk, low-impact training job.

'I'll see what happens in the next couple of days,' Gray said. 'If it gets worse, I'll bring them home.'

Vick stuck her head through the door and beckoned them into the dining room, where a huge salmon *en croute* surrounded by seasonal vegetables took centre stage. Gray offered Harvey another beer but he declined.

'Not when I'm driving. I might have a small glass of wine, though.'

Gray did the honours and they tucked in, Harvey once again complimenting Vick on another delicious offering.

'Any news from the doctor?'

'Nothing,' Gray told him. 'I'm on my sixth different medication, but I'm not holding out much hope. I guess I'll just have to live with it.'

Thankfully, Mansour's canisters hadn't contained the virulent haemorrhagic fever that the authorities had been led to believe. If it had, or the dispersal location had been more densely populated, Gray and the other victims would have died quick, unpleasant deaths, and the disease might have spread rapidly, creating tens of thousands of other casualties. As it was, Gray and some seventy thousand other Londoners would only ever father female offspring. As for actual figures, new cases were still being reported, but sporadically at best. The government hadn't come clean about the nature of the virus, except to assure the public that they faced no danger.

That was at least true. The contagion's only symptoms mimicked those of mild flu, and as long as no deaths were linked to the mini-outbreak, the health secretary would continue to spin it as an unseasonable influenza virus. The fathers of any newborn girls were still being asked for blood and semen samples to determine if they'd been affected, all under the pretence that it was a new screening test for genetic diseases.

'How's Melissa?' Harvey asked.

'She's fine,' Vick said. 'She's staying with my aunt and uncle this evening. They love having her over.' She turned to Tom. 'Speaking of which, Ken asked if you could pop round. He wants to have a word with you, something about security, he said.'

Gray nodded. 'I'll drop by in the morning on my way to town.'

'Actually, he wants you to go to his shop on Monday. He didn't say why, but he wasn't his normal self, and I get the feeling he didn't want Aunt Mina to know.'

Probably the local tearaways giving him grief, Gray thought. The location of the shop had its good points and bad points, and the proximity to the Handsworth estate was one of the latter. The security services he offered were different from Ken's needs, so he made a note to call a friend and source a CCTV unit on the cheap. He might even suggest a Mosquito alarm. These devices emitted an unpleasant sound at a pressure level of up to a hundred decibels at a frequency of 17.4 kHz, and could only be heard by people under the age of twenty-five. It was designed to prevent youths congregating in a specific area, and though not illegal, there were several human rights groups calling for them to be banned.

'Okay, I'll go round and see him at lunch time.'

'Is Melissa talking yet?' Harvey asked.

'That'll be a few months away,' Vick said, 'but she did give us her first proper smile a few days ago. I wanted to video it, but I was in the middle of changing her nappy at the time.'

They finished their meal, Harvey having a second helping.

'I hope you don't think I'm being greedy, but work usually keeps me in the office until late in the evening, which doesn't leave much time for home cooking. That's why I enjoy coming round here so much.'

'Just the food?' Gray asked.

'No,' Harvey said, trying to dig himself out of a hole. 'The food's just a pleasant addition to the wonderful company.'

Vick smiled at his deft retrieval as she cleared away the plates and began the washing up, while the boys retired to the living room once more.

'Has Boyd's article affected work?' Harvey asked.

'Like you wouldn't believe. Half of my big clients have disappeared, and I don't think that's the end of it.'

Harvey's face creased with concern. 'You're not going to do anything stupid, are you?'

Gray shook his head. 'I made my bed, I've gotta lie in it. If it hadn't been Boyd, it would have been another reporter.'

Harvey gave him a look.

'Look,' Gray said. 'I'm not going to hunt him down and skin him alive, if that's what you're thinking. I can't say I'm chuffed that he wrote the story, but I've got no plans to go seeking retribution.'

Despite Harvey's fears, Gray wasn't about to thrust himself back into the limelight.

A yawn escaped and Harvey looked at his watch. 'I've got to go, Tom. Thanks again for the meal. Vick's a real catch, you lucky sod. You take care of her.'

Gray stood and shook his hand. 'Don't worry, these girls are all I care about.'

Harvey popped into the kitchen to say goodnight and Gray saw him to the front door, hitting the button to open the gate.

'Maybe next time you bring a friend along, even if it's a work colleague. I'm not sure Vick will fall for the excuses much longer.'

Harvey smiled. 'Will do, Tom. See you.'

As Harvey drove out onto the road, Gray closed the gates and his thoughts turned back to his team in Malundi. He opened up his laptop and fired off a quick email to Len Smart before settling down in front of the TV for a late-night movie with his wife.

Chapter Ten

Saturday 5 October 2013

By eleven in the morning, a crowd of nearly three thousand had gathered outside the president's private residence in the Kingatan capital Molewe. Some carried hand-painted placards, but most just danced and chanted. A few government troops stood on the periphery, but as long as the demonstration remained peaceful, they seemed content to simply observe proceedings.

The previous day, Obi's men had travelled to the villages neighbouring the scene of the massacre to inform the residents of the attack. They told of the Agbi soldier who had been killed by one of the villagers and left behind by his men, and graphically recounted the scene they'd found that morning. Women and children raped and hacked to death, men emasculated so as to demonstrate the Agbi's intention of destroying the Kanto lineage.

'Your government sends fifty troops to the border to protect you from the Agbi invaders!' Obi had told people in the surrounding villages again and again, 'That is not enough! The president must act now and punish the murderers!'

The line had been swallowed by everyone, and with each village they visited, the numbers of outraged followers swelled until fifteen hundred set out that morning. As they passed through the suburbs and into the city, the ranks grew as more and more people learned the details of the atrocity.

The newspapers had mentioned the killings but hadn't gone into specifics, so as rumours passed like a game of Chinese whispers through the ever-growing crowd, the mob's anger mounted. With every passing minute, the chanting intensified, as did the number of protesters, until more than five thousand stood before the iron gates of the president's house.

A spokesman appeared from the mansion and walked down the drive to the throng, a sheet of paper in his hand. He gestured for silence and it took a few minutes before the noise died down enough for him to be heard.

'The president has spoken with his counterpart in Malundi, and they are both shocked and saddened by Thursday's events in Zamwetta. A full investigation is taking place and we hope to have further news tomorrow. When—'

Obi's men began the chanting once more, demanding direct action, and the rest of the crowd followed, drowning out the rest of the statement. The presidential aide tried to get the rest of the message across, but with the crowd being whipped up by strategically placed members of Obi's forces, the deafening crescendo left him with no choice but to retreat inside.

Obi himself was watching the protest from a building a quarter of a mile away, and through his binoculars he could see his men striking up conversations with the soldiers overseeing the demonstration. Kgosi had relayed the president's comments via mobile phone; all seemed to be going to plan. While the leaders tried to find a diplomatic solution, Obi and his growing army would take control of the matter and force their way across the lightly protected border.

Two of his people had been scouting the enemy for a few weeks now, and the map they'd drawn up showed every strategic target, from electrical power stations to army bases and the small airport that provided access to the international equivalents in neighbouring countries. With today's developments, he fully expected a number of Malundi troops to be moved to positions close to the Kingata border. His spies would feed him information on their strength and locations. The initial assault would flank and eventually surround any such forces before finishing them off, leaving a relatively simple journey to the Malundi capital.

He called Kgosi and reminded him to keep the crowd there for another two hours, all the time seeking out those of fighting age to help with the upcoming assault. After that, they would gradually disperse and all would return to normal for a couple of days.

The calm before the storm, Obi thought, smiling as he prepared to return to the jungle.

Chapter Eleven

Monday 7 October 2013

Tom Gray spent most of the day on damage-limitation duty, calling up his existing clients and seeking reassurances that they wouldn't be moving on in light of the recent newspaper article.

One was willing to bide its time, but warned that the company's reputation was of paramount importance, and the first sign of customer dissent would mean cutting ties completely. Another thanked him for pre-empting their phone call and announced that the contract was terminated with immediate effect. It hurt but, having spoken to his solicitor over the weekend, Gray came armed and ready for exactly that kind of response.

'If that's your decision, I quite understand,' Gray said. 'I'll expect the remainder of the contract to be paid in full within the next fifteen days.'

'Mister Gray, I don't think we'll be—'

'May I remind you that I personally visited your offices to sign that contract, and therefore you were fully aware at that time just exactly who you were dealing with. If you're going to claim breach of contract now, you'd better have a damn good reason for it. Something other than my personal history. Your own assessments gave my men glowing scores, so you can't use their misconduct as an excuse, either.'

The phone went silent for a while and Gray hoped he'd hit home.

'We'll have our lawyers look into it.'

'I think you should, because since we signed that contract, I have done nothing to harm the reputation of your company. Everything I did prior to that was in the public domain, so if you want to try to convince a judge that you didn't know who I was, I wish you the best of luck.'

As the business contact tried to respond, Gray continued. 'I'll have the outstanding figure couriered round to you this afternoon and I expect payment by the twenty-first. Otherwise, my solicitor will start legal proceedings and I'll personally make sure the case gets all the media coverage possible.'

Gray put the phone down and took a deep breath. Threatening clients wasn't the ideal way to run a business, but hopefully they'd see sense and continue to use his services. It was either that, or pay him off and hire someone else, and bean counters didn't like paying twice for anything.

He prepared the invoice, all the while wondering how the clients he'd already lost would react once they received their final demand for payment from Amos Ryan. While part of him hoped they'd rethink their position, deep down he knew the damage had been done. Any payments he received would be used as severance pay for his men, and hopefully that would give them a bit of breathing space until they found work at another agency.

His phone calls continued throughout the day, with varying degrees of success, and it wasn't until after four that he noticed the CCTV brochure on his desk and remembered the meeting with Ken. He'd promised to pop into the shop at lunchtime. That wouldn't be possible now, but if he hurried he could make it before Vick's uncle closed up for the day.

The drive through rush-hour traffic took longer than he would have liked but he still managed to get to the shopping precinct before five. He parked in a side street and walked around the corner to Ken Hatcher's shop, where four customers were waiting to be served.

Gray waited until the last one left before wandering over to the till.

'Sorry I'm late. I was swamped at work.'

'No problem,' Hatcher said, looking inordinately happy—even relieved—to see him. 'Vick told me you're having problems with your clients. I hope you're getting it sorted out.'

Gray gave him the condensed version of the last couple of weeks, though he tried to paint a positive picture.

Ken nodded sympathetically and wished him luck.

'Vick tells me you have some security issues yourself,' Gray said, handing over the brochure. 'I spoke to the owner of this company and can get you a fifty per cent discount on anything you need.'

Ken's face fell as he nodded again, then went on to recap his encounter with William Hart and son. He told Gray that he'd spoken to the neighbouring shop owners, one or two of whom had confirmed the arrangement.

'Have you paid him anything?' Gray asked.

Hatcher shook his head. 'No-one's been back since.'

It wasn't a pleasant situation to be in, and the fact that it involved a family member angered Gray. He decided to get in touch with Andrew Harvey to see what information was available on the Hart family. He hit the speed-dial on his phone and was waiting for it to connect when Hatcher tapped him on the arm and looked towards the door.

Gray hung up the phone as two men entered. Both were dressed in designer jeans and could have been twins, though one appeared to be a few years older. They stopped at a display of strawberries and pretended to browse.

'Can I help you?' Ken asked.

'It's all right,' the younger one said. 'Serve this guy first.'

'I'm not a customer, I'm his business partner,' Gray lied.

The pair came over to the counter.

'Then you'll know about our arrangement,' the elder one said.

Aiden Hart, Gray guessed, as the young man gave him a once-over.

'I know this guy from somewhere,' said the other, whom Gray suspected was Aiden's younger brother.

'My name's Tom Gray. I guess you've heard of me.'

Aiden nodded. He had a confident manner, and didn't seem overwhelmed by his present company. 'Yeah, we know you. In fact, we all cheered when that bomb went off. Shame you managed to live through it.'

'Sorry to disappoint you,' Gray said. 'Ken's explained your proposition to me.'

He pulled his wallet out and extracted a bundle of twenty-pound notes. He counted some off and handed them over.

'Glad you're seeing sense,' Aiden said as he accepted the money, but Gray held on to it.

'Here's my counter offer. That's five hundred. Take it as a token offering, but I don't want you coming back here. Ever.'

He let go of the money and Aiden toyed with it for a while before putting it in his pocket.

'We're not the bunch of petty criminals you're used to dealing with, Gray. I know your history, but compared to us you're just a boy scout.'

While he spoke, his brother slowly eased around his sibling, but Gray had half an eye on him, and when the punch was thrown he was ready for it. He ducked his head to one side and the blow failed to connect, and while little brother remained off balance, he delivered an uppercut which caught him square on the chin. He didn't have time to see him fall to the floor as his brother joined in.

While the younger Hart was all muscle, Aiden added speed to the equation. His punch connected with the side of Gray's face and stunned him, but he knew that if he went down the fight would be over. He managed to keep his feet and threw a punch of his own but Hart dodged it easily and body-slammed him onto a table laden with potatoes.

Gray had the wind knocked out of him and was struggling to breathe as blow after blow landed on his rib cage. He managed to swing a leg and connected with Aiden's crotch, but the strike didn't halt the onslaught for long. More punches landed, with Aiden switching skilfully between Gray's head and midriff as he lay almost helpless on the display table. Gray did what he could to protect his body and lashed out whenever possible, but the fight was getting away from him.

Ken had been stunned into inactivity by the sudden attack, and it took him some time to react. He grabbed the pole used for retracting the awning outside his shop and swung it as hard as he could. It hit Aiden on the back of the head and he slumped forward before collapsing to the floor.

Gray struggled upright, his face already badly bruised and swollen.

'I'm not sure that was a good idea,' Hatcher said, shaking slightly as adrenaline coursed through his body.

Gray agreed, and dug into Aiden's pocket to retrieve his money.

'I think you'd better call the police,' he said, and Hatcher pulled out his mobile while Gray dealt with the Harts. Sean Hart, according to the ID that Gray found in his wallet, was trying to get to his feet. He got a kick in the ribs for his effort, which quickly changed his mind. The older brother was out cold, and Gray hoped he'd remain that way until the authorities arrived.

After telling Gray that the police and ambulance were on their way, Hatcher began picking up vegetables from the floor.

'Leave them,' Gray told him. 'This is a crime scene now. Plod won't want you touching anything.'

It was another eight minutes before the patrol car pulled up, closely followed by the paramedics. During that time Gray had cleaned himself up, but blood still seeped from the wound above his eye and his face had puffed up considerably.

While the ambulance crew tended to the Hart brothers, Gray gave one of the officers his account of what had happened. Hatcher also gave a statement and, as instructed by Tom, told the whole truth, including the initial visit by Hart senior.

After the Harts were led away—Sean to a police car in cuffs and his brother on a stretcher—Gray was given an exam by a paramedic. He initially declined the offer of a visit to the hospital, but when told that he'd probably cracked at least two ribs, he knew he had to get them seen to.

First, though, he had to make a phone call.

'Aw, come on!'

Three minutes into the game and Frank Wallace's team were already a goal down. He cracked open his third can of lager just as his mobile phone started ringing, tearing him away from the Monday night football. The ringtone told him it was his backup phone, which meant only one caller.

'Wallace.'

'What the fuck are my sons doing in your cells?'

Not many people spoke to the Detective Inspector in such a manner—his ex-wife being the first to learn that lesson—but William Hart was the exception.

'I had no idea they'd been picked up, Bill. What are they supposed to have done?'

'Aiden said they got jumped by Tom Gray, of all people.'

'*The* Tom Gray?'

'No, his next door neighbour. *Of course, the Tom Gray!* Christ, Frank, for a top copper, you're not too fucking smart.'

Wallace let the remark slide. 'There's not a lot I can do tonight. If I turn up at the station, questions will be asked. It won't hurt the boys to spend a night in the custody suite.'

The response almost shattered his eardrum. '*If I wanted them to spend a night in the cells I wouldn't be on the phone to a fucking moron right now!*'

William Hart could be a cultured conversationalist, but when angered, his East End roots began to show.

'Tell me what they're supposed to have done,' Wallace said, trying to defuse the situation.

Hart calmed down slightly, but the rage was still obvious in his voice as he gave Aiden's account of what had happened earlier in the evening.

The DI knew Bill's son wouldn't be telling the whole truth. If there was one thing he knew about Tom Gray, it was the man's animosity towards the criminal element. Having said that, he thought it unlikely that Gray would launch an unprovoked attack on two men who were, by Aiden's account, simply shopping for apples.

'So what was he really doing there?' he asked, knowing he risked angering Hart once more. 'If Gray had kicked this off, he'd be the one in the cell, not Aiden.'

'He was doing a collection,' Hart admitted.

That made a lot more sense.

'I can't go down to the station,' Wallace reiterated, 'but I'll go and have a word with Gray and see if I can get him to drop the charges.'

'You'd better,' Hart said. 'Try St. Michael's hospital. He was still there when Aiden was discharged.'

The phone went dead and Wallace hit a button on his remote to record the football game while he was out. After a quick wash and toothbrush he locked his flat and climbed into his car, a six-year-old

Ford. With the money Hart was paying him to keep the family out of prison, he could easily have afforded something better, but stupidity like that got you noticed. Instead, the money was squirrelled away for his retirement in a sunny climate; meanwhile, he lived on his police salary.

Gray was just finishing up his statement when Wallace arrived at the hospital. It was just after nine when the detective flashed his badge at the A & E receptionist, who directed him to Gray's cubicle. A row of beds lined one wall of the unit, each separated by plastic curtains, and Wallace found Gray in the second from the end.

A uniformed officer was nursing a vending machine coffee. Wallace introduced himself to both of them.

'Fetch us a coffee, son.'

The policeman knew it wasn't a request and disappeared down the hall.

'National Crime Agency?' Gray asked, when they were alone. 'Why would you be interested in a punch-up?'

Wallace took a seat next to the bed. 'The people you had a ruckus with are currently the subjects of a sensitive investigation, and your little exchange couldn't have come at a more inopportune time.'

Gray felt the bruising around his right eye. 'I'm sorry if this was inconvenient for you, but it wasn't exactly something I had planned when I woke up this morning.'

'I quite understand, but if you proceed with your complaint, it could put us back eighteen months.'

'You want me to drop the charges?' Gray asked, astounded. He pointed to his face. 'Am I supposed to pretend this didn't happen?'

'If you press charges, we'd have to prosecute with the evidence we have, and that's not enough to guarantee a conviction. If you do as I ask, we'll get them eventually, and your testimony will prove extremely helpful when the time comes.'

The idea didn't sit well with Gray, but he appreciated the detective's stance. He'd seen enough news reports to know that taking down criminal gangs could take years, and he couldn't afford to let his personal feelings hamper their investigation. However, one thing troubled him.

'Okay, let's say I drop the charges,' he said. 'What guarantee do I have that they won't come back to the shop tomorrow?'

'Trust me, I know how these people operate. To them, crime is a business, but they only prey on the weak and vulnerable. When someone stands up to them, they back off rather than draw attention to themselves.'

Gray wasn't convinced. From what he knew of Britain's criminal gangs—admittedly not much, and that mostly gleaned from movies—they earned their reputations through intimidation and violence. He thought it highly unlikely that they'd allow someone to stand up to them, a concern he shared with Wallace.

'These guys are smarter than your average thug,' the detective said. 'They grew up around some of the toughest gangs in London, and over the years they've seen them dismantled as the leaders were sent down, one by one. William Hart, the father, has avoided many of their mistakes. He runs a legitimate business which brings in a decent amount, but the majority of the family's wealth comes from, shall we say, other means. That's rather hard to prove in court as most victims are unwilling to testify against them, but we're slowly building our case.

'In the meantime, their one weakness is publicity; they do their best to stay under the police radar. Hart's a pragmatist, and he knows when to walk away from a fight. From what we've seen, he's not the type to push a bad position as he knows what the unwanted attention will do to his little empire.'

Gray was partly assuaged, but made a note to have one of his guys keep an eye on the shop for a few weeks. He certainly had plenty of manpower available, and it would feed one of them for another month at least. After all, he couldn't think of a better way to spend the diminishing salary funds his company possessed.

'Okay, I'll let it go. I can't speak for Ken Hatcher, though. He might want to pursue this, and it's his shop in the firing line.'

'Then I'd appreciate it if you could have a word with him. It would be better coming from you.'

'I suppose so.'

'Thanks. If you could do it soon, it should convince them that we've got nothing to go on. The longer they're in custody, the more suspicious it will appear when we let them go.'

Gray nodded just as the officer returned with Wallace's coffee. The detective took a sip, and his face suggested it wasn't the best he'd ever tasted.

'Mr Gray isn't going to be taking the matter any further,' Wallace told the duty officer. 'Let the station know, will you?'

He didn't wait for a response. His coffee consigned to a shelf, Wallace walked out, leaving Gray to explain his decision.

William Hart answered the phone on the first ring.

'Well?'

'Gray has agreed to drop the charges,' Wallace said. 'The boys will be out within the hour.'

'Good. I'll speak to you soon—'

'Bill,' Wallace interrupted, 'I think you should let this one go.'

As the seconds ticked by, he knew Hart was building up to another eruption, and he had to defuse it before the man went off half-cocked. Despite what he'd told Gray, Wallace knew that Hart's first thought would be to bury the people who'd defied him, and he couldn't allow that to happen, for both their sakes.

It had been many years since he'd first done Hart the simple favour of finding the address of his estranged uncle. The sob story in the pub had been convincing, and Wallace had agreed to try to locate him. It had taken a few seconds on the Police National Computer system to find the house in Exeter, and his reward had been five hundred pounds in a plain envelope.

As a fledgling detective constable, the money had been a welcome bonus, but once Hart showed him a video of the handover he knew he'd been set up. For a few days he'd considered going to his superiors and owning up to the indiscretion, but when Hart's uncle was killed in an apparent hit-and-run later that week, the realisation dawned that he hadn't helped with a simple family reconciliation. He'd set up Hart's uncle for a hit, something Hart was all too happy to spell out.

The deal Hart offered was simple: start providing information that kept the family out of trouble, and he would receive a healthy stipend. Try to back out, and the video would be shown at any subsequent trial.

With no way out, Wallace had done everything within his power to get transferred to the now-defunct Serious and Organised Crime Agency so that he would have first-hand knowledge of any intelligence gathered on the Hart family. Being inexorably tied to them, his fate rested with theirs, and so he fed Hart information that kept them all out of prison. When a wiretap was placed on Hart family phones, Wallace warned them to talk about the legitimate business only and use untraceable mobiles for their other dealings. When a raid was planned, he tipped them off to ensure nothing incriminating was found. Now and again he would advise them to have a little cocaine lying around, though just enough to be classed as for personal use. The Harts dabbled in the drug market but kept their distance from the product and worked merely as financiers, investing their money for a two hundred per cent turnaround. They would find the people to finance, and Wallace would warn them if their new partner were on any radar.

So far, he'd managed to keep them out of any serious trouble, but as time went on, Hart seemed more and more convinced that he was untouchable. This meant more brazen acts, such as the crippling of the Singh boy the previous year. He'd used hired muscle from the north for that job but bragged openly that it was his own work.

The collections used to be done by cheap hired muscle, who made a few quid per client, but in recent months Hart had started sending his own sons to do the job. Wallace had warned against it, but as was happening with increasing frequency, Hart had ignored the advice.

Now his boys had a fresh allegation of extortion on their files, and Wallace knew that Gray was at the top of Hart's to-do list.

'What do you mean let it go?'

'I mean forget about Gray and forget about the shop. Chalk it up to experience and move on. You know his history, and if you push this, it could get very messy.'

'Of course it's going to get messy! They'll be finding bits of him for years!'

'Bill, think about this. You're angry, I understand that, but you're already too close to Gray to get away with this. They'll look at his allegation and it will point to you and the boys.'

Silence took over again, though Wallace could hear deep breathing on the other end of the line.

'Okay,' Hart eventually said. 'I won't lay a hand on him, and I'll steer clear of the shop.'

William Hart put the phone down and launched into a tirade capable of turning a nun to stone. He needed Wallace, that was a given, but the man was increasingly forcing decisions on him, and that went against every principle. To be told which dealers you could work with was one thing, but to have him dictate the people he could hit was something completely different.

His business had been built on fear, his reputation as merciless cementing his place among the most notorious gangsters in the country, and the moment he let someone slap his sons around and get away with it, his power would be gone overnight. Word would spread, and people would start refusing to pay protection money. Then other crews would start trying to steal his business, and . . .

It didn't bear thinking about.

He'd promised Wallace he wouldn't hit Gray or the shop, and he would stick to that.

However, accidents happened every day, especially if he threw in a financial incentive.

'Oh my God! What the hell happened to you?'

It was just after ten in the evening when Gray arrived home, and his plan of not worrying Vick was unravelling quickly.

'I told you, it was a scuffle with a couple of yobs.'

'Tom, you look like you've been hit by a bus! This was more than a little pushing and shoving.'

'It looks worse than it is,' he lied, thankful for the Tramadol he'd been given.

He winced when Vick wrapped her arm around his chest and led him into the living room, where he gingerly took a seat on the sofa.

'Tell me what happened,' she said, and Gray stuck to his story of two local hard cases who wanted to cause a little trouble.

'I politely asked them to leave the shop and one of them swung for me. What was I supposed to do?'

Vick was sceptical and voiced further concerns about reprisals against her uncle, but Gray assured her that his attackers were being dealt with by the police and wouldn't be troubling Ken again.

A wail broke up the conversation and Vick padded upstairs to attend to their daughter, while Gray turned on the TV and switched over to the news channel. His eyes began to droop as the anchor rehashed the same stories he'd seen earlier in the day, and by the time Vick returned he was fast asleep.

Rather than try to get him upstairs, she arranged the cushions and gently laid him down on his back before covering him with a patchwork throw. As she sat and caressed his hair, she hoped that Tom was telling the truth. After just over a year together, it finally looked like things were settling down and they could begin to enjoy a normal life together, just the three of them. No more adventures or excitement except of their own making, which was all a family could ask for.

After ten minutes, she kissed him on the forehead and went up to bed, hoping the gnawing sensation in her stomach was due to a disagreement with her dinner rather than a warning of trouble to come.

Chapter Twelve

Tuesday 8 October 2013

'That's right, keep coming . . . '

The darkness was shattered as gunfire erupted from the jungle and the four men on the narrow track immediately took hits. One took a leg shot but managed to dive into cover and scramble away, while the other three were confirmed kills.

'Too early,' Smart cursed quietly, and when the injured man took the full force of the improvised Claymore mine that had been hidden under a pile of dead leaves, he knew the ambush had been a complete disaster.

The team of six emerged from the undergrowth and began prancing around the dead, taunting them and laughing. Smart looked at Sonny Baines, who shook his head, both of them knowing what was about to happen.

The dancing was cut short as more fire burst through the trees, from the very positions the men had left. All six registered hits and the screaming from their web belts signalled an end to the exercise. Smart and Sonny left their position and strode over to offer their critique.

'The odds of anyone sending an attacking force of four men is a gazillion to one, which means you just took out a scout party. What you did afterwards was completely unnecessary, not to mention fatal. All you succeeded in doing is alerting your enemy to your position.'

'But what if there *had* only been four of them?' one of the men argued.

'That's why we told you to spread out. If there's just four, you let them through and those at the far end of the trap can take them out. Silently, if possible.'

The soldier who'd been hit with the Claymore struggled onto the footpath, a round of laughter greeting his appearance. Thankfully, the training mine contained white powder rather than the standard ball bearings. As he dusted himself off, Smart considered how to explain why the trainees' ambush had gone pear-shaped.

It wasn't as though the Malundians didn't know the basics. They'd gone over and over it again in the classroom. Perhaps it was the mobilisation to the border and the prospect of actual combat that had made the men forget the basics. If so, that wouldn't be good news. The whole point of training was to make their actions second nature, so that when they went into battle they'd be able to keep their heads in a firefight.

To get to that stage, however, took a lot longer than the week they'd had so far, and Smart hoped the deployment to the border would be purely precautionary.

If it weren't, a lot of these men were going to die.

He called in the rest of the soldiers and arranged them in a semicircle in a clearing.

'You guys were chosen because you're the elite fifty troops in Malundi, hand-picked to become the most effective unit in the region.' Smart looked at their faces and saw pride, and in a few places arrogance. That would soon change.

'You're fit, you're strong, and you're all fighters, but you don't listen, and that's going to get you killed.'

One soldier started to protest and Smart threw his hands up in frustration.

'There you go again,' he said. 'I'm trying to tell you how to stay alive and you don't want to hear it. You'd rather add your own perspective and do things your way.'

The soldier took the hint and held his tongue.

'Gentlemen, we moved our training down here because of the tensions between Malundi and Kingata. It might turn out to be nothing, but we can't take that chance. You need to start focusing, and more importantly, listening.'

Smart spent another few minutes trying to instil a sense of urgency into the men before he chose another six soldiers to lay the next ambush. He gave Carl Levine the location of the next checkpoint, which lay three miles away, and told him that his small team would lay up somewhere along the route.

'Give us an hour's start,' Smart said, and he set off, followed by the others, Sonny taking up the rear. They'd managed to cover less than a kilometre when Jeff Campbell's voice came over the headset and Smart ordered the team to stop. Sonny Baines was also hearing the same message, and he trotted up from the rear of the formation to get Smart's take on the situation.

'Roger that,' Smart said into his throat mic, and gathered the men together. He dropped to one knee and pulled out his field map.

'In the last thirty minutes, two border posts have been attacked. Reports number the enemy in excess of three thousand.' He indicated their current location, and drew a vertical line either side. 'They're heading north in a flanking movement, and if their two forces manage to join up, we'll be cut off. Not only us, but garrisons here, here and here.'

He marked the locations of the other Malundi troops in the area, all of which lay inside a semicircle created by the advancing army.

'They have a large convoy of vehicles, though most are infantry, and the majority of those are in civilian clothing. Their mechanised troops are expected to get behind us within a couple of hours, so we can expect them to start pressing soon after that.'

'Doesn't give us much time,' Sonny noted, and Smart agreed. According to Campbell, the orders that had come over the net were for the trainers to lead their charges north at a clip, joining up with the other Malundi troops on the way, and attack the motorised advance party before the infantry caught up, punching their way through any defences. Once they reached the capital, they were to set up a defensive perimeter.

Unfortunately, that would leave a couple of villages in the south at the mercy of the advancing force. They shared the news with the troops, who were also less than eager to leave civilians in harm's way. One of them had family in the local area and wasn't about to run in the opposite direction.

'We must go south and protect our people,' he said, to the approval of the others.

'That's not our decision to make,' Smart reminded them. 'Let's get back to the others and see what Sergeant Okeke has in mind.'

They jogged back and found the rest of the unit involved in an animated discussion. Campbell and Levine were clearly keeping out of it, sharing a bottle of water between them while watching impassively from the sidelines.

Sonny and Smart joined them, and Sonny asked if there'd been any further updates.

'The other garrisons are already clearing out,' Campbell said, 'and we'd better start moving soon, too. Johnny wants to follow orders and move north, but most of them are more interested in protecting their families in the region.'

'What's your call?' Levine asked.

'That's an easy one,' Smart said. 'We're here as non-combatants, and if the head of the armed forces says we go north, we go north.

We didn't come here to run their army, we came to make a few quid.'

'And if these guys want to head south?' Sonny asked.

Smart thought about it for a few moments, then shrugged. 'Then I guess we let them.'

'And you're happy with that decision?' Campbell asked.

'Not really,' Smart admitted, 'but our rules of engagement are clear, and if we ignore them, the shit flies Tom's way, not ours.'

Though the four men were officially equals within the team, Smart was the *de facto* leader based on both age and experience. Whenever a big decision had to be made, each of them got a vote, but despite this, Smart's was usually the deciding one.

Johnny came over and sat down among them.

'We've come to a compromise,' he said. 'We will go south and collect the people from the villages, then take them north. Once we fight our way through the enemy ranks, we'll escort them to safety.'

'There isn't time,' Smart said, consulting the map. 'They crossed the border less than forty minutes ago, which means they could be at the first of the villages in the next hour. We're still an hour and a half away, and we don't know how fast they're travelling.'

'We have to try, Mister Len.'

'Sorry, it's just too risky. Even if we get to the village first, we won't be able to outrun them. We'll have women, children and the elderly to look after, and that will slow us right down. They'd have us surrounded in minutes, and apart from the blank ammunition we've only got one clip of live ammo each.'

'We should call Tom before we do anything,' Sonny said, and Smart agreed, despite the late hour. He pulled out the satellite phone and put it on speaker. Gray answered on the second ring. Smart apologised for the timing and gave him the condensed version of recent events, as well as their current predicament.

'What do you suggest, Tom?'

'Len, my only concern is getting you guys out of there. In fact, I should have done it a few days ago.'

'Appreciated,' Levine said, 'but if you *were* here . . . ?'

'It doesn't matter. I'm not there, and you can't go into a battle with thirty rounds each. Get back to base, arm yourselves, and get out of the area as quickly as possible.'

'One sec,' Sonny said. 'Len told us about the contracts collapsing. How's it going to look if word gets round that we run at the first sign of trouble?'

'That's my problem,' said Gray, 'not yours.'

'I disagree,' Campbell said. 'If your contracts run out, we're out of a job, too.'

'But at least you're alive, right? What would your family want, Carl?'

Levine thought for a moment. 'Sadly, it should be noted that whether we go north, south, east or west, we're still going to have to fight our way through their lines. Personally, I'd feel a lot better saving more than just my own arse.'

Levine's words suddenly made their decision a lot easier, and one by one, they nodded in silent agreement. They'd all joined the armed forces to make a difference, and while that hadn't always been the case, this was an opportunity to make up for it, despite no longer wearing the uniform.

'We're going to try and save the villagers,' Smart said.

They waited for Gray's reply.

It was a long time coming.

'How long will it take to get them to safety and make your way to the airstrip?'

Smart worked it out as an hour and a half to get there, twice as long to get back to their current position, and another ten hours to the landing strip.

'If we can avoid contact, we should be there by five in the afternoon. If we run into trouble . . . '

'I'll have a plane on standby waiting to lift you out. Call me when you're an hour from the airfield and I'll send it in.'

'Thanks, Tom. Talk to you later.'

Smart ended the call and gathered everyone around. He could see the men were eager to get going, and as time was precious he kept the speech to a minimum.

'There are two villages in harm's way, and we're going to try and get everyone out before the enemy arrives. I need fifteen volunteers to head back to the camp, pick up our heavy weapons and grab as much ammunition as they can carry. Sonny, you'll be leading them. The rest of us will use the sentinels to distract the enemy while we guide the civilians out of the area.'

A number of hands went up and Sonny chose a team to help him fetch the ordnance. He told them to hand over their magazines, which they left with Smart; then, after confirming the coordinates of the rendezvous point, he led his team north at a pace comfortable enough for a five-mile run.

Campbell distributed the live ammunition Sonny's group had left behind while Smart gave one last pep talk.

'We're going in with little ammunition, so I want all rifles on semi-automatic.' He used his right forefinger to flick the selector on his AK-47 to the down position and waited until everyone followed his lead.

'We're hoping to avoid any contact with the enemy, so no-one shoots until I do. Is that understood?'

He got nods from the men, but wasn't convinced that they would maintain discipline.

'Pick your targets and use single shots. We don't know the enemy numbers, so conserve your rounds.'

More nods.

He told them the next step was to remove their electronic webbing and the laser apparatus from their rifles. The equipment was expensive, but they didn't have time to hide it properly, so it was thrown into a pile at the base of a tree and covered with some vegetation.

Campbell settled in at the rear position while Smart and Levine took point. They formulated a series of plans as they led the men south, hoping that Plan A—grab the civilians and run—was the only one they'd need.

'Still reckon we're too old for this shit?' Smart asked.

'We'll find out soon enough.'

Tom Gray eased on his trousers and T-shirt and crept out of the bedroom and down the stairs to his office, all the time cursing himself for not pulling the guys out sooner. He made a cup of coffee while the laptop booted up and the first page he visited showed him a map of Malundi. Much of the area between his team's last location and the 'airport'—in truth, no more than a dirt strip cut into the jungle with one building serving as immigration and air traffic control—was dense jungle. A road ran up from the south, but he knew Len would avoid that at all costs. Thankfully there were no rivers to cross, and the terrain was largely flat all the way, so it shouldn't prove too difficult for anyone in the party.

Even though it was barely two in the morning, he knew one man who would be wide awake. The Malundi defence minister, the man he'd personally negotiated the contract with, would no doubt be overseeing the mobilisation of his armed forces to counter the threat.

He pulled up the man's details and placed the call.

'Minister, this is Tom Gray.'

'Mr Gray, I'm sorry, you've caught me at a bad time—'

'I know, sir. My men are in the south of the country and told me about recent events. I was wondering if you had any updates.'

'In that case, I have, Mr Gray. Your men have disobeyed orders. Instead of heading north to protect the capital, they have taken our best troops south to engage the enemy.'

'From what I understand, minister, a large number of civilians are in the path of the enemy and my team has joined up with your troops to rescue them. They felt they could do that and still make it to the capital before—'

'I don't care what they think, Mr Gray, they had orders. My men had orders. They don't have the big picture, and now they are going to be cut off and annihilated. Of the three companies in the area, one has already been wiped out, Mr Gray. We lost over two hundred men. The other two managed to get out in time, but they were pursued and have taken heavy casualties.'

'I'm sorry to hear that, sir.'

'Don't be, Mr Gray. Be sorry for your friends. We estimate a thousand men already lie between them and the capital, with another four thousand moving up from the border. I'm afraid they stand no chance.'

'Aren't you going to send anyone to help them?'

'No, Mr Gray, we are not. Your men are gone, and with them went any further need for your services. Good day.'

Gray almost slammed down the phone, but realising how early it was, he placed it back in the cradle with a shaking hand, not wanting to wake his wife and daughter.

His friends might be heading into danger, but they certainly weren't gone. He'd put one of them up against fifty any day of the week, but the numbers the minister had mentioned meant it wasn't looking favourable. Malundi's armed forces had only six thousand serving members, which meant they were currently looking at an equal fight, but if the enemy ranks had swelled by sixty per cent in an hour, they could soon be vastly outnumbered.

His friends certainly were, and the scale of the problem was growing all the time, though they might not know it.

Gray called Smart's satellite phone and got a whispered response.

'Smart here.'

'Len, it looks like the cavalry won't be coming any time soon. The Malundians are pulling everyone out of the area, so you're on your own for now.'

'Yeah, we got the same message from the top brass, though not so eloquently put.'

At least spirits were up, Gray thought, despite the enormity of the battle ahead. He shared the minister's update with his friend, who confirmed that the enemy numbers had already been relayed to them.

'For the record, I'd have done exactly the same thing,' Gray said.

'I know, and you'd swap with any one of us. Now get off the line, you soppy sod. I've got to save the batteries and we're getting close.'

Gray managed a smile and wished his friend the best of luck, asking him to get in touch again when they were on their way out.

While making a fresh coffee, he thought about Len's words. Even though he'd spoken them in jest, Smart was right. Gray would gladly have traded places with any of them right now, but that wasn't going to happen.

What he *could* do, he decided, was try to offer a helping hand.

It was still far too early to rouse Andrew Harvey from his sleep, so he made a mental note to call him just before sunrise. He knew his friend would be unable to provide any direct help, but perhaps he'd be able to get word to the foreign secretary's office. If they knew British nationals were in the firing line, they might be able to exert some pressure on the Malundi government to send reinforcements.

It was a long shot, but at that moment, it was all he had.

Chapter Thirteen

Tuesday 8 October 2013

The barest sliver of a crescent moon offered the only illumination as the party stopped short of the first row of houses representing the outskirts of Selena, which lay in silence a few hundred yards away. According to one of the soldiers who had relatives in the area, there were approximately forty dwellings in all. Smart gathered the men round and they took a knee, a few blowing hard from the rigorous journey.

'Jeff, take two men and set up a couple of sentinels along the side of the track. Use a mixture of live and blank ammo. If they come through this way, we'll make them think we're moving west.

'Carl and I will go through the back and provide covering fire, while the rest of you clear the houses. It needs to be fast and quiet. Send them this way and keep them moving. If anyone objects, you leave them and move onto the next house.'

Before anyone could respond, Smart turned and jogged towards the buildings, Levine in close support. The rest followed, fanning out as they entered the communal square and starting with the houses nearest to the approaching—though as yet unseen—enemy.

At the rear of the outlying buildings, Smart and Levine hit a wall of darkness. They pushed on, putting a hundred yards between themselves and the hamlet, watching and listening intently for the slightest sign of their foe.

It wasn't long in coming.

The horizon seemed to shimmer as first tens, then hundreds of heads appeared above the bush line, advancing menacingly towards the settlement. Smart reckoned they had four minutes at the most, and he ordered Levine to follow him as he retreated. Back among the buildings he searched out Johnny, who was organising the evacuation.

'How many left?'

'Maybe one more minute,' Okeke said. 'We are clearing the last of the houses now.'

Levine gestured for the men to get a move on, urging them to get their charges out of the area as quickly as possible. Many of the villagers were doing as they were told, but the sound of raised voices came from a nearby house, and Smart went to investigate.

Inside, he found two soldiers arguing with a woman, who was clutching two young children to her chest. They looked no more than four years old, one boy and one girl, both terrified at being woken up at such an early hour by armed men.

'What's the problem?' Smart asked one of the local soldiers.

'She is refusing to leave. She says this is her home and she won't abandon it to anyone.'

The woman was in her late thirties, Smart guessed, which meant she had the right to make her own decision. The kids, however, were a different matter. They couldn't appreciate the dangers they were facing, and he couldn't leave them with a mother who valued her humble dwelling above the lives of her children.

Smart had read enough about the genocide in Rwanda in 1994 to know that kids weren't given any special dispensation in tribal disputes, which is what this was looking like. Close to a million Rwandans had been slaughtered, a large number of them children, and eyewitness accounts suggested bad things were in store for these two if he didn't get them out of the area sharpish.

He explained the need to move, but the woman responded in her native tongue.

'We haven't got time for this,' he said, turning to one of the soldiers. 'Tell her these people will chop her children's arms and legs off and disembowel them in front of her if she stays here. She's got five seconds to get moving or I shoot her and take the kids.'

The message was relayed and the woman stared at him wide-eyed, turning slowly to face Smart.

'One!'

She gripped the children closer and let rip another stream of incomprehensible howls.

'Two!'

The soldier shouted back, gesturing towards Smart and shaking his rifle in an effort to reinforce the fate that awaited her if she didn't comply.

'Three!'

The woman stared at Smart, defiant in the face of death, her anger palpable. She spoke slowly, deliberately, and although Smart couldn't understand the words, the message was clear.

'Four!'

He raised his rifle and aimed between her eyes, but the mother remained resolute. She pushed the children aside and spread her arms wide, eyes closed as she awaited her fate.

Smart weighed her up and made his decision.

'Five!'

He took a step towards her and reversed his grip on the rifle before clubbing her to the side of the head. She collapsed, dazed, and he ordered the soldiers to carry her out. The youngsters started crying; Smart shouldered his weapon and grabbed one of them around the waist, using his other hand to cover the boy's mouth. He left the house and ordered two more soldiers to go in and help with the mother and daughter.

The woman was brought out, her feet dragging the ground as she was half-carried through the streets, Smart and her son in tow. They were the last to reach the dirt road out of the village, and he handed the child off to another soldier, urging him onwards and into the darkness that would provide them with a little protection, though not for long.

Campbell came to the rear of the formation to update Smart on the retreat.

'We've got over a hundred non-combatants, and several are going to find the going tough. I've ordered the able-bodied to help as much as they can, but it'll still be slow going.'

For the moment, that was all they could do. The priority, though, was getting out of the area.

'What about the defences?' Smart asked.

'The sentinels are set up and we've got remote control and video enabled. Once they reach the kill zone we'll keep them busy while we open up a lead on them.'

Smart nodded. The rendezvous point was a dense area of jungle to the north-east, and they would head through that while the enemy were pinned down from the west. On their own, they'd be clear of the area in no time, but with their new charges, he knew it was going to be a game of cat and mouse until they were out of the danger zone.

There was no time to try to reach the other village. To do so would be suicidal, and the locals would have to fare as best they could on their own. Many, if not all, would die, but Smart and his team had their own responsibilities now. He watched the line of humanity as it snaked into the darkness, and he and Campbell took up the tail position, their eyes and ears focused on the rear for signs of pursuit.

They didn't have to wait long.

The first they heard was shouting as the frustrated attackers found the buildings empty, followed by a mounting rumble as a multitude of feet jogged down the dirt path in search of the inhabitants.

Smart and Campbell urged the tail-enders forward and ran back fifty yards so that they could see the dirt trail from the edge of the forest. The first of the enemy came into sight, wearing a mishmash of civilian clothes and army fatigues. Some carried AK-47s, though most wielded blades of varying lengths. The one thing all had in common was the desire to use their weapons on someone.

Campbell switched the display of the remote control to red-light mode so that it didn't give their position away, and once he had a couple of hundred people in the kill zone he toggled the screen and activated each of the sentinel devices.

The weapons opened up and the reaction was instant. A couple took hits from the live rounds, but the majority dropped to the ground and began returning fire. Campbell used the on-board cameras to target those with rifles, though he was frustrated by not knowing if the next round was live or blank. At least it kept them pinned down, and every passing second meant the friendlies managed another yard towards safety.

'We'll give them a five-minute head start, then set the sentinels to automatic and follow them,' Smart whispered.

Campbell nodded agreement, but the plan was blown out of the water moments later. From further up the trail, one of the villagers lost her footing in the pitch darkness, twisting her ankle and letting out a scream as she fell.

One of the Kanto turned towards the sound, and pointed up the trail into the trees, shouting orders to others who began opening up at nothing in particular. One or two rounds flew too close to Smart for comfort. As he was trying to decide whether to engage them, he saw a few men heading his way.

His mind made up, he told Campbell to switch the sentinels to automatic and catch up with the others. 'I'll keep them busy for a while. You get the tail-enders to form a defensive line a few hundred yards in. Just make sure they hold their fire when I come through.'

Campbell slapped him on the back and disappeared into the night while Smart picked the first of his targets. Like Campbell, he initially selected those carrying firearms as they posed the most immediate threat, and when he squeezed off the first round he saw his target stagger and eventually fall. Rather than halting them, it seemed to galvanise the horde, and they soon turned their attention on him. Thankfully, their aim was poor, though he knew one lucky round could ruin his day.

As each of his bullets brought another man down, ten more took his place, until hundreds were advancing on Smart's position. They seemed to sense that they faced a lone gunman, and fancied their chances based on safety in numbers.

Smart knew it was time to bug out. After his first clip ran dry he inserted the other and fired off a quick salvo before sprinting deeper into the trees. Bullets whizzed through the air, striking trees and shredding branches all around him as he ran at a crouch towards the safety of his own lines.

It was two agonising minutes before he came across Campbell, who was waiting to lead him back to the others.

'I thought I'd better escort you in,' Campbell said. 'The guys are so jumpy, if you'd come tearing in they'd have cut you in half.'

'They'll get some targets soon enough,' Smart said. 'I reckon we've got about a minute to get our shit sorted.'

Campbell called out a password, which was answered immediately, and having been identified, they walked for twenty yards before he signalled for Smart to halt, pointing to the ground.

'I've set up flares,' he said, indicating the fine wire stretched across the narrow track. Both men stepped over it and trotted another forty yards before taking their place along the defensive line. Campbell had the ten troops spread out with at least eight yards between each man, giving them a large enough field of fire that they didn't hit their own during a staggered retreat.

Everyone was told to hold their fire until Campbell gave the signal, and the two instructors prayed that the men would heed the instructions. The last thing they needed was a trigger-happy maverick giving the game away.

A faint *tat-tat-tat* sound permeated the forest, and Smart cursed his luck as he noted the change in weather. A fat raincloud had drifted over their position and begun depositing its load. The rain would cause him only minor discomfort, but he was concerned that the going underfoot would slow down the main body of the party as they tried to escape the area. He had to give them more time, which wouldn't be easy with just a dozen men and thirty rounds of ammunition each.

He didn't have time to reflect on the situation as all extraneous thoughts left his head when the first of the silhouettes came running down the path, closely followed by the next wave. Smart could make out the occasional profile of a machete, but he was more concerned with the AK-47s bearing down on them.

The point man was fifty yards out. Smart held his breath, determined to wait until he reached the trip wire.

Just as he'd feared, one of his men opened up early, setting off a chain reaction as the rest began spraying the area with long bursts of automatic fire.

'Single rounds!' Smart screamed, but no-one was listening. Now the enemy had gone to ground, and the battle immediately became one of attrition. A dozen men against hundreds, and with ammunition pitifully low and running out fast.

Time to disappear.

'Pull back!'

He looked over at Campbell and gestured for him to take the first wave with him, while the rest provided covering fire.

'Even numbers, fall back now!' Campbell screamed above the noise, and four of the five men followed his instructions, one deciding to stay and continue the fight. Campbell retreated fifteen yards and spun round to offer covering fire while the front rank leapfrogged them.

'Len, go!'

Smart ordered the others to follow him and he sprinted past Campbell for another fifteen yards before throwing himself to the ground, looking for the next target. Two of his men continued past him, their weapons empty. It was turning into a clusterfuck, with death only minutes away.

He held his fire, waiting for another clear shot, when the man next to him took a bullet to the shoulder, his screams drowning out the chatter of gunfire. Smart ignored him and continued to search for his next hit, managing to take down a man who'd stepped just a little too far away from the tree he was using as cover.

Another figure appeared in his sights, and he squeezed the trigger.

Click.

Smart threw down the empty rifle and crabbed his way over to the screaming soldier. The man thought he was going to get some first aid but Smart rolled him onto his front and grabbed the rifle he'd been lying on. The man cried out in pain but Smart was already looking for his next target.

If they made it out alive, then perhaps he'd apologise.

Outgoing fire dwindled rapidly as Campbell pulled his men back, and soon Smart was the only one putting up any kind of fight. A bad day got even worse when he spotted someone carrying a long tube on their shoulder. He immediately recognised it as a Soviet-built RPG-7. Though primarily used as an anti-tank weapon, the rocket-propelled grenade could do a lot of damage to ground forces.

He got a bead on the man holding the launcher and took him out with a bullet to the chest, but the weapon was quickly retrieved by another. Smart once more aimed for centre mass, but again the firing pin fell on an empty chamber.

By this time, all of the fire was incoming. He scrambled to his feet, ordering a swift retreat as he ran. Bullets chased them through the trees, one of them catching the man to Smart's right.

A *crump* resonated through the trees, and Smart awaited the inevitable, but the round thankfully fell well short.

Crump!

Crump!

More explosions landed, each one further away than the last, and as Smart turned he saw a round take out a dozen of their attackers, the fountain of dirt and flames sending bodies flying in all directions. Small arms fire erupted behind him and Smart swivelled to see Sonny and a dozen others joining the fray.

Sonny ran to Smart, weapon up. He handed over a couple of magazines and began picking off those who still fancied taking on the light artillery. As more men collected ammunition and rejoined the fight, the battle swung their way. The enemy had been emboldened by the lack of resistance, but the introduction of the mortars was a game-changer. Coupled with the resumed small arms fire, it was enough to make the marauders fall back and regroup.

Once the sound of incoming rounds died away, Smart ordered everyone to pull back and catch up with the main party. Three men had fallen; their bodies were collected while the more seriously wounded were treated at the scene. The walking wounded would receive first aid once they had some breathing space, during which time the dead would be buried. Smart wanted to leave them where they lay, but the local custom dictated that the bodies be laid to rest in a proper and decent manner, and the Malundian soldiers refused to leave them behind.

Acquiescing, Smart took up the rear with Sonny and put Levine and Campbell on point with instructions to make it a decent pace.

'You cut that a little fine.'

'Sorry,' Sonny smiled, 'we stopped off for a burger on the way back.'

With the tension of battle dissipating, Smart managed a chuckle, glad his friend had turned up while he still had all his limbs.

'We got to the RV point but you weren't there, so we thought we'd come and find you in case you needed help.'

'Good thing you did,' Smart conceded. 'We were down to rocks and harsh words. Did you pass my main party on the way?'

'Yeah, they're about a click away and moving fast. Amazing how the sound of a firefight can spur people on.'

'I hope they can keep it up,' Smart said. 'The sooner we get out of this country, the better.'

Chapter Fourteen

Tuesday 8 October 2013

Sese Obi slumbered as best he could in the back of the Land Rover as his convoy rested up thirty miles inland, the initial assault having gone exactly as he'd planned. His men had taken out the two border posts with ease and had moved up country while the foot soldiers swept through, destroying anything in their path. The power station was spared, though the majority of workers had been killed; only the most important technicians saved in order to keep it operational. When the time came, power to the capital would be cut, as would the water supply. The latter facility had yet to be taken, but he was confident it would fall into his hands later in the day.

The troops in the south had been rousted and were fleeing north, but there had been a report of a small pocket of resistance that was being hunted down. It was a minor setback, and one that hadn't troubled him until he was shaken awake by his lieutenant, Baako.

'Sir, Kgosi has called in.'

Baako would not have disturbed him for something as trivial as a progress report, so it had to be an urgent matter. Obi came instantly awake.

'What is the problem?'

'We lost over two hundred men near Selena. The village had been cleared out and our forces came under attack when they tried to track them down. The stories we heard about *abazungu* training the Agbi appear to be correct. At least one was seen before our men had to break off the attack.'

The fact that white men were among the defending numbers didn't concern Obi. Rather, it was the decision to disengage that brought his anger to the surface.

'What do you mean, break off the attack?'

He glared at Baako, who, despite being only the messenger, was clearly worried. With good reason: being awakened with bad news did nothing for Obi's mood.

'They pulled back when the Agbi began using mortars,' Baako told him, nervously. 'They were taking huge losses and decided to—'

'My men do not retreat!'

The scream woke everyone in the temporary camp, and all heads turned to see what had angered their leader.

'You tell Kgosi to track them down and kill every single one,' Obi said, jabbing Baako in the chest with a beefy finger. 'I don't care how many people it takes, just do it!'

The lieutenant quickly got Kgosi on the phone and shot off the instructions. After a few seconds, Baako suggested his counterpart relay the message himself and handed the phone to Obi before taking a step backwards.

'I don't want excuses!' Obi screamed into the handset after listening for a moment. 'I don't care if they outnumber you a hundred to one and have nuclear weapons. You will find them and destroy them!'

He couldn't allow anyone in the region to survive if his advance north were to continue unimpeded: having enemy forces to his front and rear would be suicidal. Six hundred men had been tasked with clearing Selena, and now a third were gone, wiped out in a single exchange. He'd allowed for casualties, but not so many in one hit, and it looked like he'd have to bring up the reserves a lot sooner than planned. It was either that, or halt the advance north to send men back to finish the job, but that would throw off his timetable and give the rest of the Agbi forces time to regroup.

Obi pulled out a map and asked Kgosi in which direction the enemy were moving. He scanned the map for possible destinations in the north-east but apart from the airstrip he saw nothing but forest. That meant they must be trying to fly out of the area. If so, they were in for a surprise. His men had already captured the strip, the four personnel who ran it having easily been overwhelmed and killed.

'I'll send some help,' he growled into the phone. 'I want you to drive the Agbi north where reinforcements will be lying in wait. Once you've eliminated everyone, join up as originally planned. You've got twenty-four hours.'

He jabbed at the disconnect button and thrust the phone into Baako's chest.

'Move the boys up,' he said. 'Have them drive to the airfield and then head south. Kgosi can drive the Agbi towards them until there is nowhere left to run.'

'But sir, they are not all ready. Only a few of the boys have been in the camp long enough—'

'I know the situation,' Obi barked. 'I've been watching their development. They are as ready as we need them to be. If any of them refuse, tell Fene to make an example of them.'

'Yes, sir.'

'And send five of our vehicles with twenty men to reinforce the airport. If the Agbi are heading there, it is for a reason. They must be expecting someone to pick them up.'

If, by some miracle, Kgosi managed to do his job properly, Obi would instruct him to hold the airstrip and call his motorised troops back for the push north. Five vehicles out of a hundred wouldn't be missed in the meantime.

The discussion over, Obi climbed back into the Land Rover to get another hour of sleep before sunrise.

Chapter Fifteen

Tuesday 8 October 2013

When the door was pushed open and orders barked into the dark shack, Nafari Cisse threw himself upright and immediately regretted it. His shoulder screamed in protest, his hand moving instinctively to the bloody weal where the instructor had hit him relentlessly with a cane.

The other three boys in the room grabbed their meagre belongings and stood to attention, leaving Nafari to incur the man's wrath. The last boy to follow instructions always got a little reminder, and this time it was the flat of a machete against the side of Nafari's head. From experience he knew that if he let the blow sink in, more and more would follow, so he shrugged it off as best he could and stood unsteadily next to the heavy blanket that represented his bed.

'We are leaving in five minutes,' the soldier told them, and gave instructions to form up in the centre of the camp.

The boys trotted out of their hut, one or two holding their stomachs as the intestinal pain once again took hold. Nafari tried to ignore the cramps, but only another hit of whoonga would keep them at bay for a few hours. It had become a familiar and desperate need. After a week on the drug, the withdrawal pains worsened every day.

He lined up next to the boys he shared a bed with. His original companions had been moved out a couple of days after his arrival, and these new recruits had been there for just three days. They were younger than him, ranging from eight to ten years old, but they learned faster. This meant Nafari got the lion's share of any punishment, though he was doing his best to catch up.

The previous day had been unarmed combat training, and after suffering at the hands of first a larger boy and then a smaller, younger one, the instructor had lost patience. Nafari had been dragged into the middle of the camp and whipped with the cane in front of the others, a warning for all to see. Capitulation would not be tolerated, and defeat was not an option.

Initially, he had considered escaping into the forest. That was until another boy had a similar idea and managed to slip his restraints before dashing off into the night. Since then, Nafari only had to look over to the side of the camp when the notion entered his mind. The escapee's head, sitting lopsided on a spike, quickly dispelled such thoughts.

The camp commander, Fene Adebola, was a giant of a man at almost seven feet tall. He strode purposefully towards the young troops, carrying a Kalashnikov in one hand and the obligatory machete in the other.

'Some of you have been here for months, and some for just a few days. But today, you are all soldiers.'

'Today you will meet the enemy, and as soldiers, you will do your duty.'

One or two of the boys who'd been through the long indoctrination process yelled enthusiastically, and soon the rest joined in. Even Nafari pretended to be thankful for this opportunity, though in truth all he wanted at that moment in time was another hit of whoonga.

'Most of you are ready, and I know you will do what I ask, but some of you may be thinking of running instead of fighting.'

He walked towards the first rank of boys and moved up the line, like a general inspecting his troops. He stopped when he came to one of the boys who'd arrived just the previous day.

'Are you ready to fight?'

The eight-year-old nodded, though his young faced betrayed a lack of conviction. Fene put an arm around the boy's shoulder and led him out of the ranks before handing him the AK-47 and walking away.

After a dozen steps he turned to face the boy. 'Let's see how ready you are.'

Without warning, he ran at the child, machete raised as he bellowed a blood-curdling war cry. The boy was petrified at the sight of the screaming giant, and he dropped the rifle, sending it clattering to the ground.

Sniggers drifted from the line of boys, but the commander hadn't done it for their entertainment. His intention was to shock them into obedience, and the show was far from over.

He put his free hand on the boy's shoulder. 'This one is not ready to go into battle,' he said, and casually ran the long knife over the shaking child's abdomen. There was a surprising lack of blood, just a wriggling grey mass as the intestines fought for a way out.

The commander ignored the child's agonised howls as he addressed the rest of the boy soldiers, all of them now wearing focused expressions.

'If anyone else is thinking of throwing down their weapons or using them against anyone but the enemy, you won't be as lucky as this one.'

He gestured towards the dying child, who was desperately trying to stem the flow of organs.

All were forced to watch until the boy finally lost the futile battle.

Once the tiny body lay still, the boys were led over to the ersatz armoury—a small shack with Kalashnikovs piled from floor to ceiling. Each was given a rifle and one clip of ammunition, and those who hadn't advanced to weapons training were given a crash course. They weren't shown how to strip the gun down and clean it, as the assumption was that very few would make it past their first encounter with the Agbi. Instead, they were told how to hold it, aim and pull the trigger. Anyone who lived to see the next dawn would then be shown the rest of the basics, such as using the fire selector and changing the magazine.

Once everyone was armed, they were given a whoonga reefer to share between four, just enough to take the edge off their cravings and ease the pain slightly.

'You will get one between two of you before we meet the enemy. Those who live to see the sun set will get one to themselves from that moment on.'

Incentivised, they piled aboard the trucks when ordered to do so. Those who had been at the camp longest were excited at the prospect of battle, though most were either daydreaming about their increased drug rations or just plain scared.

Nafari Cisse fell into the latter category.

The first fingers of dawn crept through the leafy canopy as Len Smart ordered a ten-minute rest break. The procession halted and everyone dropped to the ground, glad of the chance to rest their aching legs and take on what little water they'd brought along for the journey.

Red colobus monkeys chirped their annoyance at the intrusion into their domain, but the catcalls went ignored as the weary travellers spent their time fighting off the myriad insects out for a dawn feed.

Smart and his team were suffering the effects of the humidity, which made them feel as if they were breathing syrup. He wiped his brow with the now-soaking handkerchief and ordered Campbell to take ten men and watch the rear while he gathered his other teammates to check their progress using the map and a handheld GPS device.

They'd been on the go for nearly four hours and expected to be halfway to the airstrip, but the elderly had slowed the pace to a crawl at times, despite the instructors' best efforts to instil a sense of urgency.

'Best guess, we won't reach the airstrip until after midnight,' Sonny said, getting nods from the others.

'That's if we can keep up this pace,' Levine added. 'I'm not sure half of them will last another mile, never mind twenty.'

Smart felt it wouldn't have been so bad if they could simply offload the civvies in a local village and carry on by themselves, but the entire route wound through thick, uninhabited jungle. Even when they got to the airstrip, they had to hope that Gray had taken their charges into account: it would take more than a two-seater turboprop to ferry them all to safety.

Leaving them at the airfield wasn't an option, either, Smart knew. The troops trailing them from the south would soon regroup and take them on once more, of that they had no doubt. If they managed to evade the enemy until they reached the airport, abandoning the villagers at that point would render the entire journey pointless.

Smart pulled out the satellite phone and hit Gray's preprogrammed number.

'Looks like we're gonna be a bit late,' he said as soon as his boss picked up. 'If we don't have any more contacts, expect us in eighteen hours.'

'Any more? How many have you had?'

Smart gave a quick rundown of the brief encounter with the enemy. 'We lost three locals and have a few walking wounded.'

'Are you guys okay?'

'We're fine. Our main concern is what to do with the non-combatants once we reach the strip. We're hauling over a hundred.'

'I'm working on that,' Gray assured him. 'We might have to make more than one trip, though.'

That wouldn't be a problem if the airstrip were secured, Smart realised, but he'd discussed a possible scenario with the others, who'd come to the same conclusion.

'Actually, I'm afraid we might have to take the strip *back*,' he told Gray. 'If you and I were planning to take this country, we'd make sure we controlled the major installations, including the airport. We're working on the assumption that it's already in enemy hands.'

'Wise move. Have you got everything you need for that kind of assault?'

'We grabbed what we could from the camp and it should be enough . . . if we don't have to use any ammo in the meantime.'

Smart felt his words must have reached the fickle god of war. They'd just left his mouth when the rattle of small arms fire resounded through the trees, and he knew Campbell and his small squad would need help repelling the latest attack.

'Gotta go, Tom, they're back for more.' He stabbed the 'End' button. 'Carl, get these people moving! Sonny, on me.'

He led Sonny towards the sound of the skirmish, which was already beginning to peter out. By the time they arrived, the fight was over.

'A small scouting party,' Campbell said, as he flicked the safety on his rifle. 'No more than three or four. I think we got a couple.'

'Let's get moving,' Smart said. 'The rest will be on our tails in no time.'

Tom Gray sat with the phone in his hand and for the umpteenth time he wondered how he'd let things get to this stage. He cursed himself for not following his instincts and pulling them out at the first hint of trouble.

That got him thinking about Andrew Harvey, and he retrieved his friend's number on his mobile phone.

'Sorry about the early wake-up call, Andrew.'

Harvey assured him it wasn't a problem—if Tom were calling at this hour, it must be something serious.

Gray gave him a breakdown of the last eight hours and asked if he could pull any strings with the foreign office.

'I'm not sure I've got enough clout to make a difference,' Harvey said. 'I'll certainly let them know that British citizens are in the middle of it all, but whether they do anything about it is another matter.'

'Thanks, Andrew, I appreciate it.'

'Don't thank me yet. I'll do what I can, and it might help, but I wouldn't stake my house on it. Once they realise that the people stuck behind enemy lines are four of the people who held Britain to ransom, their enthusiasm might wane. Even if it were four others, you know how slow the diplomatic route is. It could be days before anything is done.'

'I can't just abandon them there.'

'I know Tom. I'm just saying, don't expect anything to happen any time soon.'

Gray knew Harvey was right. The political wheels turned slowly at the best of times, and they would virtually grind to a halt once the government learned who was in trouble. He knew that sending in troops was also a political decision, so that idea could be ruled out, too.

That left him with just one option. He'd been considering it all morning, and now that all other avenues had been explored and discounted, he knew what he had to do.

'Thanks anyway, Andrew. I'll let the guys know to keep their heads down until we sort something out.'

'What are you thinking?'

'What do you mean?' Gray asked.

'I've known you for a while, Tom. There's no way you'd leave this to the political machine, so let me know what you've got in mind.'

Gray considered lying, but Harvey always saw through his fabrications. Hiding his true feelings had always been a problem for Gray, and he'd never been much of a liar. True, he'd fooled the entire country a couple of years ago, but he'd had plenty of time to practice his speeches to make them sound convincing. It was when he tried to spin a tale off the cuff that he was usually found out.

'You don't want to know,' he eventually said. 'It's better that way.'

'Tom—'

'It's all right. Don't worry. I just have to do what I can to get them back. They're like brothers to me. The less you know, the better.'

'Now you're really worrying me. When you start thinking like this, all hell breaks loose.'

'I'm just going to provide them with an exit route, that's all.'

'It's never that simple,' Harvey said, 'and you know it. Let me help if I can. Just let me know what you've got in mind.'

'A simple exfiltration,' said Gray. 'That's all. I'm going to arrange transportation to meet them at the airfield and fly them out. Worst case, it'll be a violation of Malundi airspace by persons unknown, and given the fact that they haven't even got an air force, they probably won't even know about it.'

'I can live with that,' Harvey acquiesced, 'and I'll see what I can do from this end.'

Gray thanked him and hung up, glad his friend hadn't pushed for more details.

He opened his favourite browser and checked the BBC news website. It had picked up the story, though it hadn't quite reached the front pages, and he had to search through the Africa section to find it. The three paragraphs gave few details, which wasn't surprising. The invasion was less than eight hours old, so it would be some time before reporters had anything to share with the world. That, at least, would work in his favour, given the idea that he'd been ruminating over since waking up.

He opened up a list of his employees and filtered it to those without a current assignment. It took thirty minutes to find a dozen men with the necessary skills, and despite it being before six in the morning, he began making phone calls.

An hour later, ten of the twelve had accepted his offer. He hadn't been able to get in touch with the other two, so he searched for two alternates and had them on board by half past seven.

With the team assembled, he searched the internet for flights leaving Heathrow in the next four hours. That would give him enough leeway to let everyone pack what they needed and get to the airport at the prearranged time.

After making a fresh cup of coffee, he called his doctor and asked for an urgent letter to confirm that he was fit to fly. It wouldn't do to turn up at the airport with his injuries and be refused permission to board the plane. He arranged to pick it up from the surgery on his way to the airport, and then brought up his contact list. He found the number for a former colleague who now worked for a game reserve just a couple of hundred kilometres from Malundi's eastern border.

Frederick Rickard had served with the Rhodesian SAS until it had been disbanded in 1980, when the country became Zimbabwe. Prior to that he'd had a secondment to 22 SAS and as a consequence, he regularly attended the annual parties. Gray had been introduced to him at one such event a decade earlier, and they'd hit it off immediately.

Freddie was a likeable sort. His skin was like a chamois leather that had been hung out to dry, the result of years spent in the African sun. Add to that a facial injury he'd sustained during the Rhodesian Bush War in the late seventies, and Freddie always gave you the impression that he was smiling. Gray had never taken up the offer to go and visit him, but he was sure Freddie wouldn't hold that against him, especially in his time of need.

He dialled Rickard and waited for the answer.

'Freddie, it's Tom Gray.'

'Tom! Good to hear from you. How the devil are you?'

They reminisced for a couple of minutes before Gray got round to business.

'What are you flying these days?' he asked.

'Still got the Dakota,' Rickard told him.

'That old heap?' Gray joked, though he was glad his friend hadn't downsized. Short of chartering a small airliner, the ancient turboprop would be ideal for his purposes. He'd seen pictures of Freddie's Douglas C-47—or Dakota, to use its RAF designation— and it had been an old crate a decade earlier. He didn't want to imagine what state it was in now. He just hoped it had another half dozen flights left in it.

'She'll outlast me,' Rickard assured him, as if reading Gray's thoughts. 'What do you need her for?'

Gray outlined his plan, not bothering to mention that it was subject to change. Both knew how fluid it was on the battlefield, and even the best laid plans could turn to shit in a heartbeat. 'Obviously I'll pay well for your time.'

'No, you won't. I won't hear of it. For the last twenty years I've been playing chauffeur to privileged tourists. The closest I've come to danger was the time someone forgot to put ice in my whisky. For the opportunity to see a little excitement, I'll do it for expenses.'

'There'll be quite a few of those,' Gray said, and rattled off a list of items they'd need on arrival.

'The rigs won't be a problem,' Rickard assured him, 'but it's a bit short notice on the weapons. I'll do my best.'

'I can't tell you how much I appreciate this.'

'No worries. When will you be in country?'

'The flight lands at seven this evening,' Gray told him.

'I'll be waiting for you. We can be over Malundi by eleven.'

That was still fifteen hours away, and he hoped—no, he prayed—that his friends could hold out that long.

He thanked Rickard and put the phone down, a tinge of guilt clawing at him at the thought of betraying Harvey's trust. As promised, he had arranged a flight to take the men out, though he'd omitted the fact that he was going along with a dozen seasoned men, armed to the teeth.

That was a conversation he could put off until he got back, though, and it would be relatively easy to smooth out.

Explaining his plans to Vick was another matter.

Chapter Sixteen

Tuesday 8 October 2013

The Volkswagen Passat wasn't William Hart's preferred conveyance, though it was still a comfortable ride. One of the useful tips he'd had from Wallace was that his own vehicle was flagged on the police's automated number-plate recognition system, and every time he passed one of the cameras, his location would be noted along with the date and time. This was one journey he didn't want anyone knowing about, and so he'd borrowed the car from a local dealer. If stopped, he would claim to be on a test drive, a story the salesman would confirm.

He approached Oxford services an hour and a half after leaving his home in Sidcup, the ninety-mile journey a pain in the arse, but necessary. He didn't need Wallace to warn him about the dangers of talking business over the phone, even on a disposable handset and SIM card, so matters this delicate were usually handled in person.

It could have been worse, he thought. The man he was meeting was travelling down from Manchester, over a hundred and sixty miles to the north, not a particularly nice journey given the traffic that builds up as the M6 hits Birmingham.

Hart pulled off the M40 and followed the signs for the services, eventually pulling up in a remote spot as far from the entrance to the complex as possible. He turned the engine off, hoping that Paul Ainsworth didn't keep him waiting long.

He'd known Paul for a couple of years, ever since being introduced to him by Wallace. The detective's idea of using other muscle for messy jobs was a sensible precaution, and one that he and Ainsworth had adopted on rare occasions.

It wasn't the closest of relationships by any stretch of the imagination, but both men knew that having solid alibis when a hit went down was paramount. Having already been linked to the shop owner Hatcher, Hart needed to distance himself and his family from the upcoming violence. He'd already booked plane tickets for a couple of days away, and it would all be over by the time he and his two sons made the return journey from Gran Canaria.

Ainsworth arrived twenty minutes late. He pulled into the space next to the Volkswagen and got out, stretching his legs before joining Hart in his car.

'A'right, mate.'

Not many people got to address Hart in such a way, and fewer still were as young as Ainsworth. At thirty-five, he was twenty years Hart's junior, and wore designer jeans and a T-shirt which showed off the tattoos on his muscular neck. The rest of his frame was the same, the result of a daily workout in his home gym.

'Thanks for coming, Paul. I hope the journey wasn't too bad.'

Ainsworth ran his fingers through his close-cropped hair. 'Worth the pay we discussed, I reckon. Who's the target?'

'Whoever's in this house,' Hart said, handing Ainsworth the address of a property in the capital. He studied it for a moment and passed it back, and Hart was glad to see there were no concerns about whether the occupants included women or children. If there had been, Hart would have had serious doubts about Ainsworth's ability to see the job through, but it seemed both men were cut from the same moral cloth.

'What did you have in mind?'

'A fire,' Hart said. 'I understand you have someone who specialises.'

'He's not one of mine, but he's good. It'll cost you, though.'

Hart pulled an envelope from his jacket and passed it across. 'There's ten grand. That should cover it.'

'If you want a couple of crackheads to toss a petrol can through the window, yeah, that'll cover it. If you want guaranteed results, it'll be double.'

The cost wasn't an issue, but Hart was accustomed to getting what he wanted at the price he specified. He knew that Ainsworth was going to take a huge cut for himself, just as he himself had done on their other joint ventures, so he couldn't complain on that score. Still, it rankled, but in order to get the job done and preserve their relationship, Hart agreed to have another ten thousand pounds delivered once the house and occupants had been torched.

'When do you need it?'

'Any time over the weekend,' Hart said. 'I'm taking the boys away for a few days and want it done before we get back.'

Ainsworth assured him the timescale wasn't an issue, and they shook hands.

'See you next time, Paul.'

Ainsworth returned to his own car to start the journey north, while Hart lit a cigarette, glad that the matter had been solved. Someone else would take over the shop lease once Hatcher was gone, and he hoped they were more receptive to his offer. In the meantime, he would be losing out on twelve hundred pounds a month, a fact that irked the hell out of him as he started the car.

The fact that people would be hurt or killed didn't faze him at all.

Tom Gray sat towards the back of the Boeing 747-400, flicking through the channels on the miniature TV screen in an effort to find something that would take his mind off the conversation with his wife.

As expected, Vick hadn't been enamoured with the idea of him gallivanting off to take part in a civil war. It had quickly turned into their first ever fight, and gone downhill from there.

He was a very attentive husband, always letting her know if he was going to be late, and he didn't go out drinking with his buddies every night. His whole world revolved around his wife and daughter, and so when he saw Vick flare up for the first time, it had come as a shock.

No objects were thrown, but she'd made it quite clear how angry she was at the idea. He'd promised her that his role would be purely observational, given his current condition, but that hadn't mollified her. Instead, she'd come out with the remark that stung the most.

'You think more of your mates than you do your own family.'

He hadn't known how to handle that. It had come across like a slap in the mouth, his face the epitome of shock.

'Vick, these aren't some drinking buddies! It's Sonny and Len, the people who saved our lives!'

'Then send someone else!' Vick had screamed. 'Why do you have to go?'

Vick had stormed off to the bathroom, locking the door and refusing to come out until he'd left the house. He'd briefly wondered if he could coordinate the operation from home, but dismissed the idea. He couldn't get a proper feel for the situation if he were sitting on the end of a phone two thousand miles from the action.

And besides, he owed them.

They'd risked their lives extracting him from the Philippine jungle, and hadn't batted an eyelid when asked to go back in and rescue Vick, too. That kind of altruistic bond didn't warrant sending in less experienced men in his stead.

The team he'd hastily assembled were all seasoned veterans of the Regiment, but none had made senior NCO or led a team in battle. The majority, however, had at least seen their fair share of action. While he knew they would all do their job, he had to be there to ensure they did it right. Which, sadly, left him winging his way to the middle of Africa while his wife stewed at home.

He hoped that her reaction had been due to the short notice he'd given her, and that once he got back, she'd have had time to reflect on his words and realise how much they owed Sonny and Smart.

If not, then he was going to have a few difficult weeks ahead.

The flight attendants came round to collect the remnants of the in-flight meal, signalling their imminent arrival. Forty-five minutes later, the aircraft juddered as they touched down, the engines howling as the thrust reversers were deployed to arrest their speed. Another few minutes saw them park and the steps were wheeled up to the side of the plane.

The temperature was in the mid-twenties centigrade as they made their way across the tarmac, with heavy, charcoal-coloured cloud cover promising a downpour within the hour. The terminal building looked like it could do with a coat of paint at the very least, and Gray mentally marked the country off his holiday destination list as he wiped the sweat from his face.

Customs was cleared without hassle, and as they had no checked luggage, they hit the arrivals area less than thirty minutes after landing.

Suits mingled with the colourful local garb, and in the melee Gray saw Rickard waiting for them.

'Christ, Tom! Been bad-mouthing the wife again?'

Gray put his hand to the shiner surrounding his eye and forced a smile. 'Not far off. I'll explain later.'

Rickard led them through the terminal and down a corridor leading to the charter area.

'I'll skip the intros, if that's okay.'

'No problem,' Rickard assured him.

'Did you manage to get everything?' Gray asked.

'I borrowed the rigs from a local diving school, so bring them back if you can. As for the rifles, all I could get on such short notice was eight AKs and some M4s.'

At least all of his men would be armed, Gray thought, even though he would have preferred them all to be using the same ammunition. The AK-47s used 7.62 mm rounds as opposed to the 5.56 mm carbine, so they wouldn't be interchangeable.

'They're in the hold, along with a hundred and fifty rounds apiece and some cleaning kits.'

'Thanks a million,' said Gray. 'I don't know what we'd have done without you. Have we got time to check everything over before we take off?' he asked, as they reached the end of the hallway, where a bored-looking security guard checked Rickard's paperwork and verified the number of passengers before waving them through the gate.

'I've got a slot booked for twenty minutes from now, but you're going to have to do your equipment checks on board, for obvious reasons.'

They rounded a corner, and the men saw their transport for the first time.

'Fuckin' 'ell, Tom!' one of Gray's men laughed. 'When you said it was old, I didn't know you meant as old as time itself! Who built this? Methuselah's granddad?'

'I bet the flight manual's written in Latin,' another quipped.

Gray put up a hand for silence, but Rickard took it all in with a smile. 'I'm used to it, Tom,' he said, turning to the rest of the team, 'and I think I've found the two volunteers I need to stoke the boiler during the flight.'

'The pilot would only fly this if it was safe, or he had a death wish,' Gray said, 'and Freddie's about the least suicidal fellow I know. Let's move it, people, the clock's ticking.'

They climbed aboard through the rear door and took in the spartan interior. The aircraft had originally boasted twenty-one seats in seven rows of three, but the centre column had long since been removed, leaving a fairly wide centre aisle by modern passenger plane standards.

The interior stank, with the body odour of a thousand baked tourists mingling with oil and jet fuel, though Gray knew his men had put up with much worse in their time. The smell would prove nothing more than a minor distraction.

Once the last man had boarded, Rickard secured the door and removed a metal floor panel to reveal a storage area filled with everything they needed for the mission, even down to the disruptive-pattern camouflage combat gear. One of the men began handing out knives, rifles and munition boxes and they broke into fours, with one squad cleaning, another loading the magazines and the last repacking the parachutes Rickard had brought along: there was no way any of them were going to trust someone else to do that crucial job properly.

While the men readied their kit, Gray powered up the satellite phone and hit the number for Smart's handset.

'Tom?'

'Len, glad you're still with us.'

'Only just. We've had a dozen contacts today, and everyone's shagged.'

'What's your location?'

Gray waited while Smart extracted his GPS and read off the coordinates, then entered them into his phone. He also marked the position on a map and showed it to Rickard, who was completing his pre-flight checks. The pilot told him they could be over the area in three hours, and Gray passed the message on.

'How far do you think you can travel in that time?' Gray asked, looking to establish a rendezvous point.

'About twenty-five yards. We've reached a plateau and we're gonna hold the high ground until you get here. We've been on the go for nearly thirty-six hours, and the locals have been running on empty since midday.'

Smart explained how their pursuers had been engaging on and off for the last twelve hours, harrying them every time they stopped for a rest, though never sending more than a handful of men into the fight.

'It's like they're trying to run us into the ground, or they're pushing us towards another unit waiting up ahead.'

'It could be both,' Gray agreed. 'I agree, form a perimeter and wait for us. What's the area like?'

'Full canopy overhead, dense on the ground, a gentle slope leading up to the plateau. I've got Sonny scoping out the land beyond that.'

That ruled out jumping straight to their location. HALO jumps—High Altitude, Low Opening—were tricky at the best of times, but attempting them at night and landing amongst tall trees was a clusterfuck waiting to happen.

'In that case, we stick to Plan A. We'll take the airport, then move south to join up with you. We'll be there as soon as we can.'

Gray signed off and pulled out his mobile phone as he considered dialling Harvey's number, but thought better of it. Getting the latest intel from the Africa desk would be nice, but having to explain why he was about to violate Malundi airspace with an armed team suddenly made the information seem less urgent. He turned the phone off and slipped it into his pocket, knowing it would be useless once they got to their destination.

Gray's team went about their business for another five minutes, rotating their duties until each man had everything they needed for the mission ahead.

'Guys,' Gray said, 'hand over your passports. You know the drill: we don't want any ID falling into the wrong hands. You'll get them back on the return trip.'

His team complied, and Gray asked Rickard to stow the documents safely.

A couple of minutes later, the engines caught with a splutter, followed by a deafening roar as the Pratt and Whitney R-2000 engines came to life. Rickard was granted clearance by the tower, and they taxied down the runway, the aircraft almost shaking itself to pieces before the forward momentum finally allowed it to climb into the dark, rain-filled night.

Chapter Seventeen

Tuesday 8 October 2013

Len Smart's eyes shifted constantly in an effort to stave off sleep, but it was a losing battle. Being awake for almost forty hours was the major factor, but coupled with the ebb and flow of adrenaline from numerous exchanges with the enemy, his body was pleading with him to shut down, if only for a few minutes.

Behind him, in the makeshift camp, all were sleeping, oblivious to the rain that seeped through the treetops overhead. The Malundi soldier to Smart's right nodded involuntarily, while Johnny Okeke to his left remained, thankfully, semi-alert.

Of the fifty troops they'd been tasked with training, only a handful had shown anything near the qualities needed for a life in an elite unit, Okeke being one of them. Hansi Cisse was another, though his performance had clearly been hampered by the anxiety stemming from the disappearance of his son a few days earlier. Smart had never married, so he couldn't imagine how Cisse was feeling, but he guessed the loss was weighing heavily.

Could he have carried on, as Hansi had done? Unlikely, Smart thought. His instinct would have been to abandon everything else and find the child at all costs, one more example of how their respective cultures differed.

It wasn't so much that life in the region had little value, but kidnappings and murders—crimes which would have caused outrage back home—were a lot more common here. Perhaps the locals were desensitised, he mused, in the same way that he didn't dwell on the government taking a chunk of tax from his monthly pay packet.

He thought about Tom Gray and how he'd reacted when his son had been killed. Smart wasn't sure he'd have gone through with anything so elaborate. More likely, he'd have just taken the killer down a dark alley and exacted his revenge. As he envisaged what he would have done in Tom's place, his mind effortlessly transitioned from daydream to sleep, the efforts of the last two days finally proving too much.

He didn't know how long he was out for, but when the outgoing bullet left Okeke's rifle Smart came instantly awake, already scanning the darkness for the threat.

He saw nothing, the only sound and movement coming from the rain as it danced on giant leaves.

'What are you shooting at?' he whispered over to Okeke.

'I thought I saw something . . . '

Smart knew he was taking potshots at shadows, and under the circumstances it was understandable.

'Just keep it tight, Johnny. Only fire when you have a certain target.'

The dim illumination from his watch told Smart that he'd slept for barely ten minutes, but that was enough to clear away the cobwebs.

For the moment, at least.

He prayed for the god of war to send Tom Gray a tailwind, then hunkered down to sit out the rest of his shift.

After suffering the longest hour of his life, Smart was finally relieved by Sonny Baines.

'Get some shuteye,' Sonny said. 'Tom'll be here in a few hours and I expect we'll be moving out again.'

Smart nodded and shuffled backwards, away from the edge of the plateau, dragging his kit with him. He found a relatively dry spot underneath a sizable spread of leaves and put his head on his backpack, expecting sleep to come swiftly.

It wouldn't.

He tossed around, trying to get as comfortable as possible, but even though he tried to clear his mind to help his body shut down, something stirred in his gut. He wanted to put it down to a lack of food, bit it was more than that; a sense of foreboding, something sinister on the horizon.

After ten minutes, he gave up and pulled the Kindle reading device from his pack. He made sure the backlight was turned off and pulled out his torch, the red filter ensuring the light didn't travel too far.

He was engrossed in a story when Carl Levine walked past on his way to relieve Johnny.

'Christ, Len, is this really the time to be getting your Tolkien fix?'

'I can't sleep,' Smart whispered. 'Something doesn't feel right out here, I guess. Besides, there's no hobbits in this one.'

'What you reading this time?'

'*Take No More* by Seb Kirby. I'd hate to die without knowing how it ends.'

'So what's got you spooked?'

'I don't know,' Smart admitted. 'It's probably just fatigue.'

'Well, try and get your head down,' Levine said, and wandered off to give Okeke a couple of hours' rest.

⌣

'What do you mean, they've stopped?'

Sese Obi squeezed the phone in his hand, threatening to crush the tiny handset as his rage grew by the second. Kgosi tried to defend himself, but the excuses fell on deaf ears. Obi was seeing his plan fall apart, as hour after hour, his advance teams were reporting in with news of increasing casualties as they tried to make inroads into the capital. What he really needed was Kgosi and his men up there offering support, not floundering in a wasteland as they struggled to wipe out a handful of soldiers and some civilians.

As Obi listened to his lieutenant explain how they'd lost the high ground and were unable to get close enough to inflict damage without depleting their own ranks, he wondered how he could have misread Kgosi so completely. As a thief, he was very good, with a brutal streak and distinct lack of compassion. But it seemed that car-jacking middle-aged women marked the limits of his tactical ability and bravado. Facing a real enemy for the first time, he was showing his true colours.

Much as he'd love to leave the man to languish in the jungle, he couldn't afford to. Unplanned losses had reduced his fighting capability, starting with guards at the electricity power station putting up more resistance than initially expected. It was a similar story at the water plant and major railway stations. Reinforcements had been sent to patch the holes in the ranks, in expectation of Kgosi forming up with the main spearhead.

That plan now lay in ruins, and the longer they delayed the final push to crush the Agbi government, the more time there was to dig in and create impenetrable defences, preventing him from reaching his goal.

Obi put the phone down and grabbed a map, checking the distance between his own position and Kgosi. He once again contemplated sending troops down to assist him—in addition to Fene Adebola's boy army—but there wasn't time. Besides, there were more than enough soldiers on site already. It was just the leadership that was lacking.

'Get your men to surround the enemy to the south, east and west,' he told Kgosi, 'but avoid contact. I want you to meet up with Fene a mile north of your current position in two hours. He will explain what I have planned.'

He stabbed at the phone, then called up Fene's number.

Fene was a no-nonsense individual who made Kgosi seem like a choirboy. Unlike the lieutenant, Fene had seen his share of conflict over the years. This mission would be straightforward for him.

'Fene,' he said, once the call connected, 'Kgosi has created a mess and I need you to clear it up for me.'

Fene listened to the instructions and agreed that he could be in place at the allotted time.

'The agreement was for me to deliver the children, nothing more. This will cost you an extra ten thousand.'

It was a princely sum in a poor country, but once Obi was running it and funnelling public coffers into his own accounts, such an amount wouldn't even bear consideration.

'The money is yours,' Obi promised. 'When you get there, I want you to give Kgosi a message.'

As he relayed his orders, he could almost hear Fene smiling.

The street was virtually empty as Rob Harman drove down it in the stolen BMW. The false plates were cloned from an identical vehicle registered in Newcastle, so there was very little chance of running into the owner of the real vehicle in this particular London suburb.

Soft light shone through a dozen front windows as the residents settled in for an evening in front of the television, heavy drapes drawn to protect them from the onslaught of winter. Harman eased slowly past the target house, the engine purring gently as he looked for anything that could impede his mission. The gate looked relatively new, but he would test that later. Beyond it, he was glad to see nothing to impede his access to the rear of the property, as had been the case when he'd first scoped the premises on his phone's Street Map application. It was conceivable that the occupants might have installed a gate since the image was taken, but thankfully he could see all the way to the end of the modest garden, light from a neighbour's kitchen aiding his reconnaissance.

A woman glanced into the moving car as she ambled down the street, but her gaze fell away a split-second later. Dressed in a cheap black suit and sporting a short, black wig, Harman looked like just another sales rep, cruising for a sale. Unlike many other career criminals, Harman shunned body piercings and tattoos, preferring the ability to blend in to any environment without drawing attention to himself. It had kept him out of trouble thus far, and he intended for that run to continue.

Satisfied that there were no physical barriers to entry, he cruised to the end of the street and turned onto the main road, heading for the wine bar he'd seen earlier. After parking in a side street, he collected his briefcase and locked the car, walking the short distance to the front entrance. Inside, gentle rock music was barely audible over the myriad conversations, and he ordered a white wine spritzer before finding a quiet corner with an empty table. He opened the briefcase and removed some papers and brochures, creating the impression that he was merely another worker bee grabbing a little sustenance before the journey home.

Patrons came and went, but Harman nursed his drink and alternated between his phone and the paperwork until closing time, when he ambled back to his car. Although it was already after eleven in the evening, he decided to wait another couple of hours before getting a closer look at the target.

Mina Hatcher brought two cups of hot chocolate into the living room and placed one in front of Vick, who was dabbing at her eyes.

'I can't believe I said that to him,' Vick sniffed, fighting back another bout of tears. 'I love him, but I was just so angry.'

Mina put a comforting arm around her niece. 'He loves you too, Vick. I'm sure it'll all be forgotten when he gets back.'

'But what if he doesn't come back?'

Vick gave in to her emotions, then, sobbing on her aunt's shoulder. She'd heard Tom pack his bag and pop into their daughter's room before leaving, presumably to give her a farewell kiss, but Vick had refused his last-ditch attempt to talk it through. Instead, he'd left, promising to be back in a couple of days, and ten minutes later she'd emerged in tears, her initial anger having been replaced by concern.

She knew Tom was damn good at what he did, but after all he'd been through, she thought his days of doing anything more reckless than driving in the capital were over. For him to suddenly announce the *ad hoc* mission had thrown her completely, and it wasn't until he'd closed the front door that the revelation dawned; it was a fear of losing him that was steering her emotions, not anger.

She didn't hate him for choosing his friends over family; she just didn't want him putting himself in harm's way. While appreciating the debt they all owed to Sonny and Len, she hadn't envisaged repaying those debts by having her husband march off to another war zone. Their daughter needed a father, and there was none more loving than Tom Gray.

'You said he was just going to oversee things,' Mina said. 'I'm sure he'll stay out of harm's way.'

Vick nodded, hoping her aunt was right. She'd taken Melissa to stay with Mina and Ken after Tom had left, unable to face the coming days alone. The move was partly for the company, but more important was having another wife's perspective.

'Go and get some sleep. You'll be no good to Melissa if you don't get your rest.'

The day had taken its toll, and Vick was up well past her usual ten o'clock bedtime. She drank her chocolate, kissed her aunt and uncle, and climbed the stairs to the spare bedroom, where Melissa slept peacefully in her bassinette. She spent a few minutes stroking her daughter's hair, whispering that daddy would be back soon.

When she eventually lay down, she said a silent prayer for Tom, and the tears came flooding back.

Harman had spent the last hour and a half wandering the area, scoping the house from the back as well as the front. The rear garden backed onto a school playing field and he'd spent time in the short grass looking for an ingress point. The old, wooden fence was too high to jump over and too flimsy to climb. Going in that way would be far too noisy, so he settled for waiting in the field until the last of the house lights were extinguished. Once darkness fell, he took a long, slow walk to the school gates, then headed down the road and turned into the street where the target house, like all the others, sat silent, streetlights the only illumination.

He carefully pushed the gate open, glad to find that it didn't protest at his entry, and crept to the rear of the house. There were two ground floor windows and another two on the first floor, and all were single-glazed wooden sashes. That would afford him easier access than double-glazing, and a plan formed as he peered through one of them into the kitchen. A half-full ashtray sat next to the sink, a welcome sign that one or more of the occupants was a smoker: he would take advantage of that to make the fire look like an accident.

Harman was about to wrap up for the evening when a faint sound came from one of the upstairs windows; moments later faint light illuminated the curtains as the bedroom door was opened. The sound got louder until he recognised it as a crying child, obviously very young. He quickly dismissed it as irrelevant, his anti-social personality disorder giving him a distinct lack of moral conscience. That he would be endangering the life of a newborn baby didn't bother him one iota.

When the sound finally died down, he crept out to the front of the building, and after a quick scan of the area, walked out of the garden and back to his car.

After programming his return journey into the satellite navigation system, Harman set off for the long drive north, his work for the evening done. He would be back in a couple of days to execute the mission and earn his five-grand payday.

Chapter Eighteen

Tuesday 8 October 2013

'We're ten minutes out,' Rickard shouted over the roar of the engines.

Tom Gray nodded and went back into the hold to inform the team, a couple of whom were dozing despite the buffeting the plane was taking in the stormy sky. He passed the message on and they woke the sleepers before checking each other's kit, making sure all clasps and ties were firmly done up.

Gray wasn't sporting a rig. As he'd promised Vick, he would manage the operation from afar. He wanted to go in, there was no doubt about it, but his rib injury would take some time to heal, and the last thing he wanted to do was to exacerbate it with a parachute jump.

Gray had one of the men open the rear door, which sent a blast of chilled air into the cabin. The troopers lined up near the opening, the first man with his foot on the edge, hands gripping the frame as he looked out into the void, hoping to see the landing zone. According to the satellite view on Gray's smartphone application, it was a small area roughly a mile from the airport, a clearing just big enough to temper some of the danger associated with a night-time jump in tree country.

Gray stood to the side of the door, his eyes on Freddie as he awaited the go signal. When it came, Gray slapped the first soldier on the back and watched him disappear into the darkness, closely followed by eleven other similarly clad figures.

One after the other, they darted down through the rain towards the jungle below, and a part of Gray wanted to be among their number, but he quickly shrugged the thought aside and closed the door before taking the co-pilot seat next to Rickard.

'How long can we stay up here?' Gray asked.

The pilot checked the fuel gauge and made a quick mental calculation. 'We've got three hours' worth,' he said. 'That's enough to get us back if we set off now, but I guess that isn't part of your plan.'

Gray shook his head.

'In that case, your men have that long to clear the airport. If they can't do it in that time, we're in for a hairy landing.'

Gray was confident it wouldn't come to that. The men he'd chosen were all experienced with a 'chute and would hardly break a sweat tabbing a mile to the target. That left plenty of time to scope the airstrip out and take the bad guys down. In an ideal world, they'd have had real-time satellite coverage of the airstrip to get an idea of enemy numbers and their defences, but in the SAS they'd learned to adapt to situations and make do as best they could.

His main concern was refuelling. If they didn't have the ability to top the plane up, they would be stuck on the ground.

'Do they have fuel bowsers at the airport?' he asked Rickard.

'I was wondering the same thing myself,' the pilot said. 'We need to find out soon, otherwise it'll be too late to head back.'

That meant waiting for the men to get eyes-on wasn't an option. Gray asked if they could do a fly-past. It wasn't the ideal course of action, as it would let the enemy know they had company, but the alternative was leaving his men to fend for themselves.

'There's a set of bins in the locker,' Rickard told him. 'If we can do this without getting too close, all the better.'

Gray rummaged through the small compartment behind the cockpit and found the binoculars, a decent set with *Steiner* stamped on the leather case. They were older than Gray himself, but Rickard had obviously looked after them.

Gray returned to the cockpit and Rickard edged the nose down as he banked towards the clearing.

'I'll stay a couple of miles out. Any closer and they'll hear us.'

Gray put the glasses to his eyes and stared out of the window as they paralleled the runway, but all he could make out were vague, dark shapes against a black backdrop.

'We need to do another run,' he told the pilot, 'closer this time. I can't make anything out from this distance, and the rain isn't helping.'

Rickard eased the yoke to starboard and circled back, halving the distance to the target and dropping a thousand feet to give his passenger a better view. The manoeuvre used up precious minutes and fuel, but Gray wanted absolute confirmation before he would even consider bugging out and heading out of the country.

Rickard began the next run and Gray squinted through the lenses, trying to distinguish between bush and man-made object. As they got closer, he could finally see the distinct outline of a vehicle, followed by another and another, though none looked like a fuel truck. He saw something that might have been a stack of drums, and as he focused on it he saw pinpricks of light twinkling in the darkness.

A second later, the shells from the .50 calibre mounted machine gun reached the plane and began shredding the main cabin, slowly walking their way towards the cockpit.

'Get us out of here!' Gray screamed, but Rickard was way ahead of him, throwing the aircraft towards the treetops, ignoring screaming protestations from the engines and howls of wind coming through the punctured fuselage. They lost a thousand feet in a matter of seconds, and the pilot struggled to level out the angle, yanking back on the wheel with all he was worth. He screamed for Gray to grab the co-pilot wheel and help, but the hydraulics feeding the ailerons had been severely damaged, and even with both of them straining every sinew, the jungle loomed ever larger.

'Pull up, you stubborn bitch!'

Both men were purple in the face, and Gray's cracked ribs protested angrily at the exertion, but the nose finally began to point away from the ground and level out.

'I have the controls,' Rickard said, a polite way of telling Gray to get his hands off the wheel. Any over-compensation at this point would send them heading vertical and into a fatal stall.

Gray sat back and exhaled the breath he'd been holding for the last thirty seconds, but warning lights in the cockpit told him they weren't out of the jungle yet. To compound their woes, the right engine coughed and threw out a shower of sparks, closely followed by a trail of burning oil. The plane juddered in response as Rickard fought to control her.

'Grab the 'chute, Tom. It's under your seat. The old girl's only got a couple of minutes left in her.'

'Okay, try and gain some height and level her up so we can jump.'

'There's only one 'chute.' Rickard was still wrestling with the controls, trying to get what he could out of his injured aircraft before she met the ground for the last time. 'Get it strapped on. You haven't got long.'

'No way. We're going together or not at all. Tie the wheel off and let's go.'

'It isn't that simple. If I take my feet off the rudder, she'll yaw to the right and roll in a heartbeat. You go, now!'

Gray wasn't in the mood to accept defeat so easily, and searched the cabin for something to jam against the controls. He found a tool kit in the locker but it wasn't heavy enough by half. He continued the search, opening a second compartment but with no luck.

'Tom, grab yourself a rifle and go! You're out of time!'

A rifle.

Gray ran to the rear of the cabin and yanked the smuggler's hatch open. There was one rifle left, along with a set of combat fatigues and a few magazines. He left those, but carried the rest back to the cockpit, where he began tying one end of the trousers to the co-pilot wheel and fed the other end through a leather strap on the side of the cockpit. He then jammed the barrel of the Kalashnikov onto the rudder pedal and wedged the stock under the seat.

The controls secured, he threw on the parachute and loosened the shoulder straps so that they left a couple of inches of play.

'That'll hold her for a few seconds,' Gray shouted. 'When we get to the door, I want you to put your arms through these gaps and hang on tight. Once we're out, wrap your legs around mine and squeeze for all you're worth.'

Rickard nodded, and Gray pulled him out of the seat and dragged him towards the rear door. He opened it to the expected buffeting, the rain soaking him instantly.

'Hold tight,' he ordered, and Rickard fed his arms through the webbing and clasped the opposite straps tightly.

'You realise this doesn't mean we're engaged, or anything.'

Gray wondered how Rickard could joke under the circumstances, but there wasn't time to ask.

'Once we're out, wrap your legs around mine. I'm gonna pop the 'chute straight away.'

Rickard nodded, and Gray mouthed a short countdown. On one, they leapt into the darkness, and Gray waited until Freddie's legs were clenched around his before reaching for the release handle.

The sudden deceleration threatened to rip Rickard free from him, but the elder man managed to maintain his grip. Rickard's grimace must have matched his own, Gray thought, as the pain in his ribs almost brought tears to his eyes. Away to the right, the Dakota flew onwards, her damaged engine now spewing fire as aviation fuel met red-hot metal.

'You okay?' Rickard shouted, and got a brief nod in reply.

Gray forced himself to focus on the jump instead of his ribs, and he scanned the ground for a suitable landing zone. Unfortunately, all he saw was foliage rushing towards them.

'This is going to be rough,' he warned, trying to steer the rig away from the taller of the mahogany trees. Seconds later, they hit, thin branches clawing at them as they descended through towards the jungle floor. The branches got larger closer to the ground, and Gray jarred his coccyx against one as thick as his thigh, sending a shudder up his spine and a streak of searing pain into his skull.

Thankfully, their journey ended a second later as the 'chute snagged in the crown of the tree, leaving them dangling three metres above the sodden ground. Rickard extricated himself and dropped the final distance, then waited until Gray did the same. Far away from them, the plane finally gave in to gravity, a hollow *crump* heralding the end of her ultimate flight.

Both men stretched and felt for signs of serious damage but declared themselves good to go. The question was: where?

Gray pulled out his satellite phone and toggled to the GPS view. It showed their current location, and he brought up the last entry to see how far they were from Smart and the others.

'They're four clicks in that direction,' he told Rickard. 'Reckon you can handle it?'

The older man smiled. 'Just a walk in the jungle. Lead on!'

'Will do, but I've got to make a couple of phone calls first.'

Smart woke with a start as the phone in his breast pocket vibrated against his chest. Realising that he wasn't actually having a heart attack, he pulled the handset out and stabbed at the green button, his eyes still bleary from the little sleep he'd managed to grab.

'Tom, what's the latest?'

'The lads dropped successfully at the airport, but soon after that we lost the plane. There's no point taking the strip now, so I've told them to RV on me and we'll head in to meet you guys.'

'Is everyone okay?' Smart asked.

'Yeah, we're fine,' Gray assured him, 'but be prepared for a hell of a walk home.'

'We'll cross that bridge later. Which direction are you coming in from?'

Gray explained the route they planned to take, and Smart promised to have a couple of scouts on the perimeter to guide them in.

'Okay, we'll be there in about two hours.'

Gray signed off and Smart passed the news on to the rest of the team. Sonny volunteered to do the meet and greet when the time came, and they all settled back into their defensive positions.

Smart knew that without the plane, getting the civilians to safety wasn't going to be easy. It was at least twenty-five kilometres to the nearest friendly border, no mean trek given that they hadn't had a proper rest or meal in over a day. The soldiers had been on the go for twice as long, which made it extremely hard to maintain the required level of concentration. Reactions would be compromised, meaning they could easily stumble into an ambush if the point man didn't spot the danger signs in time.

He decided it would be best to let Tom's team take over those duties, and hopefully allow them to get a few hours of sleep once they were out of danger. He expected the enemy were doing just that, as there hadn't been any sign of them for a few hours.

He considered the possibility that they might have packed up and gone home, but knew they wouldn't be so lucky.

'What took you so long?'

Kgosi stared up at the huge figure of Fene, unable to tell whether the big man was joking or deadly serious. After the long march through rain-soaked jungle, Kgosi was in no mood for banter.

'We had to keep well clear of the Agbi, that's what took so long. Would you prefer we walk straight through their camp?'

Fene smiled and urged Kgosi towards the group of boys, who were sitting in silent expectation, seemingly oblivious to the rain and clearly hoping their next hit of whoonga wasn't long in coming.

'Men,' Fene addressed them, 'this is Kgosi. He is the leader of all the soldiers in the region.'

The children looked at the lieutenant, not really knowing what to say, simply praying it didn't drag on too long while they waited for their chemical relief.

Fene faced his counterpart, the smile still on his face. 'Would I prefer that you just walk through the enemy camp?'

Kgosi was both confused and annoyed, wanting simply to get some rest before the next engagement.

'Yes,' Fene said, 'I would have preferred that. Sadly, that would have taken courage, something you obviously lack.'

Kgosi wasn't accustomed to being humiliated, especially in front of a group of children. His hand went for the pistol he carried in a belt holster, but Fene was already on the move. The tall man's right hand went to the handle of his machete and he pulled it out, swinging it in a wide arc towards Kgosi's head.

For a moment, nothing happened. All seemed frozen in time, until a trickle of blood turned into a ribbon that ran across Kgosi's throat. The head slid forward and dropped to the ground, closely followed by the former soldier's torso.

'Not even leaders can be excused for cowardice,' Fene told the boys, before turning to address the men the corpse had once commanded.

'That message came from Sese Obi himself,' he told them. 'Does anyone want to question it?'

As he expected, the men were content to remain silent, no-one wanting to suffer the same fate. Fene gave them another moment to take in the penalty for failure, then explained their mission.

⌣

The trooper sank to one knee and held up a clenched fist, causing the party to stop in their tracks, weapons at the ready. Gray eased his way forward, his civilian clothes looking out of place among those of his uniformed colleagues.

'What have we got?'

The soldier pointed up the track, where the man on point was making a similar gesture. When Gray reached him, he could see the problem. An armed man was standing fifty yards away, his back to them as he smoked a hand-rolled cigarette. Another walked into view, their demeanour suggesting that neither of them expected to see action any time soon, confident in their roles as hunter rather than hunted.

Gray could make out more figures, most sitting on the ground, only their heads visible. It certainly wasn't a scouting party, judging by the numbers, and that meant Len and the others were sandwiched between two armed units.

Gray tapped the point man on the shoulder and indicated that they should both fall back, and they quietly slid back to the rest of the team. He shared the situation with the rest of them and asked for ideas, then called Smart to let him know the situation.

'Len,' he said, without preamble, 'you've got a large force to your north, just over a click away.'

'I guess that settles it,' Smart said. 'We were thinking of heading for the eastern border, and they've just left us with no other option.'

'Sounds like a plan. How soon can you get moving?'

'Give us five minutes.'

Gray checked their respective positions on the GPS, then read off some coordinates.

'We'll meet you there in thirty minutes.'

His team had come up with the idea of playing rear gunners, holding off any attacks with a series of ambushes. It was the obvious choice, short of teleporting back to England, so they set off at a pace that would allow them to stick to the schedule while keeping an eye out for trouble.

'Let's get moving,' Smart said. 'We've got half an hour to cover a kilometre and meet up with Tom and the boys.'

Everyone began gathering what few possessions they had and quietly formed a tired line. The rain had finally relented, the only plus in what was an otherwise miserable situation. Sonny took the lead, while Smart, Campbell and Levine took up the rear: if they were attacked again, that was the direction it would likely come from.

Aware that the majority of the group were shattered, Sonny didn't push them too hard. It was a gentle stroll as far as he was concerned, though he had little doubt some would find it taxing. That couldn't be helped, and he was certain that in the weeks to come, their present discomfort would be forgotten, replaced with the relief at still being on the planet.

He hoped.

The general consensus among the Malundians was that this was an invasion from the south, the Kanto people following through on previous threats to take back the land stolen from them when the country split. Who was leading them was anyone's guess, but it was highly unlikely that the invaders would be leaving any time soon. Their plan was obviously to take over the country, which meant the Agbi villagers he was transporting to the neighbouring country wouldn't be welcome back any time soon, if at all.

Despite their predicament, Sonny knew it wasn't their fight, and for once he was certain Tom Gray would agree. Saving a few villagers was one thing; defending an entire country was quite another.

His train of thought was interrupted as a round slammed into a tree a few inches from his head, and instantly the bush sparkled as AK-47s opened up on him. Sonny crouched and returned fire, keeping his head down while he sprinted back to the main group.

Smart ran forward to meet him and Sonny gave him a quick rundown.

'Looks like a dozen at most, but we're gonna have to break through if we want to make it to the border.'

Smart agreed, and called Campbell and Levine up from the rear. He also took Johnny Okeke to the side and explained that he was in charge of the group in their absence. 'Once we break through, I want these people running for all they're worth.'

'They cannot all run, Mr Len. Some are too old, and they have already been through a lot.'

'Then you either find people to carry them, or you leave them behind,' Smart said.

The sergeant nodded, respecting the decision. As soon as the four instructors disappeared towards the conflict, Okeke began moving the less able to the front of the queue and assigned them to some of the stronger villagers, explaining just what was required of them. His grave look told them all they needed to know about the price of failure.

Up ahead, the firefight intensified as the British soldiers engaged, their volleys infinitely more accurate and deadly. The short, aimed bursts quickly found targets, while the return fire grew increasingly wild. Sonny saw a shape appear from behind a tree, the muzzle of a rifle blinking as it sent rounds towards him, but a double-tap caught the man in first the throat, then the chin, dropping him before he even had time to register his own death.

The enemy sought deeper cover and continued the fight, spraying the kill zone in the frantic hope of hitting flesh. Smart's team were happy to let them do so, knowing that their ammunition would soon be exhausted.

As expected, the incoming chatter soon diminished to nothing, and the first of the enemy made a run for it, only to be cut down before he got a couple of yards. Others tried, mostly failing, but one managed to disappear into the bush. Seconds later, another two shots were heard from that direction, and the fight was over.

'Len, we're coming in!'

The sound of Tom Gray's voice drifted towards them, and Smart's team held their fire as some familiar faces emerged from the darkness.

Tom Gray was at their head, looking like a lost tourist in his slacks and white, long-sleeve shirt.

'I see you dressed for the occasion,' Smart quipped.

Sonny was more interested in Gray's recent injuries. He whistled long and low. 'Looks like someone set fire to your face and then beat the flames out with a shovel.'

'If only we could all be as handsome as you, Sonny.'

'I hate to be a party-pooper, but can we get the fuck out of here?'

Levine's words brought them back to the moment, and Smart began organising the defences.

'My guess is, they had us surrounded, so we can expect trouble from our flanks any time now,' he said, giving the new arrivals positions to the left and right of their current location. He sent Sonny to instruct the main party to move out, and asked more of Gray's team to take the lead.

'I'm guessing you're the pilot,' Campbell asked, seeing Rickard for the first time.

Gray made the introductions, adding how much help Freddie had brought to the rescue attempt, including the loss of his beloved plane.

'Not to worry,' Rickard smiled, 'I'll just write it off as expenses.'

The colour drained from Gray's face as he tried to calculate how much it would cost to replace the flying fossil, and Rickard saw the discomfort on his face.

'Don't worry, son, I'll leave you enough for a pot to piss in.'

Sonny returned at the head of the villagers and urged them to keep moving as he stopped to chat with his boss.

'They don't look good,' Gray observed as the people passed. Getting to the border was going to be a nightmare, and that went for everyone. Having been on the run for the best part of two days, the group already looked on the verge of collapse, and at the moment they faced the prospect of another three to four days of forced march through a jungle crawling with people intent on wiping them out.

'I think it's time we made a stand,' Sonny said, as if reading his mind.

'That makes the most sense,' Gray agreed. 'Choose the best twenty locals and send the rest on ahead with the main group. We'll dig in and show them what jungle warfare's all about.'

They were interrupted by a volley of fire from the north, the signal that the enemy were once again hot on their tail.

'Fetch the men who are staying and tell the others to clear out,' Gray said. He checked the magazine on the rifle he'd liberated from one of the enemy dead. Finding it half-empty, he took one from Sonny.

'Go,' Gray said, and ran to join the fight.

Chapter Nineteen

Wednesday 9 October 2013

Fene Adebola had been fifteen minutes away from ordering his men to advance on the enemy camp when the distant chatter of gunfire told him he'd missed his opportunity. The initial reports suggested the Agbi were trying to break out, so he'd sent everyone in the direction of the battle.

As he jogged towards the battleground at the head of a column of armed boys, he asked for the latest updates, and it soon became apparent that they were facing formidable defences. According to those already in the fight, they were facing more than a dozen foreigners, no doubt the occupants of the plane that had recently been shot down as it buzzed the airport. He was losing men at an alarming rate, but he was sure the foreigners would think twice when faced with his child army.

For years, boy soldiers had been used in armed conflicts throughout Africa, and few armies had any compunction about utilising them—or killing them, for that matter. In the West, however, Fene knew that a different mindset prevailed. Life had a higher value, and children were to be nurtured rather than annihilated. Western armies had strict rules of engagement and an inexhaustible list of battlefield taboos, but in Fene's mind there was only one way to win a war: kill the enemy. If that meant using rape and mutilation to instil fear, so be it. If boys were to be thrown into the kill zone before they reached puberty, all that mattered was that they make a contribution to the fight. In this case, their job was to force the enemy to either kill them, or run away.

He realised that after all the training, in some cases months of mental and physical conditioning, the vast majority of them would be dead before the sun rose.

Not that it mattered.

Finding new recruits wasn't all that difficult, and once he'd replenished the ranks he would once more offer them to the highest bidder. This time it had been Sese Obi, and perhaps, if the war went well, he would require some more. If not, there were plenty of others willing to pay a decent price for his services.

The sound of gunfire reached a crescendo as they approached the battle lines. Fene told the boys to wait while he consulted the men who were already engaged in the fight, and he returned a few minutes later. He told the boys the way had been cleared, and ordered them to advance on the enemy.

A few of the children obeyed him, but for the most part, the line held. Fear was etched on tear-stained faces, eyes pleading for him to change his mind, but Fene wasn't moved. He pulled out a pistol and shot the nearest child in the head.

'You will attack our enemy, or I will kill every single one of you, right here, right now!'

Despite their tender years, the children knew that the possibility of death was far more attractive than a certain bullet to the brain, and they began walking slowly into the darkness. Another shot rang from his pistol, and they picked up the pace, firing as they ran, each waiting for the inevitable bullet that would put an end to the nightmare.

When the firing stopped, Gray ordered the men to fall back to where Levine and the other half of the team had been busy preparing the first of the ambushes. They hadn't gone far when bullets once again began to thud into the trees around them, and they upped the pace to a sprint. It took a minute to reach the others, after crossing an open area the size of a football field.

The kill zone.

Gray stopped at the treeline and took the controls to the remaining sentinel from Sonny. He waited until the first of the attackers was visible across the open expanse, then he ran into cover, hoping to draw the enemy in for those lying in wait.

An armed, human wall jogged towards them, and Gray was glad to see the Malundian troops holding fire, ignoring the wild, incoming rounds and allowing the enemy to enter the danger zone. According to Smart, Okeke and his men hadn't exactly covered themselves in glory thus far. Perhaps they now realised that with the arrival of his team, one more fuck-up would see them relegated to carrying the elderly rather than defending their land.

Gray was seconds away from opening up when something struck him as wrong. The approaching figures were much smaller than he'd expected, and when the moon peeked through a gap in the clouds he could see that some had barely reached puberty.

They were well within range, and he had about ten seconds to make a decision.

'Tom,' Levine whispered into the comms unit, 'they're just kids!'

'Understood,' Gray replied. 'Wait one.'

Gray's training told him that anyone running towards them firing a weapon was a legitimate target, and during selection it had been suggested that they might one day face this very scenario. However, it was much easier to hypothesise about bringing down a child than it was to actually do it in the heat of battle. Then again, he realised that you didn't always get to choose your enemy, and if they were to leave this country alive, a tough decision had to be made.

Thoughts of his son Daniel came flooding, unbidden, into his mind. He would have been six years old now, if he hadn't been stolen from him so cruelly three years earlier, the incident that had driven Gray to actions no-one could ever have predicted. The pain he'd felt since Daniel's death was something he would wish on no man, so filling dozens of tiny body bags was not going to happen.

That said, they had to be stopped.

'Shoot low,' he advised the men. 'Go for the legs only.'

The troops adjusted their aim, lowering the sights a couple of feet from centre mass. Like Gray, many were uncomfortable with the idea of cutting kids down, but the weapons the boys were carrying were no toys, and it was self-preservation that caused the first of the rounds to fly from the men's rifles.

Youths began to collapse a split-second before Hansi Cisse could scream out his child's name.

'Nafari!'

Hansi stood and broke from the treeline, ignoring the hot metal whizzing around him as he ran towards his son. The boy stopped in his tracks, screaming children surrounding him, the gun held across his chest looking huge in his tiny hands. Hansi had tears in his eyes as he sprinted into the kill zone. More children fell as his friends laid down covering fire and he scooped his son into his arms and dropped to the ground, his body offering the child protection from the flying bullets.

The remaining children took flight. The sight of the huge soldier bearing down on them and the screams from the fallen enough to make them turn and run for their lives.

It was the worst decision they could have made.

Bullets flew from their own ranks as Fene kept his promise to kill those who fled from the battle. Unlike Gray's team, none of his men aimed to wound, and child after child dropped to the ground, their brief sojourn on the planet at an abrupt end. Those that remained standing were stuck in no man's land, with death facing them no matter which way they ran. On the journey into the area, Fene had told them tales of what would happen if they were ever captured by the enemy. Their limbs would be chopped off and their torsos thrown into open graves, to be buried alive; the more fortunate would have their stomachs split open and they would be hung by their own intestines.

All lies, but enough to deter them from capitulating.

With no real choice, they once again ran towards the enemy lines.

'Cease fire!' screamed Gray. 'Johnny, tell them to drop their weapons and we won't fire!'

Okeke conveyed the offer, but the boys kept coming, Hansi and his son running twenty yards ahead of them. The soldier and his boy made it safely back to the cover of the trees, thanks to some extremely inaccurate fire. Clearly, many of the children were using AK-47s for the first time.

Cisse dropped behind a large trunk and hugged his son with every ounce of strength in his body, the battle raging around them forgotten. Nafari reciprocated, tears streaming down his cheeks, having been convinced that he'd never see his family again. Johnny left them to their reconciliation and continued shouting at the oncoming horde, urging them to lay down their arms, but the onslaught continued, his words going unheeded.

Nafari extricated himself from Hansi's grip and ran out into the open.

'Kwame!' he shouted, spotting one of the boys he'd spent a few days with in the hut. 'It's okay, it's my father!'

Kwame hesitated, clearly unsure what to believe. Like Nafari, he hadn't spent much time in the camp, and his indoctrination wasn't as complete as Fene would have liked. Most of those who had been under the commander's care for months were already down; they'd followed orders and had been the first casualties. That left the newcomers, but for them the prospect of freedom was tempered by Fene's warnings of atrocities committed by the enemy.

Nafari continued to stare at Kwame, projecting a sense of calm and safety as best he could. He saw the expression on Kwame's face change: no-one was pointing a gun at him, no-one threatening to disembowel him.

Decision made, Kwame dropped his rifle and ran, sprinting furiously until he reached Nafari's side. Once behind enemy lines, he turned to face the battlefield, and saw dozens of unarmed children swarming towards him.

In less than a minute, the last of the boy soldiers had reached the Agbi lines and taken cover behind whatever they could find. Without exception, they all wondered what lay in store. Was Nafari telling them the truth? Were they really free? Or was it just an elaborate ploy to lure them into a nightmare of pain and torture?

Their fears were allayed somewhat when they were told to follow Hansi, who would lead them to join the other refugees heading for the border, though some were still apprehensive. Was this part of some diabolical plan, or were they actually safe?

They certainly weren't being fired at, so they took it as a good sign and followed Cisse and Nafari, who were walking hand in hand into the darkness.

The sudden capitulation meant a lull in the fighting, only the cries of the wounded carrying in the darkness. Gray knew that no-one else would be coming across the open ground—at least, no sane person—and so the likely tactic would be a flanking manoeuvre. That meant taking the long way round in the cover of the jungle, which gave Gray and his team the advantage. They could easily fall back to the second ambush point before anyone caught up with them, and this time the sentinels would also be lying in wait.

To do that, though, meant leaving a few dozen children screaming in the darkness. He could only estimate the extent of their injuries, but he knew many would die without urgent treatment, and there were surely indigenous animals that would make short work of them.

Abandoning them was not an option.

'On me,' he said over the comms, and in seconds his team had gathered around him, some taking a knee as they awaited instructions.

'Options?' Gray asked, looking around the group.

Each man was entitled to his own take on the situation, but he figured there would only be a couple of suggestions between them: fall back to the next ambush point, or take the fight to the enemy so that the injured could be treated. The sensible option was to retreat, but they all knew the fallen children would be unlikely to receive medical attention from their own side.

'I'm not saying we leave them,' one of the new arrivals said, 'but even if we take them with us, we've only got rudimentary medical supplies, and certainly not enough to go around.'

'And it's not like we're likely to stumble across a hospital any time soon,' another agreed.

Others chimed in, suggesting that it would take hours to fashion field stretchers for the wounded and that infection would set in long before they managed to get them to safety.

'Okay, so we know what we can't do,' Gray conceded. 'How about what we *can* do?'

'We could ask Hansi's son how they got here,' Sonny suggested. 'If they arrived in transport, we could use that to get to the border a lot quicker.'

Gray nodded, and Sonny got on the comms to relay the message. A minute later, they had confirmation that three trucks were parked close by, likely with enough capacity to carry everyone in the ever-growing party.

'There's also bad news,' Sonny added. 'Hansi's son estimates the enemy strength to be at least four hundred.'

'So it takes us a few minutes longer,' Gray said. 'Divvy up the ammo and let's get going.'

'Not so fast, Tom,' Smart said. He gave Gray a gentle dig in the ribs and saw his boss wince as the pain racked his body.

'Thanks for that,' Gray grunted. 'What's the problem?'

'You're in no state to be frolicking in the jungle. Join up with the others and we'll be back with the trucks soon.'

Gray started to protest, but looks from Sonny and the others told him Len was right. His injuries could slow him down, and there were plenty of men to complete the mission without having to worry about an invalid.

'Point taken.'

'Glad you're seeing sense,' Sonny said. 'Besides, if you die, who's gonna sign my pay cheque?'

Gray smiled at the joke, knowing full well that self-interest was the last thing on Sonny's mind.

Carl Levine was holding the handset that controlled the sentinels on either side of the ambush area. He'd turned the cameras one-eighty, pointing them into the jungle, and could see people moving across the screen. 'They're on their way,' he told the group, pointing towards the treeline to the left of the open ground.

Gray asked if they were coming from both sides, but Levine shook his head.

'Okay, you guys have some fun and let me know when you've secured transport.'

Gray trotted away as best he could, leaving the men to prepare for the next encounter.

———

Fene Adebola wasn't surprised that most of the boys had decided to abscond. He'd cautioned Obi that not all were ready, though the number of boys who lay screaming on the battlefield was a testament to his work. Every single one of them had been through the entire induction, whereas those who lay dead or had vanished were the late arrivals.

He'd been paid for the boys and had delivered them. Caveat emptor, as far as he was concerned.

Still, there was an extra ten thousand dollars to be earned, and that meant wiping out what remained of the Agbi resistance.

Fene gathered the men and led them around the clearing rather than taking the suicide route across open ground, hundreds of soldiers forming a thick column behind him. He led them at pace towards the enemy, the time for subtlety gone. He had the numerical advantage and was confident that he could win a war of attrition, so there was no need for the silent approach.

He'd covered barely fifty yards when a rifle on full automatic opened up, cutting down two dozen soldiers from the middle of the column before anyone could react. Belatedly, his men fought back, sending thousands of rounds into the jungle at an unseen enemy.

'Hold your fire!' Fene yelled, and the message was passed down the line.

The shooting eventually petered out, and silence returned. Fene strode down the line towards the carnage, enraged at his men's profligate consumption of ammunition.

'What are you firing at?'

'We were attacked,' one soldier replied, gesturing towards the bodies littering the ground.

'By one man, if my ears serve me right!'

The soldier looked sheepish, but Fene didn't have time to teach him basic weaponry. He turned and stood with his hands on his hips, peering into the darkness, but saw no sign of a threat.

'At least you got him,' he said bitterly. 'Now, move out!'

———⌣———

Levine had the giant in his sights, but unfortunately one of the incoming rounds had destroyed the sentinel's firing mechanism, rendering it unable to take the shot.

'Looks like they brought King Kong along,' he whispered to Smart, who glanced at the screen. The man filled the frame and looked menacing to say the least, but both knew he would bleed like anyone else.

'I'll leave that one to you,' Smart joked. 'Let's do this.'

He rose to a crouch and moved slowly towards the head of the line. Levine swapped the handset for his rifle and followed, eyes straining to adjust to the darkness once more.

The diversion had given the rest of the team the opportunity to flank the enemy, and two others were covering the open space in case anyone broke cover. They were all in place, just awaiting Smart's signal.

It came from the muzzle of his AK-47 as a round tore through the air and embedded itself in an unsuspecting skull, closely followed by scores more as the team opened up in full take-down mode. A quarter of the enemy were wiped out before they could organise themselves and return fire, but the assault was too well-coordinated. More fell to the superior accuracy of the ambushers, who started moving in to finish the job.

One of the British soldiers took a stray round to the shoulder, kicking him out of the fight, but the remainder pushed the attack, colouring the jungle floor crimson with the blood of their victims.

The coppery aroma mixed with the cordite to create the heady odour of death, and Sonny was savouring the familiar smell when the firing pin fell on an empty chamber. He ejected the magazine and reached for the last one in his pocket, slamming the half-empty clip into the port and picking out the next silhouette. Two shots dropped the target and he moved on to the next, keenly aware that the incoming rounds were diminishing rapidly.

They'd blitzed the enemy, but after taking out two more he was once again left with an empty magazine. He screamed out for more, only to find that everyone else was in the same boat. The only way they were going to find more rounds was to get in amongst the enemy and steal them from the dead.

Sonny switched the rifle to his left hand and pulled out his knife, the six-inch serrated blade feeling comforting now that his primary weapon was empty. He ran at a crouch, eyes peeled for danger as well as some more ammunition.

Sonny spotted a fallen figure and made a beeline for him, but from out of the shadows came the biggest man he'd ever seen, with a coal-black face and flaring nostrils.

The apparition looked to be twice Sonny's size, and wielded a machete that made his own knife look like a potato peeler. He swung his rifle like a club at the giant's head, but a raised arm harmlessly deflected the blow while at the same time slicing at Sonny's head with an already-bloodied weapon. Sonny dodged the strike, glad that the huge man wasn't equally matched in speed and height, but as he took a step back he tripped on a tree root and tumbled backwards, just as the machete came flashing towards his head.

Sonny tried to scramble to his feet, but in two enormous strides, Fene was standing over him, machete raised above his head. Sonny feigned terror, but he knew that the big man would have to stoop to deliver a killing blow, and he timed his moment perfectly.

Fene bent double as he brought the cleaver down towards Sonny's head, but the smaller man rolled to the left and brought his right boot up, connecting with the giant's happy sack. A groan erupted from Fene's throat as pain exploded in his groin. Sonny used the moment to roll quickly to the right, his left leg bent so that his knee collided with the big man's skull.

Fene collapsed to the ground, clawing the dirt blindly, hoping to catch hold of Sonny. The last thing he saw was the knife as it arced towards his head and came to rest in his ear, the blade entering his skull up to the hilt.

Sonny rolled away, the fight forgotten as he concentrated on arming himself. He found an AK-47, quickly checked the magazine and saw that it was half full. After dispatching another fleeing figure, he searched the pockets of a corpse and came out with more ammunition. He was instantly up and chasing the survivors, who now numbered less than fifty. It was a figure that dropped rapidly as they fled the scene, their leader slain and nothing left to fight with, their reckless shooting having expended all ammunition.

The team converged as they continued the clean-up operation, and minutes later the battle was over. They'd won a tremendous victory against an overwhelmingly superior force—if only numerically—and the only tinge of sadness they felt was that it would never be officially recognised.

Still, very few SAS missions made it into the public domain, and they would at least have bragging rights on their next visit to the mess in Hereford.

'All clear,' Smart said over the net. 'We'll let you know when we find the trucks.'

Tom Gray acknowledged the transmission and told Smart to move the vehicles up to their current position as quickly as he could.

'Did everyone make it?' Gray added.

'John Sharp took one to the shoulder, but he'll live.'

'Send him out,' Gray said, 'and we'll treat him along with the others.'

Smart signed off and ordered the men to grab as much ammo as they could, just in case they came across any more surprises. As he trudged through the undergrowth towards the coordinates he'd been given, the first rays of the African sun painted the clouds an appropriate shade of red.

Smart barely noticed the spectacle; he was simply relieved that the end was finally in sight.

Chapter Twenty

Wednesday 9 October 2013

The grey sky promised a turbulent flight as William Hart ducked through the entrance into Luton Airport, sons Aiden and Sean trailing in his wake. His preferred departure point would have been Gatwick to the south of London, but the only direct flight from there left just before six in the morning. The trade-off of a lie-in for a budget flight meant no free food on board, but on a four-hour flight it was no real inconvenience. He'd paid the few extra pounds for priority passes, and that allowed them to jump to the head of the queue for check-in, security and boarding.

The trip was uneventful, and they landed at Las Palmas airport ten minutes ahead of schedule. Their priority passes didn't work so well on arrival, and the trio had to queue with everyone else to get through immigration and collect their luggage. An hour after touching down, they left the terminal and basked in the heat as they walked to the hire car, a clear, blue sky the perfect antidote for the windy, wet weather they'd left behind.

Hart senior climbed behind the wheel and pulled out of the airport and onto GC1, the main highway that would take them to the southern resort of Puerto De Mogan. His sons looked sullen as they drove past the more laddish resort of Playa Del Ingles towards what was, to their mind, one of the more boring spots on the island. Still, they knew it was only a short taxi ride to their preferred playground, and William Hart didn't exactly set curfews for his kids.

It took forty minutes to reach the villa, which was built into the old, volcanic cliffs, overlooking a harbour filled with sailing boats of all shapes and sizes, as well as the obligatory fishing charters. Beyond that, the beach was already packed with tourists from a dozen nations, united in their quest for sun, sea and relaxation.

Hart parked the car in his private garage and his sons retrieved the suitcases from the boot, following their father up the gently winding stone stairway. Fifty steps later they arrived at the door and were met by Judy, an ex-pat who looked after a few of the holiday villas and apartments on the island, making sure everything was ready for the owner's arrival and cleaned again once they'd left.

'Here you are,' she said, handing over the keys with a smile. 'I filled the fridge and the receipt's on the table. I also put a dozen towels in the bathroom closet.'

Judy had no idea what Hart did for a living, nor did she care, happy to earn a few hundred euros a month to supplement her husband's army pension and afford them a decent lifestyle in the sun.

Hart thanked her and handed her a small bundle of twenties before going inside and picking up a cold beer on his way to the bedroom. The interior of the building was surprisingly cool, the open French windows allowing a gentle breeze to blow through the room. He changed into shorts and smeared himself with factor-fifty sun cream before walking out into the blazing heat of the veranda.

His sons joined him a few minutes later, armed with fresh beers, and the men relaxed on the recliners.

The fact that they were there to avoid implication in an upcoming murder was a million miles from their thoughts.

Sese Obi wasn't often overcome with nerves, but the lack of communication from his people in the south had him distinctly on edge. After thirty minutes of failed attempts to speak to Fene Adebola he'd sent some men from the airport to investigate, but that had been an hour ago and he still hadn't heard back.

His scheme was unravelling quickly. Despite the months of preparation, only the first twenty-four hours had gone to plan. Since then, he'd stalled fifteen miles from the capital and was losing men at an astounding rate. The Malundian forces were stubbornly resisting every probe, inflicting casualties beyond his already-generous predictions. And without the hundreds of men who were now under Adebola's control, it was unlikely that his bid for power would succeed.

He almost dropped the phone as it vibrated in his hand; after composing himself he pressed the green button.

'It's about time!'

The caller hesitated, clearly dreading the reaction his message was likely to cause.

'Sir, Fene is dead,' a voice eventually said.

The news was unexpected, but Obi knew these things happened in battle. Adebola was a good warrior, but he was but one man, and unlikely to influence an entire campaign.

'Who is in charge now?' Obi barked. 'And why haven't they been updating me?'

Another pause, and Obi sensed the bad news piling up. 'Speak, man!'

'There is no-one to lead, or follow. We found them all dead. There are no survivors.'

Obi felt like he'd been kicked in the stomach. How could a few Agbi soldiers wipe out hundreds of his men, especially while shepherding women and children? It didn't make any sense at all. Could they have had outside help? If they had, he imagined it had to be a sizeable force, one that was sitting not too far south of him. They could even be powering their way towards him at this very moment.

Was it something to do with the plane that they'd shot down during the night? He'd been told that a transporter had ventured too near the airport for comfort and had been blown out of the sky, but could there have been more of them? If there were, they weren't landing, so that meant paratroopers, which pointed to the Americans or Europe.

It still made no sense, though. He racked his brain for a reason for those superpowers to intervene in an African skirmish and found none. Rwanda, almost twenty years earlier, was a classic example of western apathy, with all countries condemning the genocide but doing little to help prevent half a million people dying. Like Rwanda, Malundi had no oil or mineral interests to entice the big boys into the fight, so why were they here?

Whatever the reason, he knew it wasn't to shake his hand.

Much as he hated to admit it, he couldn't continue with his quest for power. It would have been hard enough with Adebola's men at his disposal, but with them gone and an unknown and evidently powerful force to his south, the war was lost.

He realised that he was still holding the phone, and he considered the best way to extricate himself from the situation. The men could sneak back over the border with Kingata in dribs and drabs, returning to their former lives as if nothing had happened. For Obi, though, there would be no return. If he was a wanted man last week, the price on his head would have increased by several orders of magnitude now.

To reach the western border meant crossing miles of inhospitable ground, leaving him the only real option of heading east and slightly north. The adjacent country had an unstable regime and power plays were a regular occurrence. He'd fit in nicely there, and after surveying the lay of the land, he'd affiliate himself to whichever faction was most likely to take the reins when the next, inevitable coup manifested itself.

With that thought in mind, he decided to take the remaining men with him. Offering his own services wouldn't be that big a draw to the various rebel outfits, but if he had two thousand men at his disposal . . . .

After consulting the map, he put the phone to his ear and gave instructions for the men to abandon the airport and head for a point a couple of miles from the border, where he would meet up with them later in the day in preparation for a night crossing. He then called Baako and Themba over, entrusting his lieutenants with passing on the order to regroup at the assigned location.

On reflection, his capitulation wasn't the end of the world. It hadn't cost him his life, valuable lessons had been learned—not least, to make sure he had more reliable commanders in place— and he still had a considerable army behind him.

Obi sat back in his seat and let out a sigh, his hand fiddling with the victory cigar in his breast pocket. Looking down at the five-inch tube, he considered lighting it, but decided not to.

There was nothing to be gained from tempting fate.

Chapter Twenty-One

Wednesday 9 October 2013

'What is it, Johnny?'

Okeke squinted through the windscreen and pointed at a group of figures blocking the road a couple of hundred yards ahead.

After hours in the stifling cab of the ancient truck, Gray had thought the worst was over. They'd met no resistance on their way to the border, and had crossed into the neighbouring country unimpeded. At that point, their destination had been just one hour away: a small town with a rudimentary hospital and the chance to grab some much-needed food and rest.

The two vehicles blocking the highway ahead, not to mention the dozen armed men, effectively meant their respite was on hold. Although the troops appeared to be wearing military uniforms, it was quite possible that they were one of the militia groups vying for control of the troubled country.

'They look like army, Mr Tom, but I can't be sure.'

'And if they're not?'

Okeke mulled the question over. 'Then make every round count.' *Great*, Gray thought.

'Any suggestions?' Johnny was gripping the steering wheel, preparing to flee or stop on Gray's command.

'Pull over twenty yards from them,' Gray told him. Into the comms net, he added: 'Heads up. Keep your weapons hidden until I give the word.'

In the open flatbeds of the trucks, the word was passed on. Everyone had a round in the chamber and safeties came off, but they kept their rifles out of sight.

Johnny pulled up and climbed out of the cab. He walked slowly towards the two approaching soldiers, and Gray strained to hear the exchange between them. All seemed calm, the soldiers carrying their rifles across their chests as they chatted.

Another three soldiers emerged from the roadblock, taking a casual stroll around the trucks. At the sight of the white men, they started shouting in a language Gray couldn't understand, but the tone was universal. His finger moved to the trigger of the AK-47, ready to bring the weapon to bear as he watched Johnny trying to placate the sentries.

The discussion quickly descended into a one-sided shouting match, and Johnny walked submissively back to the truck. He opened Gray's door and gave him the bad news.

'They want us to go with them,' Johnny said. 'I think we should do it.'

'There's not many of them, and—' Gray began, but Johnny stopped him in his tracks.

'They've already radioed this in. There will be an entire army after us if we fight our way out of this. Besides, they think you're mercenaries, here to help overthrow the government. Once we prove them wrong, they should let us go.'

Gray wasn't itching for a fight, and if a quick conversation could speed them on their way, he was up for it.

He climbed down and shouted for the others to drop their weapons and dismount.

'Tell them we have wounded,' Gray told Johnny. 'They need to get to hospital as soon as possible.'

The message was conveyed, and the foreign soldiers began the job of segregation. The British and Freddie Rickard were told to stand to one side of the road while everyone else was lined up facing them, the dirt road separating the groups.

When the AK-47s were discovered, tensions increased immediately.

One of the soldiers, evidently their leader, raised his rifle and aimed at Johnny's head. He began pointing at Gray's team and then to the trucks, all the time screaming at Johnny for explanations. Okeke did his best, but it soon became obvious that his words were falling on deaf ears. He was ushered over to stand next to Gray.

'Just do as I do,' he said from the corner of his mouth, before dropping to his knees and clasping his hands at the back of his head. Gray followed his lead, and soon the entire party were on the ground, staring up at weapons held by some seriously pissed-off soldiers.

They remained in place for twenty minutes while the Malundian villagers and the wounded boys were placed into two of the trucks, and those wearing military clothing were herded over to Gray's side of the road.

Hansi Cisse was frantic at the thought of losing his son again, and it was only after much pleading and begging that the boy was allowed to remain behind with him.

The old Bedfords departed, and as they disappeared in a cloud of dust, Gray hoped they were heading towards medical help. After all the effort his team had gone through, it would have been nice to personally deliver the occupants to safety, but that was out of their hands now. They had their own safety to consider now, and judging by the look on the faces of their captors, it was fifty-fifty as to whether any of them got to see their own homes again.

The leader ordered one of the prisoners to stand, and he was brusquely frisked before being ordered onto the remaining truck while the next member of the team was called forward. The process took twenty minutes, and the flatbed was jam-packed by the time everyone was on board. Most had to stand, while the unlucky ones were sardined onto the wooden benches lining the sides of the truck and had to spend the entire journey with their faces stuck in various stinking crotches.

After an hour of bouncing along dilapidated roads, they came to a small town. Yelling children ran alongside the truck as it motored along the semi-tarmacked streets, scattering dogs and chickens as it made its way towards a walled compound. They passed through large, wooden gates and into a courtyard framed on three sides by buildings. Stairs ran up the walls to the fort's defensive positions, making the place look like the stronghold in a Beau Geste film set. The men were ordered to climb out and line up against a stone wall and assume the kneeling position once more.

The patrol commander disappeared into a building and returned five minutes later with an African man who wore the insignia of a British Army colonel. The officer stood with his hands on his hips, chest puffed out as his eyes wandered up and down the line of prisoners.

Gray knew his type: full of self-importance and a chip on his shoulder, traits he'd seen in more than one officer in his time. It meant an ego that had to be massaged, and Gray knew he'd have to play the man carefully.

'Which one of you is in charge?' the colonel barked.

Gray raised his hand and was ordered to step forward. He stopped a couple of yards from the officer, who took a step closer.

'What is your name and rank?'

'Tom. Tom Gray. I have no rank, sir.'

The colonel looked sceptical. 'What are you and your men doing in my country, Tom Gray with no rank?'

The colonel's English was good, thankfully removing the need for an interpreter who could inadvertently twist his words. The accent was refined, as if he'd spent time in England. Perhaps a university, Gray thought.

'Sir, we have just escaped from Malundi. Armed insurgents attacked a village and my men launched a rescue mission. We were hoping you could offer our sick and wounded medical assistance and sanctuary, sir.'

'And what were you doing in Malundi?'

Gray explained his role in the security industry and the team's remit across the border, though he embellished the truth by saying that they'd all been there for months. It wouldn't do for this man to know they'd illegally entered the country and killed hundreds of men as part of a rescue mission. Their passports would have painted a different picture of events, but as all documentation had gone down with the plane, that base was covered.

The officer spoke in his native language to the patrol commander, who verified that there were indeed several civilians and a few wounded among the party they'd come across.

'My men have taken them to the hospital, Mr Gray. Their wounds will be treated and the rest will be found temporary accommodation until they can return to their own country.' The colonel paused, looking along the line of men. 'However, medical supplies are hard to come by, and when we can find them, there is always a price to pay.'

Gray got the message—if you want me to take care of the injured, it's going to cost you—and he didn't imagine it would be the same price as an NHS prescription.

'Sir, I'm afraid we have nothing of value to offer you.'

That didn't please the officer, who barked an instruction. The patrol leader disappeared and returned with a bag containing the items that had been confiscated at the road side. The colonel rummaged through, picking out objects at random. He took a fancy to Gray's satellite phone, along with a few Samsungs and Nokias.

'This might pay for the medicine,' he said, dropping the items back inside the bag, 'but we will need more for their recuperation. They will have to be fed and housed until they can return to their homeland, will they not?'

Gray nodded, but didn't know what more they could offer. Their combined possessions consisted of the clothes on their backs, everything else having gone into the bag hours earlier.

'I can arrange to have a payment sent to you,' Gray offered. 'More than enough to cover the cost of their rehabilitation.'

The officer smiled and handed the bag to Gray. 'Make the call.'

Gray hadn't seen that coming. 'I meant when we got back home,' he said. 'No-one I know has the authority to access my accounts.'

'Not even your wife?' The colonel asked, looking at the wedding band on Gray's left hand.

Gray sighed. The last thing he wanted to do was worry Vick with his problem. His plan had been to pretend it had all gone smoothly and put the matter behind them, and that wasn't going to happen if she knew he was being held to ransom.

'She's away on holiday,' he lied. 'She won't have access to my business account.'

'Then call a friend and ask them to lend you the money. Otherwise, I will have to assume that my captain was correct when he suggested you might be mercenaries.'

The smile was gone, signalling an end to negotiations. Gray fished in the bag for his satellite phone, wondering who he could contact to wire the money. His solicitor was the obvious choice.

As he prepared to start typing the number into the handset, he asked the colonel, 'Which account do you want it to be transferred into?'

'I'm a lowly soldier, Mr Gray. I have no need for bank accounts. Just have twenty thousand dollars delivered here.'

Gray was stunned when he heard the amount. He'd been expecting to pay a thousand at the most, and immediately deduced that the colonel planned to line his own pockets first. In fact, it was more likely that he would keep the lot, without a single cent being spent on the injured. That said, they'd done all they could for the villagers, and his priority had shifted to getting his men home. If that meant playing along, so be it.

It also meant he couldn't ask Ryan Amos for help. The amount wouldn't have been a problem, but asking his solicitor to venture into the African heartland was out of the question. That left just one option, and Gray dialled the number from memory.

'Hi, Andrew.'

'Tom! How're you doing?'

'Not so good, mate.' Gray explained the situation, leaving out anything incriminating due to the close proximity of the colonel.

'That's a tough ask.'

'I know, but something tells me we're going nowhere until the money arrives.'

Gray glanced at the officer, whose smile confirmed his suspicions.

'Well, the government won't fund it, and I can only raise half of that myself. Is there anyone who can provide the rest?'

'The money isn't the issue,' Gray said, 'it's getting it here. It has to be a cash deal.'

He told Harvey to contact Ryan Amos for the money, and asked if Harvey could arrange delivery.

'I can ask Kyle Ackerman,' Harvey said. 'You remember him?'

'From Durban? Sure, I know Kyle. How soon do you think he could be here?'

'I'll have to check. Can I call you back on this number?'

Gray assured him he could, and asked Harvey to keep an ear to the ground regarding Malundi. He then dropped another bomb.

'We lost our passports. Any chance of getting us replacements?'

'Jesus, you don't do things by half measures, do you?'

Gray felt sheepish, but Harvey agreed to arrange for temporary travel papers. After giving the names of the team members, Gray thanked him and hung up, handing the phone back to the colonel.

'Arrangements are being made,' he said. 'They will call back once everything is in place. Can you please let them know where to deliver it?'

'Of course. In the meantime, please re-join your men.'

Gray started back, but hesitated and turned. 'We haven't eaten for a couple of days. I was wondering if you could spare some food and water.'

The officer pointed to the corner of the courtyard. 'There is a well over there,' he said. 'As for food, I will send someone to the market when your money arrives.'

Without waiting for a response, he turned and walked back inside, leaving Gray with an empty feeling.

He knew it wasn't just a product of his hunger.

Andrew Harvey put the phone down and wondered how many more times Tom was going to spring these surprises on him. Barely forty-eight hours after promising to take a purely observational role, Gray was now virtually captive in a foreign nation, and Harvey could feel an international incident brewing. He should really kick this upstairs, he knew, but there were several in the hierarchy who were waiting for Gray to make exactly this kind of mistake so that they could hang him out to dry. Gray certainly hadn't made many friends in the upper echelons of power with his crusade two years earlier, and there were plenty who would love to see him rot in an African prison.

Harvey decided that until Gray's name was mentioned in any official dispatches, he would deal with it on the quiet. He looked up the contact details for Kyle Ackerman. They'd been introduced in South Africa a year earlier, when the ex-marine had been instrumental in saving the lives of Gray, Vick, Sonny and Smart. Ackerman worked out of the UK Trade & Investment department in Pretoria, and had stepped into the shoes of Dennis Owen, who had been shot and wounded during the rescue attempt.

Despite having the title of Senior Advisor, Ackerman was a British Intelligence operative, though with a more limited area of responsibility than Harvey's. Ackerman's cover allowed him access to the major companies in the region under the pretence of helping forge trade ties with Britain, but his real job was to dig deep and uncover information not found in annual reports. The British government had been scarred by dealings with companies purporting to be legitimate, only to be embarrassed as ties to groups such as Al-Qaeda and German neo-Nazi groups were uncovered by investigative journalists. It was Ackerman's job to follow every thread and ensure there were no skeletons. Every company had to be whiter than white before Ackerman would recommend them to the trade and industry secretary back in the UK.

'Kyle,' he said, when the call was answered. 'It's Andrew Harvey.'

'Andrew! What can I do for you? Not looking for another truckload of fugitives, I hope?'

'No, not this time. At least, we know where they are, but I need someone to drive up country and make an exchange.'

Ackerman was intrigued, and Harvey laid out the bones of the mission, including the need to process some travel documents for the team.

'Tom certainly has a way of finding trouble,' Ackerman noted.

'You don't know the half of it. If I can arrange for the money to be transferred to you this morning, when can you get up there?'

Ackerman checked his schedule. 'I'm swamped until five this afternoon, but I can shift tomorrow's meetings and travel up this evening.'

It wasn't as soon as Harvey would have liked, but short of fly-ing over in person, there was little he could do. He confirmed the receiving bank account and promised to have the money in there by lunchtime, so that Ackerman could send someone out to with-draw it from the bank in preparation for his journey north.

'I'll get back to you later with the exact location of the meet,' he told Kyle, then hung up. His next call was to Gray's solicitor, Ryan Amos. He'd met the man a couple of times, once at one of Vick's dinner parties, and he was a likeable man, if a little short on conversation. After reaching Amos's secretary, Harvey was put on hold for a few seconds before the familiar voice came onto the line. Harvey gave a quick rundown of the situation and asked if he could accommodate Tom's request. Amos was only too happy to help, and once Harvey recited the account in Pretoria, he promised to have the money wired immediately.

After hanging up, Harvey put in a call to the Africa desk and asked for all recent developments in Malundi to be sent to his screen, then called Tom back. The phone was answered by a stranger.

'Can I speak to Tom Gray, please?'

'Who is speaking?'

'Andrew Harvey. I'm calling about the . . . delivery he arranged.'

The voice started rattling off instructions for the drop, but Harvey interrupted him.

'I want to speak to Tom first.'

'You can speak to him when the money arrives, not before.'

'Then it looks like we have a standoff,' Harvey said. 'Either I speak to Tom Gray, or the deal's off.'

Harvey held his breath, hoping he hadn't just condemned Gray and his team to an impromptu firing squad, but he had a feeling their captor wanted the money more than the satisfaction of offing some foreigners.

'Wait!'

It was over a minute before he heard Tom's voice.

'Andrew, please tell me you've got good news.'

'Kyle will be setting off at five local time,' Harvey said. 'I don't know when he'll get there, but he'll have the money and your temporary passports.'

'Any chance you could ask him to grab a few pizzas on the way? We're starving and these guys refuse to feed us. We've also got a boy who's cramping up and may need medical attention. He said he was given something to smoke, and it looks like he's going cold turkey.'

'I'll let Kyle know,' Harvey promised. 'Just keep your head down, don't do anything stupid and we'll have you out of there as soon as possible. Now, let me have a word with this guy.'

Gray handed the phone over.

'You've spoken to him,' the voice said. 'When will the money be here?'

'In the next twenty-four hours. In the meantime, I want you to ensure they're not mistreated, and that means feeding them and offering any medical attention they require.'

'We are a poor nation, Mr Harvey. We can't waste food and medicine on every armed transient we come across, especially if they're in the country illegally.'

'They've explained their reasons for being in your country. They put their lives on the line to save civilians, and I think they deserve some respect for that.'

'You can show them all the respect you want when they get back home,' the voice said. 'Now take down these instructions, or your friends might be here for a long time.'

Harvey realised he wasn't going to change the man's mind, and jotted down the details. Once he'd read them back, the call was abruptly terminated.

There wasn't much more he could do for Gray, and he wondered once again if he should inform his superiors about the incident.

Word was sure to spread that British soldiers had been active in the region, and it would only need a little digging to come up with some names. Any further investigation would certainly reveal his involvement, and he had no real excuses for acting outside of his authority.

He opened a document and began typing up a report, which he saved to his hard drive. He would eventually have to pass it up the chain, but decided to wait until Ackerman had confirmation that they were in his custody before sending it to his boss.

In the meantime, he would also prepare a nice surprise for Tom's captor.

Chapter Twenty-Two

Thursday 10 October 2013

Night had already rolled in by the time Kyle Ackerman navigated the bus towards the old fort. Armed guards approached as he pulled up at the gates and he leaned out of the window to state his business. One of the guards climbed aboard and walked the length of the bus. Then, satisfied that it wasn't a Trojan horse, he instructed the other to open the gates.

Ackerman drove through them and into the courtyard, where he saw a few dozen men lounging against one wall, most of them asleep. As he climbed down from the conveyance, the first face to jump out at him was Gray's, but before he could walk over to greet him, a trio emerged from one of the buildings and made their way towards the bus.

'You have the money?' the one with the scrambled egg on his epaulettes asked.

Ackerman walked to the rear of the bus and opened the engine compartment. A metal briefcase was strapped to the inside door. He extricated the case and handed it over.

'Just a little precaution,' he said, 'in case I got stopped along the way.'

'A wise decision,' the colonel said, opening the case and thumbing the bundles of twenty-dollar bills. 'This country can be dangerous for those travelling alone.'

Ackerman motioned for Gray to join him, but the colonel held up a hand.

'Not so fast,' he smiled, a toothy grin devoid of warmth. 'Someone with such easy access to money might be useful to have around.'

Ackerman had expected something like this. Having spent over five years on the continent, experience told him that not everyone could be taken on their word. Certain traits were easily recognised, with greed amongst the most common. This man, who'd demanded twenty grand for basic medical supplies, fell into that bracket.

'I think you should reconsider,' Ackerman said, his voice steady despite the precarious situation. 'The person you spoke to yesterday works for British Intelligence, and these men are his close friends.' He checked his watch. 'I spoke to him ten minutes ago to say I was here, and if I don't call back in the next sixteen minutes, he will be on the phone to President Lwami. I'm sure your leader would be interested to know why four heavily armed Apache helicopters are roaring through his airspace and heading for this location. Mr Harvey will explain that not only did you hold British citizens hostage, you also demanded that money.' Ackerman pointed to the case. 'Now, you can either keep the cash and enjoy it, or hold us for another quarter of an hour and see who gets you first: the British, or your own president.'

The colonel's smile disappeared, indicating to Ackerman that he'd guessed right when he'd assumed the man was working for his own benefit rather than the country as a whole. Now, Ackerman hoped, the colonel could acquiesce without losing too much face, given that none of his companions likely spoke English. In truth, the colonel had no other option, apart from losing his life in one of several uninviting ways.

The colonel turned and walked towards the building, barking an order as he went. Guards ordered the prisoners to their feet and pushed them towards the waiting vehicle, while Ackerman shouted after the departing officer, who turned once again to face him.

'Don't forget the wounded and the other civilians. We expect them to make it back home safely. If they don't . . . . '

He put his hand to his ear in the universal phone-call signal, then turned to join the others as they made their way onto the bus. By the time everyone was on board there was barely room to breathe, with half a dozen forced to stand in the aisle.

Kyle took the wheel and reversed out of the fort, pointing the bus towards the road out of town, with Gray sitting next to him in the jump seat.

'Good to see you again, Tom.'

'You, too,' Gray said, 'though I wish it was under different circumstances. Did Andrew mention food?'

Ackerman nodded, and told Gray to lift the floor panel behind the driver's seat. Inside there was a variety of tinned meats and several loaves of bread, along with a couple of can openers. Gray started passing them down the bus, saving a tin of Spam for himself. A cooler contained three dozen beers, and although the heat had got to them, the bottles were emptied in no time.

'Where are we heading?' Gray asked with a full mouth.

'Pretoria,' Ackerman told him. 'Your travel documents will be ready when we get there. I tried to rush them through, but without an official request it takes time.'

'What about the others? How will they get back to Malundi?'

'We're stopping off on the way,' Ackerman said. 'Andrew told me that the fighting has stopped. One minute there were a couple of thousand hostiles poised on the outskirts, the next, nothing.'

'They pulled out? Why?'

'No-one knows,' Ackerman grinned, 'but they think it might have had something to do with a horde of hairy-arsed Brits slaughtering everyone in sight.'

'I think we got one or two of them,' Gray admitted.

'I'll bet. I'd love to sit in on the debrief.'

'Not much to report,' Gray said with a shrug. 'They shot at us, we shot back. We just did it a lot better.'

Gray proceeded to doze while the bus ploughed its way to the Malundian border. He woke at the crossing, which was heavily armed, the stable door firmly bolted long after the horse had gone. And despite there being close to fifty of their Malundian soldiers on board, it was thirty minutes before the sentries allowed the bus through.

It was approaching four in the morning by the time they hit the outskirts of the capital. Smart and his team spent a few minutes saying their farewells to their charges. Johnny Okeke came in for particular praise. On the side, Smart told Gray that he hoped Okeke and his men didn't get into too much trouble for disobeying orders. Gray promised to put in a good word for them with the defence minister, highlighting the role the local soldiers had played in the civilian rescue.

Heavily embellished, of course.

'I've booked us into a hotel,' Ackerman said once the men had climbed back on board. 'It isn't the Holiday Inn, but you'll be able to get a good night's sleep.'

'Can't we just head back?' Gray asked, but Ackerman explained that he'd been driving for ten hours, and it was at least another ten back to Pretoria.

'Best to get our heads down for a few hours and set off just before lunchtime.'

Gray yielded, though the thought of a comfortable bed didn't quite match his desire to see Vick and Melissa again. He'd been gone nearly three days, not the longest he'd spent apart from them, but the first time they'd parted under such acrimonious circumstances. Vick had never complained about the time he spent abroad setting up a new contract or visiting existing clients, but her fury at his latest jaunt was understandable. What made it worse was that she would beat him about the head with a sackful of 'I told you so.'

Gray was still thinking about his family when they pulled up at the two-storey building, a solitary sign hanging over the door proclaiming it to be the Majestic Hotel. Gray's first thought was that the place should be sued for false advertising, but he let it go. A bored night porter dealt with their reservations and took the bundle of notes from Ackerman before handing over four room keys and returning his attention to the portable black-and-white television behind the counter. The fact that the majority of his new customers wore combat dress was clearly none of his concern.

When they got to their rooms they found that each had just two single beds, meaning they would have to sleep two to a bunk, but most were out cold before they could raise the energy to object. Gray went to the room next to his to check on John Sharp's shoulder wound. The bullet had only grazed the skin, cutting a two-inch furrow through the flesh, and while it had bled like a bitch, there were no signs of lasting damage.

'You'll live,' Gray said, 'but you might want to visit a hospital before you fly home.'

Sharp agreed, and Gray returned to his own room to find Sonny fast asleep on the bed, doing his best impression of a starfish. Not having the heart to disturb him, Gray took a pillow and found a relatively clean spot on the floor.

Sleep came easily, his dream taking shape with the vision of Sonny sleeping morphing into his daughter reaching her starfish-shaped hand up to him . . . .

Chapter Twenty-Three

Friday 11 October 2013

Rob Harman parked his car three streets away from the target and walked the few hundred yards with one gloved hand in his pocket while the other held a plastic bag containing a sandwich box. The lunch container had been sterilised and all prints wiped clean before a few breadcrumbs were added. If he were stopped by the police, it would add to the illusion that he was just another night-shift worker heading home.

He slowed his pace as he neared the objective. The lights were out, which was what he expected given that it was two in the morning. After a final glance round, he eased through the gate and gently placed the bag behind a bin, ready to collect on his way out to continue the subterfuge while he made his way back to the car.

At the rear of the house, all was quiet, though a bitter breeze was picking up. He checked the upstairs windows, but all the curtains were drawn, the occupants hunkered down for the night. Having checked the fittings on his previous visit, he knew the tools for the job, and he pulled a flexible strip of metal from his sleeve. In seconds he had neutralised the sash lock; now he teased the bottom frame open, wary of making a sound. The window was decades old and it initially resisted his efforts, but eventually he had a gap wide enough to squeeze through. After moving some plants aside, he stole through the tiny entrance and onto the floor, his rubber-soled shoes landing silently on the tile-effect linoleum.

One of his main concerns was leaving any sign of entry, and the only way to avoid that was to exit via the front door, closing it behind him. He spent a minute closing and locking the window before rearranging the plants in their original place, all the time listening for signs of movement in the house.

Confident that he hadn't woken anyone, he crept into the living room and waited a few moments for his eyes to adjust to the darkness. He soon made out the outline of the furniture, and began looking for a packet of cigarettes. It was entirely possible that the occupants had taken them upstairs at bedtime. Because of this, he'd brought one along just in case. He much preferred to use the brand the householder smoked, just in case it survived the fire, but as he hadn't been able to ascertain what they used, he'd brought along one of the more popular packs.

He didn't find any cigarettes, but spotted a liquor cabinet, stocked with several spirits. The bottle of sambuca was half-empty, suggesting it was a popular tipple in this household. He crept over and poured a generous measure into a glass.

A sound caused him to stop in his tracks, and he strained to recognise it. All was quiet, and he could hear nothing but the sound of the wind tormenting the ill-fitting windows.

There it was again!

Above the faint and irregular rattling, a baby's cries reached him from the upper floor, followed soon after by adult footsteps.

———

Vick woke up as soon as she heard Melissa cry for her feed, her ears attuned to the sound after four months of motherhood. She prayed that her daughter would go back to sleep, and for a while it seemed her wish had come true, but then the tiny voice once more demanded milk.

She sat up and rubbed her face, trying to energise herself for the chore ahead, knowing that if she didn't make a move, her daughter would soon wake her aunt and uncle as well.

The last evening had gone much the way of the previous three, with Vick crying and her aunt doing the comforting. The worst part was that she hadn't heard anything from Tom since he'd left. His phone went instantly to voicemail and she had no other way of contacting him, so all she could do was sit and wait for him to get in touch.

Vick turned on the bedside lamp, padded over to the travel crib and gently lifted Melissa out, the unpleasant aroma indicating that there was more than feeding to be done before either of them would get back to sleep. As she rocked her child, cooing, she decided that the nappy had to be the priority, for both their sakes. She placed the changing mat on the floor and laid Melissa down, all the time making comforting noises in a vain attempt to silence the cries. The nappy came off and Vick searched around for the changing bag, then realised that she'd left it downstairs.

'Shhh, darling. I won't be long.'

She left Melissa on the mat. The little girl wouldn't be going anywhere as she hadn't quite reached the crawling stage. Vick put her robe on and walked out onto the landing, closing the door behind her so that Melissa's screams didn't carry. She carefully walked down the stairs, and at the bottom she turned and entered the living room, flicking the light switch as she did so.

Straight ahead of her she caught her reflection in the mirror over the fireplace, and a look of horror spread over her face as she glimpsed a man dressed in black hiding on the other side of the door.

She tried to run, but the door slammed into her, throwing her sideways into a cabinet. Vick fell to the floor, winded, and the man ran at her. Instinctively, she lashed out with her foot and caught him in the chest, forcing him backwards into the doorway. Vick struggled to her feet and ran around the front of the sofa, searching for a weapon. She hadn't even had time to consider screaming, her natural survival skills kicking in and forcing her to flee. She reached the fireplace and grabbed a thick vase, but by the time she turned around, the stranger was on her.

She tried to swing the vase but a strong hand gripped her arm and pulled her into the middle of the room before pushing her backwards. Vick tried to maintain her balance, but gravity won the battle. As she fell to the floor, she twisted, throwing her hands out to protect her face. The corner of the coffee table met her head before she could bring her arms around far enough, and Vick was out cold before she could even register the pain.

<hr />

Harman knew he had very little time. The impromptu violence was sure to have woken someone. If it hadn't, the crying child soon would, and he needed to get a decent flame going before anyone had a chance to extinguish the fire. If the householders managed to put it out, any pretence of it being an accident were over.

He quickly lit the cigarette and picked up the glass of sambuca, which he carried over to the prostrate woman, splashing it around her head and placed the vessel in her hand. He thought about how little time he had, and picked up the bottle, pouring the contents over her clothes and the nearby furniture, then put the bottle in her other hand before lighting the Zippo and holding its flame to the strong alcohol's vapour.

As the flames caught, he threw the cigarette next to the woman's head and moved into the hallway, closing the door behind him. He could hear footsteps on the floor above, and he quickly opened the front door before sneaking out, closing it with a *snick* behind him.

He picked up his bag on the way out and strode purposefully in the direction of his car, only slowing his pace once he reached the end of the street.

He caught his breath, knowing how close he'd come to being caught. Adrenaline surged through his body as he tried to focus on normalising his breathing and maintaining a casual posture as he walked. He didn't look back, but his ears strained as he listened for cries for help.

When Harman reached his car, the night was still quiet, only the wind snapping at the trees and a couple of fighting cats disturbing the silence. He quickly started the BMW and pulled out into the road, his job done. He'd been paid to start a fire, and he'd done that. The unspoken intention had obviously been to roast everyone inside, though that was beyond his control now. At least the woman was dead, of that he was sure.

It would have to do.

Mina Hatcher once again woke to the sound of little Melissa screaming. She eased herself out of bed and went to empty her bladder, passing the spare bedroom on her way to the toilet. The cries intensified, but she guessed Vick was doing all she could to pacify the girl.

Mina had dreamt of a child all her life, but her best efforts had proven fruitless. She and Ken had tried many times and had several courses of IVF years earlier, but it wasn't to be. Her sterility meant a life without being able to cuddle their own young, and adoption didn't hold any appeal to them; they just didn't feel they could offer the same love to a child who wasn't a product of their union. Having Melissa around was the next best thing, but she hoped her father returned soon so that she could get a peaceful night's sleep.

Once she'd finished her ablutions, Mina walked back to her bedroom, stopping outside the door to the spare room. She put her hand up to open it, but suddenly thought better of it. Vick was a good mother, and would be able to get her daughter settled without an old busybody interfering. Besides, she had to go to work at the supermarket in a few hours, and she needed all the sleep she could get.

Once in her room, Mina slipped into bed next to her husband, who was still snoring like a diesel engine. She pulled the heavy duvet over her head, sleep already returning.

Chapter Twenty-Four

Saturday 12 October 2013

Tom Gray sat in the hotel room looking out over Pretoria. The view was a lot better than he'd seen from the bedroom of the Majestic twenty-four hours earlier, but having a double bed to himself had been the biggest bonus.

As promised, temporary travel documents had been waiting when they arrived at the offices of the Trade & Investment department the previous evening. Flights to Heathrow had also been booked, though the earliest they could get was late morning due to the short notice and an international conference disgorging its customers and vendors the day before.

Gray had spent Friday evening staring at the hotel phone, wondering if he should call Vick. There was a chance that she could still be angry, and trying to make peace over the phone wasn't the most intimate way of reconciling their differences. After long deliberation, he'd decided to leave it until he got home, but with the new morning came the longing to hear her voice.

He dialled the number for her mobile but it went straight to voicemail, and when he tried the landline it rang for several minutes. Frustrated, he tried the landline for Vick's aunt and uncle, but got no response. As with most people he knew, he hadn't memorised their mobile numbers. Instead, he'd just entered them into the contacts library on his mobile phone, which was probably sitting in an African pawn shop by now.

All sorts of thoughts began clambering for centre stage in his mind, not least of which was that there had been some kind of accident, but he preferred to think of the positive. Perhaps Vick had taken Melissa out for the day in the countryside, something his daughter loved. That would explain why she couldn't get a signal. Or maybe they were at the shops, where the reception was terrible, or the battery had simply run down on her phone.

Despite his best intentions, the negative feelings kept creeping into his head. In an effort to banish them, he left his room and went down the corridor to see Rickard.

'Morning, Freddie,' Gray said, as the door was opened by a bronzed figure wrapped in a towel. 'I just thought we could get a few things sorted out before we head home.'

Rickard bid him enter, and Gray took a seat at the foot of the bed.

'I need you to put a figure to what you've lost over the last few days.'

Rickard rubbed his chin, deep in thought. 'Well, there's five thousand dollars for the rifles, ammo, parachutes and clothes,' he said. 'But the big one is the bird. She might have been old, but she had a few more years in her and will cost close to four hundred grand to replace.'

Gray felt like he'd been hit by a train. He would have to downsize the house to bankroll a new plane, and Vick was certainly going to have an opinion to share. He could imagine the scene, and it involved objects flying at high speed towards his head.

'Jeez, Tom, the look on your face!' Rickard burst into laughter and slapped Gray on the back. 'The plane was insured, matey. I'll get back enough to buy another with plenty to spare.'

'You miserable bastard!' Gray said. 'I almost shit my pants!'

'Serves you right, Mr "Can-we-do-a-quick-fly-by?"'

'Are you sure they'll pay out?' Gray asked. 'We weren't exactly on a sight-seeing mission.'

'No doubt about it. The flight plan I filed took us over Malundi, and as we had no warning to deviate from a war zone, there was no reason to expect anyone to open up on us.'

Gray breathed a sigh, glad that his friend hadn't lost his livelihood, though he wasn't crazy about Freddie's sense of humour. He rose from the bed and offered Rickard his hand.

'Thanks again. We couldn't have done it without you.'

'My pleasure. And don't you be a stranger. Bring the family over, they'll love it.'

Gray promised to get in touch and plan the get-together, then said his goodbyes and headed down to the lobby to check out. The rest of the team were gathered, kitted out in the jeans and T-shirts Ackerman had purchased for them earlier that morning. Not all were perfect fits, but they would attract less attention than if they were still dressed in their combat gear.

Ackerman approached Gray and told him the transport to the airport would be arriving in the next few minutes. 'I'm afraid we're going to have to bill you for the hotels, clothes and flights. We can't ask the taxpayer to pick up the tab.'

Gray had no issues with the arrangement. He would be out of pocket by about thirty-five thousand overall, but that was a small price to pay to get his friends home in one piece.

'If it's any consolation, Andrew Harvey contacted me this morning,' Ackerman said. 'It seems the colonel who was holding you was picked up on the president's orders late last night. Looks like someone tipped the big man off about a large amount of cash.'

'No less than he deserves,' Gray shrugged. 'Did Andrew mention what's being done with the civilians we rescued?'

'They're being looked after. The president is looking to strengthen military ties with Malundi in an effort to stave off another coup attempt, so he promised to make sure they were well looked after.'

'Thanks, Kyle. Sorry we had to meet again under these circumstances. Hopefully, the next time we meet, our biggest problem will be a grumpy barmaid.'

They shook hands as the bus arrived outside the main entrance, and Gray followed the team on board. During the ride to the airport, Gray reflected on the last few days, and apart from sorting out the issue with Vick, he reckoned things had turned out well.

When they arrived at O.R. Tambo International an hour later, they had a brief delay while their papers were verified, then made their way to the departure lounge. The plane took off just before midday, with an expected ETA at Heathrow just before ten in the evening.

During the flight, Gray tried to busy himself with the in-flight entertainment and even accepted the offer of the insipid airline food in an attempt to take his mind off Vick, but he couldn't shake the concern he felt. He once again tried to focus on the obvious explanation that she'd just been out and had a bad reception when he called earlier, but something had soured his stomach, and it wasn't the economy-class Chicken Supreme.

Despite managing ten hours of sleep the previous night, Gray eventually dozed off halfway through the journey, and was shaken awake by Smart as the Boeing 747 started its descent.

After touching down in a rain-lashed London, their travel documents once again faced scrutiny, but after a couple of phone calls they were cleared through immigration. Having no luggage, they walked through the baggage claim area and out into the arrivals hall, where Gray was none too surprised to see Harvey waiting for them.

'Andrew, I'm so sorry—'

Harvey cut him off and took him by the arm, leading him away to a quieter area, his expression grim.

'What is it?'

'Tom, while you were gone, there was a . . . . ' Harvey sought the appropriate words, but didn't have time to find them.

'Tom Gray!'

Both men turned to see Danny Boyd rushing towards them, a young photographer in tow. Harvey moved to intercept the journalist, trying to usher him away, but Boyd was intent on getting his story, shouting his initial question over Harvey's shoulder.

'Tom, what's your reaction to the fire?'

Gray was confused by the question, and the incessant flash of the camera didn't help matters.

'How does it feel to lose a second wife, Tom?'

Harvey's face was contorted with anger as he pushed the journalist backwards, sending him sprawling to the floor. 'You're a real piece of shit, Boyd!'

'Maybe,' Boyd said from the ground, 'but I've got you on film, assaulting a reporter. Andrew Harvey, isn't it?'

The photographer continued to take pictures, clicking away frantically as he sought an angle for the perfect shot of Boyd and his attacker. He was suddenly slammed up against the wall, and a hand began searching his pockets. It came out with a wallet, and Sonny Baines said between clenched teeth, 'If just one of those pictures is published, I'll be round to . . . . ' Sonny checked the address on the drivers licence. ' . . . Twelve Tennyson Road. Your shit-heel friend here obviously knows us, so he can explain what we specialise in.'

Sonny stepped back and tossed the wallet at the shutterbug's head. 'Now I suggest you walk away before I get really pissed off.'

The shocked photographer quickly decided that a hasty retreat would be the shrewdest move. He dragged Boyd to his feet and pulled him towards the exit. The journalist initially resisted, but when Sonny turned his attention toward Boyd, he immediately thought better of it.

Gray turned to Harvey, praying that he'd misheard Boyd. But the look on his friend's face said it all. 'What happened?'

'There was a fire at her aunt and uncle's place. Vick and Melissa had been staying with them while you were away, and . . . I'm sorry, Tom.'

Gray's instinct was to picture the scene, something he'd done when his first wife, Dina, had ploughed into a concrete overpass a few years earlier. This time, he saw Vick, screaming for help as flames licked around her, hugging her daughter to her chest.

He grabbed Harvey's shoulders. 'What about Melissa?'

'She's at the hospital. They said she's stable but not out of danger yet.'

Gray turned to Smart and the rest of the team, who were just catching up. Tears had begun welling in his eyes. He needed to fashion a quick exit.

'I'm sorry. I have to go . . . ' he managed, his voice cracking on the last syllable.

Concerned, Smart put a hand on Gray's arm and asked what was happening, but even as he formed the words in his head, the tears flowed unabated.

'Vick is dead.'

Smart looked stunned, as did the others. Few of them had met Gray's family, but they all felt his pain. No words were wasted, and Gray didn't expect any. Death happened, a fact they'd long ago accepted. Everyone knew fellow soldiers who'd lost their lives in the service, but when it was someone so close it always offered a different perspective.

'Go,' Smart said.

Gray nodded, suddenly unable to move.

Harvey put an arm around his shoulder. 'Let's get you to the hospital.'

Chapter Twenty-Five

Saturday 12 October 2013

The familiar antiseptic smell assaulted Gray's senses as he and Harvey entered the intensive care unit.

Neither man had said a word on the way to the hospital, Harvey wanting to let his friend handle things his own way while Gray descended into a black hole filled with self-loathing. On the flight back to England he'd been looking forward to holding his wife and child in his arms again, to say sorry, to promise never to abandon them again.

And now it was too late.

He'd never see her smiling face, or know the smell of her hair, the gentleness of her kiss . . . .

The next thing Gray knew, he was following Harvey into the hospital building, time having shrunk the journey to what felt like seconds. Staff seemed to be few on the ground as they walked to the reception desk, where the nurse on station directed them to Melissa's room. They followed the directions and came to a locked door, which buzzed open once Gray identified himself.

A nurse stood over the child's incubator, making notes on a clipboard.

'How is she?' Gray asked as he gazed down at his daughter. She didn't appear to have sustained any burns, but a tube was taped over her mouth, helping her to breathe, while an assortment of sensors covered her tiny frame and an intravenous drip fed her a clear liquid.

'She's stable, bless her,' the nurse said, looking down at Melissa. 'The doctor will be round in a few minutes.'

She left before Gray could ask any further questions, and he had to satisfy himself with watching his little girl's gentle breathing. He wanted to rip the plastic cover off and sweep her up into his arms, but somehow managed to restrain himself.

'How did this happen?' he asked Harvey.

'I don't know the details. I got a call from Ryan, your solicitor, to say Ken Hatcher was looking for you. I spoke to Ken and he told me about the fire. They're okay, by the way. Both are being treated upstairs for smoke inhalation but they should be released in the morning.'

'Do you know what caused it?'

'Not yet. The fire investigation unit are still sifting through the debris.'

The door opened and a doctor entered, the look on his face telling them it had been a long shift. He introduced himself as Roger Duckitt and looked over Melissa's notes, adding his own comments.

'Is she going to make it?' Gray asked.

'Yes, she's going to live,' the doctor said, comparing the notes with the digital readout on the screen next to the incubator, 'but we won't know the effects of the cerebral anoxia for a while. Melissa had to be resuscitated at the scene, and we simply don't know how long the brain had been starved of oxygen. Brain cells start to die within about five minutes of the oxygen supply being cut off, and at this stage we simply cannot tell how much damage has been done. The EEG scan looked reasonable, which suggests there isn't too much injury.'

'When will you know?'

'She'll be having an MRI scan in the next hour, and that should give us a better indication.'

'Why are you waiting so long?' Gray asked, his concern palpable. 'Can't you do it now?'

'I totally understand your anxiety, Mr Gray, but we only managed to stabilise Melissa a couple of hours ago, and there have been other tests to carry out. We're doing everything we can for her at the moment, and the MRI won't cure her; it will just tell us how to manage her recovery going forward.'

Gray pressed for more information, but the doctor assured him there was nothing more to be done.

'Go home, Mr Gray. There's little point in being here right now.'

'I want to be here when she wakes up,' Gray said, defiantly. 'She needs her daddy.'

'That won't be any time soon,' Duckitt said. 'She's in a medically induced coma. It was necessary to prevent further damage to the brain. Go and get some rest. You look like you could do with it.'

'Come on,' Harvey said, 'I'll take you home.'

Gray shook his head, never taking his eyes off his daughter. She looked so peaceful, despite all the medical equipment attached to her tiny frame. Tears flowed as he recalled hearing of his son's death all those years ago, and he knew he wouldn't be able to cope if he had to go through it all again.

'I can't, Andrew. She needs me.'

'Come on,' Harvey said, 'you're staying at my place tonight.'

Gray found himself being led out of the room, and after initial resistance, he allowed himself to be torn away from his daughter.

⌣

Harvey thanked the consultant and handed over a card, asking him to call if there was any change in Melissa's condition in the next few hours, then led Gray back through the building to the deserted car park. The roads were quiet at one in the morning, and

Harvey made it back to his flat in record time. Once inside, he got Gray settled on the couch before making up the spare bedroom, throwing a sheet and duvet onto the single bed. When he got back to the living room, Gray was sitting in silence, staring at the faux-fireplace.

'Your bed's ready, Tom. Go and get your head down.'

Gray nodded imperceptibly, but didn't move.

It was heart-breaking for Harvey to see his friend in such a state. He'd personally known Vick for over a year, and the news of her death had come as a huge shock. He simply couldn't imagine what Gray was going through, but he knew Tom wasn't in a good place right now. The tough façade had cracked, and Harvey saw a helpless man on the edge of a breakdown.

He thought about sitting down and talking things through, but decided against it. He could see that Gray needed time and space to himself.

'Can I get you anything before I turn in?'

A slight shake of the head answered his question, and he reluctantly left Tom Gray to deal with his loss.

Chapter Twenty-Six

Sunday 13 October 2013

'It's me,' said Detective Inspector Frank Wallace. 'Buy yourself a burner cell phone and call me back on this number.'

Wallace ended the brief call and rubbed his head, wishing he'd stopped at just half a bottle of whisky the night before. While he waited for Hart to get back to him, Wallace forced himself into the shower, the hot needles of water helping to soothe away the dull ache from the previous night's overindulgence.

Reinvigorated, he dressed in jeans and a T-shirt before making his third coffee of the morning. He was pouring the water when his pay-as-you-go phone chirped.

'Bill, what the hell have you done?'

'I don't know what you mean, officer,' Hart chuckled into the phone. 'I was here the whole time.'

Wallace gripped the handset until his knuckles went white, again cursing his luck at being saddled with such a stubborn imbecile. He'd seen the initial news report that a house fire had killed a woman in London, which was nothing noteworthy, but when the morning newspaper revealed the identity of the victim, he knew Hart had to be behind it.

'Are you telling me that Tom Gray's wife is dead and you know nothing about it?'

'People die all the time. Get over it.'

'This is no joke, goddamn it. Your sons have a run-in with Tom Gray and a few days later his wife is dead. You don't have to be a genius to join those dots.'

'Then make it go away,' Hart said, his voice suddenly serious. 'That's what I pay you for.'

'That's not the point. You're drawing unnecessary attention to yourself. The idea is to stay off the radar, not stamp your name on every crime you commit.'

'Who says it was a crime? Are they calling it arson?'

'Not yet,' Wallace admitted, 'but it's standard practice to investigate the cause of all domestic fires, and given the high-profile victim, I think this one will be thorough.'

'Listen, the boys and I will be back from Gran Canaria in a few days. If it turns out to be arson, you bring us in, we provide the perfect alibi and that's the end of the matter.'

You wish. Wallace wasn't concerned with Hart being put in the frame for the fire. The alibi was cast iron, irrefutable. No, that wasn't what disturbed him at all.

The problem was Tom Gray himself.

The last time Gray lost a family member, he'd used his military know-how to bring the country to a standstill. With that kind of prior record, would Gray simply let this lie just because Hart had a rock-solid alibi?

Unlikely. It had taken Wallace about three seconds to tie Hart to the crime once he'd heard the name Vick Gray, and her husband was no fool. Hart may not have lit the match himself, but he sure as hell had a hand in it, a conclusion Gray was certain to reach if the investigation showed the fire was no accident.

Armed with that knowledge, what would Gray do? He might be content to rely on the police to handle it, Wallace thought, then immediately dismissed the notion. Gray had baulked at dropping the assault charges against the Hart boys, so there was no way he was going to sit back and let his wife's killers carry on while the force quietly went about the task of gathering evidence.

Would Gray take Hart out? Possibly, if he was one hundred per cent convinced of Bill's involvement.

A light went on in Wallace's head as an idea began to take shape.

'Okay, Bill. We'll play it like you say, but you have to tell me everything. I don't want any surprises coming across my desk, so you need to give me all the details you have about the fire.'

Hart told him about the meeting with Paul Ainsworth, stressing that he didn't know who had carried out the actual deed.

'Is there any way you can find out?' Wallace asked. 'I can look up a list of Paul's known associates when I get to the office, but every search made on the PNC is recorded. Unless this turns into a murder investigation, I'd have a tough time explaining them away without a crime to pin them to.'

Hart promised to get in touch with Ainsworth on his return to the UK that evening, and with nothing else to discuss, Wallace ended the call.

The seed of an idea that had planted itself in his mind began to grow. While the money he got from Hart was nice, Wallace wanted nothing more than to be rid of the thug. It was only a matter of time before the idiot made a mistake that landed them both in hot water, or more specifically, the rest of their lives in prison. Over the years, Wallace had hoped for a young pretender to move into Hart's territory and remove the family from power, but it hadn't come to pass.

Perhaps it was time to use the false passport he'd acquired the previous year, one of the benefits of working with criminals every day. He could take the money he'd saved and say goodbye to Frank Wallace, Detective Inspector, and start a new life as Herman Ulrich, German national. With his sizeable bankroll, he could live comfortably in South America for the rest of his life.

Southeast Asia was also an option—lazing on a beach while the young local women catered for his every whim.

It was a daily dream, but Wallace knew he would only disappear as a last resort, when all other options were exhausted. He needed someone to deal with Hart, and if anyone could, it was Tom Gray.

All Wallace had to do was push the right buttons . . . and that was easily done.

By the time Andrew Harvey surfaced, Tom Gray was long gone. His bed hadn't been slept in, and there was no note of explanation.

Harvey didn't need one.

After a quick shower, he drove to the hospital and found Gray standing over Melissa's incubator. He was about to tell his friend that he looked like shit, but figured Tom already knew and didn't particularly care.

'Any news?' Harvey asked.

Gray looked up, finally acknowledging his presence. 'The doctor said she has a thirty per cent chance of making a full recovery.'

As Tom's gaze returned to the plastic cocoon, Harvey knew his friend was close to losing it completely. Facing up to the death of a wife and child was hard enough for any man to bear, and a few years earlier it had driven Gray to extreme measures, but to then lose Vick and see his daughter teetering on the edge . . . .

'Have they found out what caused it?' Gray asked, never taking his eyes off the tiny figure.

'I haven't been into the office,' Harvey admitted, 'but I'll go and check in now.'

He left Gray alone with his thoughts, bleak as they were, and once in the hallway he dialled Thames House. He asked his colleague, Hamad Farsi, to get what information he could from the emergency services, the cause of the fire in particular.

As he waited for a response, he saw a couple approaching the room. Their hollow expressions told him they were Vick's aunt and uncle. They ignored him and entered the room, closing the door quietly behind them, and Harvey watched through the window as the woman hugged Gray like a long-lost son.

Farsi came back on the line and gave Harvey what they had, which wasn't very much, though it did leave a few questions in Harvey's mind. After promising to be in within the hour, he went back into the room, where the woman was recalling the events of the fateful night.

' . . . . and I heard Melissa crying, but I thought Vick was in there with her, trying to get her to sleep. When I finished in the toilet I went back to bed and was just dozing off when the fire alarm went off.'

'We jumped out of bed,' Ken interrupted, 'and I went to get Vick, but when I opened the door there was just Melissa, lying on the floor, screaming. I told Mina to grab her while I went looking Vick, but I couldn't find her upstairs.'

'I took Melissa,' Mina said, taking up the story again, 'and wrapped her in a blanket, but by the time I got halfway down the stairs, the hallway was already filled with thick smoke. I couldn't even see an inch in front of my face. There were flames coming out from under the living room door, so we couldn't get to the front door.'

Harvey had his eye on Gray, who was listening intently as the story unfolded. He had a feeling Tom was picturing the scene, walking through the building with them as they fought the dense smoke.

'We tried for the back door,' Mina said, tears beginning to well, 'but the kitchen was so dark, and Ken couldn't find the key. It took forever to get the door open, and by that time Melissa had stopped crying . . . . '

She trailed off and looked down at the plastic crib, tears running down her face.

Gray hugged Mina once more, assuring her that she'd done as much as she could for the little girl.

'Tom, I have to go,' Harvey said. 'I'll give you a call later.'

Gray nodded, then remembered that his phone had been confiscated a few days earlier. 'I haven't got a mobile.'

'No problem, I'll get one and bring it round this evening,' Harvey said. 'I take it you'll be here?'

'I'll be here.'

As Harvey opened the door, Gray stopped him. 'What did you find out about the fire?'

'I haven't seen all the details, but it appears to have been accidental.'

He could see it was little comfort to Gray. His wife was gone and his daughter was fighting for her life, all down to happenstance.

'Get something to eat, all right? I'll be back soon.'

Harvey left, wishing he could stay and try to bring his friend back from the brink of despair, but unfortunately life went on for the other seven billion people on the planet. He reached Thames House an hour later, having stopped off to buy Gray a phone and shaving kit. Hamad Farsi was sitting at his desk, and Harvey took a seat opposite him, a bank of monitors dividing the pair.

'How's Tom taking it?' Farsi asked.

Harvey shrugged. Farsi had met Gray a couple of times, most recently when Harvey had helped bring him safely back from Durban. 'About as well as you'd expect, under the circumstances.' Harvey logged into his terminal and brought up the fire report that Farsi had sent to his station. He read that the investigation was still in the early stages, with crews having just finished the damping-down process. Initial checks showed no sign of forced entry, and no accelerants were found near any of the doors or windows, usual indicators of an arson attack. The fire appeared to have started in the living room, where the single fatality had been found.

Harvey cringed at the impersonal description. It was easy to dismiss the detached narrative when the victim was a stranger, but when it was someone you'd known, had spent many an evening with, it seemed so cold. He felt sure Gray would react the same way if he saw it.

The report went on to say that the flash point had been next to an empty bottle of sambuca, and a cigarette was deemed to have started the fire, with the alcohol acting as an accelerant.

That struck Harvey as wrong, just as it had when Farsi had mentioned it over the phone. Vick didn't smoke—hadn't smoked, he corrected himself. She had enjoyed a drink, though he'd only ever seen her drink wine or the occasional beer, never spirits.

Perhaps she'd gone for sambuca as that was all there was in the house, but it didn't explain the cigarette. Could she have been smoking in anger at Tom's absence, or because of it? He didn't think so. She was a healthy girl who'd loved her exercise, and there was no way she'd inflict the second-hand smoke on her infant daughter.

He decided to have a word with Vick's aunt and uncle to see if they could shed some light on it.

One thing he wouldn't do, however, was question them in front of Tom. Much as he liked the man, he knew Gray would jump on the inconsistencies and start seeing phantoms that might not be there. He made the decision to withhold those details from Gray for the time being, though he knew Tom would eventually get a copy, for insurance purposes if nothing else.

When that happened, the shit was sure to fly.

Chapter Twenty-Seven

Tuesday 15 October 2013

Tom Gray woke at five in the morning and threw on his running gear, hoping to get a few miles in before his house guests rose for the day.

He'd offered Ken and Mina a place to stay while their housing issues were sorted out, and Vick's mother and father had arrived from Australia the night before. To say the atmosphere had been solemn didn't even begin to describe the mood of the house.

He jogged out to the street and did a few stretches to loosen up his muscles, then began pounding the streets, pushing harder than he normally did on the opening circuit. Sweat soon soaked his T-shirt, and his breathing grew increasingly laboured, but he maintained the pace, the discomfort taking his mind off recent events.

He finished the second lap of the area, but instead of heading home, he continued on, pumping harder and harder. After another mile, he slowed to a stop, leaning against a wall as he caught his breath. As he closed his eyes, gulping oxygen, a vision of Vick drove into his head, flames licking at her as she screamed his name . . . .

Gray vomited, dry-heaving after what little bile that lined his stomach had been expunged. He knew the visions would continue until he sought closure, so he promised himself he'd again ask

Harvey what had happened. According to Andrew, the report deemed it an accident, and he hadn't offered any further details.

To Gray, it just didn't add up. What was Vick doing downstairs at that time of night? Ken and Mina thought she'd gone to get the changing bag, because Melissa had been half-dressed when they'd found her. If that was the case, why did she stay in the living room and close the door?

Gray wiped his mouth and walked home, making the decision to go to the office that morning. Burying himself in work would perhaps take his mind off things, and as he hadn't been there for a week, there was bound to be plenty to do.

When he arrived back at the house he took a shower and dressed before forcing himself to eat a meagre breakfast. He'd had no appetite for days, but knew the importance of keeping himself fuelled.

Ken surfaced just before seven and joined him in the kitchen, helping himself to a coffee. Conversation was light, neither of them in the mood for idle chit-chat, though they did discuss the funeral arrangements.

The ceremony was scheduled to take place the coming Friday, leaving them just a couple of days to finalise the preparations. Gray was grateful that Ken and Mina were taking on most of the responsibility, leaving him time to be at Melissa's side, and although he now realised that his presence made no difference, he felt like he was abandoning his daughter every time he left her room.

Gray left the house before eight and struggled through the rush hour traffic to the office, where he found a pile of mail in his in-tray. Taking centre stage on his desk was a bouquet of flowers sitting in a vase, along with a message of condolence from his secretary. He was touched by the gift, but it immediately brought back memories of his wife, and he sat for some time with his face in his hands.

Get a grip, Tom!

He forced the memories aside and made a start on the correspondence, mostly bills and invoices. His secretary Gill appeared just before nine.

'Tom, I'm so sorry. I can't believe this happened to you again. How's Melissa?'

Gray explained his daughter's situation, his voice shakier than he would have liked.

'Bless her. Why did this have to happen?' She handed over the day's mail and disappeared without waiting for an answer, wiping her eyes as she went.

At the top of the small pile was a plain, white envelope with the address printed on the front. He opened it, expecting more marketing crap, but inside was a single sheet of A4 with a succinct, typed note:

Your wife was murdered by Robert Harman on William Hart's instructions.

Gray was stunned by the brief message. He read it over and over, not quite believing his eyes. Under the message was printed an address in Manchester. Gray assumed it belonged to Robert Harman.

He reached for the phone and started dialling Harvey's number, but halfway through, he stopped. If Vick had been murdered, then surely there would have been something about it in the fire report, which Andrew had a copy of.

It was no secret that the government didn't like Gray, given that he'd held them to ransom a few years earlier and further embarrassed them since by exposing one of their kill squads, but would Harvey take their side? Gray refused to believe it. Harvey had put his life and career on the line to help Gray escape from James Farrar's clutches in Durban, so it was unlikely he'd withhold anything this important.

If Andrew had information that the fire was no accident, he would have shared it.

Wouldn't he?

Gray was going round in circles. He grabbed his jacket and strolled along to the café, where he bought a latte to go, all the time trying to figure out why Harvey was withholding information from him. When he arrived back at the office, his mind was no clearer, so he decided to call the detective who had asked him to drop the assault charges against Hart's sons. He found the calling card in his desk drawer and dialled the number.

'DI Wallace.'

'Hello, Inspector, this is Tom Gray. Is it possible to meet? I may have some information regarding William Hart.'

'What kind of information?' Wallace asked.

'It relates to the fire that killed my wife. I think he may be involved, but I need something from you first.'

'You have my condolences, Mr Gray, but I can't give you anything relating to an on-going investigation.'

'That's fine. I just need a copy of the report into the cause of the fire. It may be important, and as it has been classed an accident, there's no reason for the police to investigate it, is there?'

Gray waited while Wallace digested the request. 'Okay, I can spare you fifteen minutes. There's a pub called the Sandford in Battersea. I'll meet you there at eleven.'

Wallace hung up, leaving Gray wondering if he'd made the right choice. If it was true, and this Harman character had started the fire on Hart's orders, was it possible that Harvey knew about it?

More to the point, if he showed Wallace the anonymous letter he'd received, would the detective do anything about it?

Gray hoped so, because if the report turned up anything suspicious, Harman had a lot to answer for.

Gray took a tube to the Sandford and was sitting at a table with a pint when Wallace arrived. He gestured to Gray's half-empty glass, but Tom shook his head. Once armed with a neat whisky, he joined Gray at the table.

'What can I do for you, Mr Gray?'

'Did you bring the report?'

Wallace handed over a manila folder and Gray extracted the three-page document. He took his time, digesting the information and skipping nothing. When he got to the cause of the fire, he stopped and re-read the paragraph three times before placing the report on the table.

'My wife was murdered, Inspector.'

'Call me Frank,' Wallace insisted. 'What makes you say that?'

Gray pointed to a section on the second page. 'My wife doesn't drink spirits, and she certainly doesn't smoke.'

'Perhaps she took it up without your knowledge,' Wallace offered. 'Postnatal stress can do that.'

'Not Vick. She hated cigarettes. And even if she was going to have a drink and smoke, why would she do it halfway through changing her daughter? Why would she leave Melissa crying in the bedroom?'

'It does seem strange,' Wallace admitted, 'but the fire investigator found nothing to suggest a forced entry, and the only accelerant was the alcohol your wife was drinking.'

'So what are you saying? She's in the middle of changing her daughter's nappy and decides to go to the living room, take up smoking and immolate herself?'

'Tom, I know you want to blame someone for her death. It's only natural. But it was an accident, and I don't see what else I can do.'

'You could bring Hart in for questioning,' Gray said, steel in his voice.

'I already checked, Tom. He was in Gran Canaria the night of the fire, as were his sons. Speaking of which, you mentioned that you had some information about him.'

Gray pulled out the envelope and handed it over.

'Not really a lot to go on,' Wallace said, after reading the brief note. He looked at the post mark. 'Looks like it was posted locally, so based on that I'd say it's one of Hart's competitors trying to frame him. If I can come to that conclusion after a few seconds, I'm sure Hart's solicitor could eventually come up with another feasible explanation.'

Gray was beginning to regret his decision to involve the inspector. 'So you won't do anything?'

'I'll run the name and ask Greater Manchester Police to pop round and have a word with this Harman bloke, but I wouldn't get your hopes up, Tom. The CPS is unlikely to take this on unless they had some forensic evidence or eyewitnesses. It's especially hard to get a conviction when the alibi is irrefutable.'

Gray snatched the letter back and shoved it into his pocket. 'Thanks for nothing. *Frank.*'

He rose and left the pub, his anger mounting as he walked back to the tube station. Vick's death was no accident, he was convinced of that, and yet once again the authorities were going to do nothing.

He considered doing an interview with the newspapers, shaming the police into action, but soon saw the futility of those actions: Hart might be pulled in, but with a cast-iron alibi, nothing would be done. Perhaps it would prompt a more thorough investigation of the fire scene, but by then the house would have been cleared out, with any forensic proof long gone.

Gray thought for a moment about Robert Harman. A large part of him wanted to drive to Manchester and confront him with a baseball bat, but he knew that was now out of the question, as Wallace would finger him for anything that happened to the man.

He needed something more subtle, a way to gather evidence against Harman, and that meant involving Harvey. Gray still wasn't sure if he could trust Andrew, especially after he'd withheld the details about Vick smoking and drinking at the time of her death. Harvey knew full well that Vick wouldn't have done those things, especially with Melissa crying upstairs, so there must have been a damn good reason for not sharing the information.

Gray pulled out his phone and hit a pre-set number.

'Andrew,' he said once the call connected, 'we need to talk.'

Frank Wallace savoured the remains of the whisky as he sat back in the chair. The meeting had gone quite well, but when Gray had pulled out the letter, he'd thought the opportunity had gone. He'd hoped Gray would set out to find Harman and beat a confession out of him before going after Hart, but Gray was nobody's fool. That way lay trouble, and Gray would soon realise it. At least Wallace had managed to stress that a conviction was unlikely if Hart could prove he was elsewhere at the time of the offence. Hopefully Gray would be able to make use of that fact.

Wallace emptied his glass and decided to give it a few more days. If Gray hadn't made his move by then, he'd press a few more buttons.

Chapter Twenty-Eight

Tuesday October 15th 2013

Gray watched Harvey pull up outside the offices of Minotaur Logistics and ring the bell. The door buzzed open and the secretary took his name. She was about to place a call to Gray's office when he opened his door and gestured for Harvey to follow.

'What's so urgent, Tom?'

Gray locked eyes with his friend. 'How did Vick die?'

'I told you, it was an accident.'

'Okay, then what started the fire.'

Harvey paused. 'A cigarette,' he eventually said.

'And you didn't think that strange?'

'Of course I did—'

Gray exploded. 'Then why didn't you tell me?' he demanded, rising from his seat.

Harvey was visibly shocked at the sudden rage. '*This* is why I didn't tell you. Right now, you look like you'd kill anyone who looked at you.'

'And how do you expect me to react? My wife's death is suspicious and my daughter is in a coma, but nobody is going to investigate it. Am I supposed to just shrug it off and move on with my life?'

'Tom, you need to—'

'Don't you dare tell me to calm down, Andrew. You knew about this, and you didn't tell me. I thought we were friends.'

'We are. It's just . . . '

Gray glared at Harvey, waiting for him to finish the sentence. It was a long time coming.

'Don't you think it odd that after all you did, kidnapping those kids and getting one over on the home secretary, I'm still allowed to hang out with you? If I want to date a woman, she has to go through a thorough vetting programme, yet they allow me to spend my Friday nights with you.'

Harvey waited for the penny to drop.

'You're spying on me?' Gray asked.

'Not so much. I'm more . . . Jiminy Cricket to your Pinocchio. My job is to make sure you stay out of trouble, and certainly don't start any.'

Gray sat back in his chair, stunned at Harvey's revelation. He was overwhelmed as a myriad of feelings assaulted him, each fighting for dominance.

One bubbled its way to the surface.

Betrayal.

'I want you to leave.'

Harvey didn't move. 'I can't, Tom. Trust me, I wanted to tell you a couple of days ago, but you weren't ready.'

'What do you mean I wasn't *ready*?'

'I mean you were emotionally unstable. Giving you information that may or may not suggest foul play would have pushed you over the edge, and you can't afford to lose it. Your daughter is in the hospital, and when she gets out she's going to need her daddy. She can't have that if you're dead or locked away in a cell.'

Gray turned and stared out of the window. Harvey was right, whichever way he looked at it, and that made him even angrier. He wanted to argue the point, but couldn't think of anything rational to counter Harvey's statement.

He resumed his seat behind the desk and exhaled loudly. 'You're right. I'm sorry.'

'No need to apologise,' Harvey assured him. 'You've been through a lot, and you still have Melissa to worry about. I can't pretend that I know what you're going through, but you need to focus on your daughter right now. If this wasn't an accident, I'll help you get to the bottom of it.'

Gray nodded and thought of the letter he'd received, but decided to hold on to that ace for the time being.

'I have to go and see her,' he said, looking at his watch.

'I'll drive you there. It's on the way.'

Harvey accompanied Gray to Melissa's room and stayed with him until the duty consultant came to do his rounds. Her condition hadn't changed, but the long-term prognosis was positive.

'Her MRI was encouraging, so we expect to bring her out of the coma in the next few days,' the doctor told them. 'Her most recent ECG looks good, though it will be some time before the full extent of the injury is understood.'

'What's your opinion?' Gray asked.

The doctor shrugged. 'It could be anything from permanent vegetative state to a full recovery. We simply won't know until she's conscious and we're able to perform some rudimentary tests. However, her recovery is progressing much better than expected, which points to the more optimistic end of the scale.'

Gray thanked him as he left, then took his usual seat next to her incubator. The book he'd brought in a couple of days earlier was where he'd left it, and he opened it at the dog-eared page.

'She loved it when Vick read to her at night,' he explained, and felt the rush of blood that usually preceded tears. He looked at Harvey. 'I'm good here. You go catch some bad guys.'

As the door closed and he was left alone with his daughter, Gray put the book down and began thinking about the next steps.

Melissa was his sole responsibility now. That meant looking after her twenty-four-seven, so work was out of the question. There was the option to put her into a nursery once she was a year old, but for the moment he couldn't imagine letting her out of his sight.

He thought about selling the business once more, but he'd need a monthly income for the foreseeable future rather than a lump sum. He'd have to get a manager in and do what he could from home, but there would always be trips overseas to consider. Len Smart was as level-headed as they came, and he'd ask him to take on the role of manager-stroke-ambassador.

The house would definitely have to go. Not only was it bigger than they needed, it would hold too many memories. He would downsize and pay cash for a smaller place, and use what remained to kit it out for Melissa's needs, whatever they might be.

He looked at her again, and wondered how anyone could do such a thing to an innocent. His mind wandered as he thought of the other children he'd seen killed and maimed while on tour in Iraq. One perpetrator had been caught and dealt with by the locals, and Gray imagined doing the same to whoever had devastated his family.

Only he couldn't. He'd tipped his hand to Wallace, and so any attack on Harman or Hart would soon have the police knocking at his door.

Gray picked up the book in an effort to force the thoughts aside, and began regaling Melissa with the story of Little Red Riding Hood. He was almost done when his phone rang.

'Tom, it's Andrew. I just got back to the office and found the autopsy report on my desk.'

Gray held his breath, wondering if he was ready to hear the details, but Harvey spared him.

'There was no sign of alcohol in her system. There was some trauma to her head, so it looks like she was unconscious when the fire started.'

'Someone hit her?'

'It doesn't look like it. The official line is that she was holding the sambuca bottle and glass when she fell against a table and knocked herself out.'

Gray recalled the heavy oak coffee table Ken had in the living room. If she had tripped and banged her head against it, that would explain the way she'd been incapacitated, but he still didn't accept the fact that she'd neglect her daughter to have a drinking session.

His heart was still convinced that Vick had been murdered.

Which brought him back to the note. Who had sent it, and why? Wallace may have been correct in suggesting it was one of Hart's rivals, hoping Gray would do them a favour. But then they'd have to have known that Vick's death wasn't an accident, as had been reported on the news. He tried to list anyone who would know the details of the report into the fire, but he could only think of himself and Harvey, plus the police and fire service. The latter two saw nothing suspicious in Vick's death, and it seemed highly unlikely that Harvey would taunt him by sending the letter, only to talk him out of taking any action.

That left just one possibility: someone else knew Vick was murdered. Not a rival to Hart, but someone close to him.

If Gray was going to find out who had killed his wife, he needed Harvey's help, and that meant opening up to him.

Having taken that decision, he told Harvey everything, from the arrival of the letter to his meeting with the detective.

'What did Wallace say?' Harvey asked.

'That he'd contact the local police and get them to look into Harman.'

'Then I suggest you let him. The police can handle this now. I'm sure that if there's any way Harman was involved, they'll get to the bottom of it.'

Gray didn't share Harvey's confidence. He still wanted to give Harman a napalm enema, but with one glance at his daughter he knew he couldn't do anything that might mean losing her.

'Okay. I'll call Wallace in a few days to see how things are going.'

Gray ended the call and returned to the book. When it got to the part where the woodcutter cut the wolf open, he swapped it for a more subtle ending.

There was no need for his daughter to be exposed to such violence: he would save that for someone more deserving.

Chapter Twenty-Nine

Friday 18 October 2013

The grey October sky reflected the mood of the party gathered around the open grave as the vicar said a final few words before laying Vick to rest.

Harvey glanced at Tom and wondered how the same shit could happen to the same guy twice. At least he was taking it better than expected. Though understandably not the life and soul of the party, Gray wasn't showing any untoward signs of anger or malevolence. Harvey was thankful that his friend had decided to focus his attention on his daughter rather than thoughts of retribution.

As the coffin was lowered into the ground, Harvey said his own private farewell, then joined the other dozen mourners as they trudged through the rain-soaked grounds to the waiting cars. They drove back to Gray's home, just Ken and Mina, Vick's parents and a handful of close friends.

A spread of sandwiches and finger food had been prepared, though few were in any mood to indulge. Instead, they stood around, drinking tea and coffee and remembering the good times they'd shared with the dearly departed.

Harvey felt uncomfortable, though he assumed everyone else did, too. What could be said that would offer comfort to a grieving family? He did his best, then grabbed Gray and took him to one side.

'How are you holding up?'

'I've had better days. The main thing is getting today out of the way so that I can start thinking about Melissa's future.'

'What's the latest news?' Harvey had been in daily contact with Gray and knew every detail of her progress, but thought it might help if he forced his friend to concentrate on the living for the time being.

'She'll be brought out of the coma on Monday. We should know more about her condition in the coming weeks.'

Harvey nodded. 'How's Len doing?'

Smart had been given the role of interim manager while Ryan Amos drew up a contract that would allow Gray to resign from his position as company director, yet retain an interest in the business. His new role would be that of technical advisor, which came with a generous monthly stipend. It was hoped that removing Gray's name from the register at Companies House would relieve the stigma and prevent more clients from bailing.

'If I didn't know better, I'd say he was born to be a desk jockey. I swear it's the first time he's ever worn a suit, but he certainly looks the part.'

Harvey chuckled at the thought of the tough ex-soldier playing office manager.

'What about you? Are you . . . you know . . . okay?'

'I'm not going to march off and start a war, if that's what you mean. I promised I'd leave it to the police, and I will. In fact, I'm going to give that copper a call, see how things are progressing.'

They walked out to the garden where Gray pulled out his mobile and the detective's business card. He dialled the number and put it on speaker.

'DI Wallace.'

'Frank, it's Tom Gray. I was just wondering if you had any news regarding Robert Harman.'

Wallace asked him to hold, and when he came back on the line a couple of minutes later, Gray heard traffic in the background.

'I just checked the database. Harman was pulled in for questioning yesterday but they got nothing from him. He knows half a dozen people who'll swear he was at a party that night.'

'And that's it? Didn't they check his wardrobe for forensics or something?'

'We can't really do that unless we're invited in or have a warrant, and those aren't easy to come by unless you have a crime to link it to, which we don't.'

'Well, what about previous? Has he got a criminal record?'

'I can't go into details, Tom. Let's just say he's no choirboy.'

The look on Gray's face as he hung up betrayed his anger. 'They have to be totally inept to see Vick's death as an accident. I hand them clues on a plate, and they still won't do anything.'

'It's frustrating, I know,' Harvey said. He, too, felt there was enough to start an investigation and couldn't understand Wallace's apathy. 'I'll head to the office and see if I can dig up anything on Harman that might shake them into action.'

He didn't know what he expected to find, but he had to show that something was being done. If he didn't, Gray might start thinking of taking the matter into his own hands, and that wasn't likely to end well.

Harvey said his goodbyes and left, arriving at Thames House an hour later due to a lorry spillage *en route*. After making himself a coffee, he signed into his work station, then logged into the Police National Computer and began searching for Robert Harman.

There were very few matches, which made it easy to find the one linked to the address in the letter Gray had given him. Harvey opened the file and was surprised to see just one conviction for a motoring offence. He was hardly the career criminal Wallace had painted him to be, and that set alarm bells ringing.

What possible motive could Wallace have for feeding Gray misleading information? He looked for the most recent entry on the file and saw that it had been recorded four years earlier, around the time of his arrest for speeding. He certainly hadn't been pulled in for questioning in the last few days.

What are you playing at, Wallace?

He made a mental note to follow that up and in the meantime looked for Harman's known associates. Harvey was surprised to find several, and they all linked back to one man: Paul Ainsworth. A quick scan of his file showed a particularly nasty character, with a long list of arrests but very few convictions. It was a common scenario: victims were harassed or bullied into withdrawing their statements and refusing to press charges.

Further digging revealed no known ties between Ainsworth and Hart, other than the fact that both were suspected of being involved in organised crime. That set Harvey thinking of Wallace once more.

As one of the senior figures in the newly formed National Crime Agency, Wallace would surely be familiar with both men, and he would certainly want to follow up any leads.

So why had he lied to Gray about checking on Harman?

The thought nagged him like a truculent spouse. Gray had explained why he'd dropped the charges against the Hart boys, and it might simply be that Wallace didn't want to tip his hand and let Hart and Ainsworth know they were being watched. If that was the case, there would surely be some mention in Vick's file.

Harvey searched for Gray's wife and the mystery deepened. Her death was still noted as accidental, with no recent updates, which meant Wallace was either extremely sloppy when it came to procedure, or he really wasn't interested in pursuing the case.

Harvey rose and walked around, trying to piece the puzzle together, but there was something missing.

He strode to Veronica Ellis's office and knocked, entering when commanded.

'I'd like to do a check on someone,' he told her.

The assistant director general gave him a quizzical look. 'Since when do you need my permission?'

'When it's a detective inspector in the NCA.'

'So you've got my attention,' Ellis said. 'Spill it.'

Harvey told her about the suspicious circumstances surrounding Vick's death, as well as Gray's altercation with the Hart boys a few days prior and the note pinning Robert Harman to the fire.

'Not exactly conclusive,' Ellis said.

Harvey agreed, but pointed out the alternative, which made Ellis cringe. She stood and smoothed her pencil skirt before wandering back and forth, arms folded across her chest.

'The thought of Tom Gray on another crusade chills my blood,' she said. 'I've been in this position for eighteen months, and still nothing scares me more than the thought of a pissed-off Tom Gray going on another rampage. That's why I tasked you with keeping an eye on him.'

She pondered a little longer, then came to a decision. 'If you think it's the only way to mollify him, I'll play along. Tell me what you need.'

'For the moment, just your say-so. Gerald can provide everything else.'

Ellis nodded, and Harvey went to the technician's office, where he found Gerald Small tinkering with a fibre-optic camera.

'You got a minute?'

Small put the device down and offered Harvey a seat. 'What do you need?'

Harvey normally worked on a need-to-know basis, but Small had a habit of finding gaps in the plan when shown the bigger picture, and he didn't disappoint when Harvey told him the entire story of Gray, his family, his wife's death, Hart, and Wallace's role in it all. Before Harvey could explain the mission, Small interrupted.

'If he said he checked up on Harman but didn't, it sounds like this Wallace guy is trying to help Hart rather than put him away,' the specialist said, 'You want me to put a trace on his calls, is that right?'

Harvey could have smacked himself. Of course Wallace was protecting Hart. Once Small had suggested it, it seemed obvious.

But he still needed proof.

'If I can get you a mobile number, can you get me a history of calls?'

'Sorry, we don't have that capability, but I can give you everything from this moment on.'

'Okay,' Harvey said. 'That'll have to do.'

He rose to leave, wondering how he could force Wallace's hand, but Small stopped him.

'There's something else you'll need to consider, Andrew.'

'What's that?'

'If you were selling secrets to the Chinese, would you conduct business using your mobile?'

Harvey laughed. 'Of course not!'

'Then perhaps Wallace isn't, either. You don't get to rise so high in the force by being stupid, so if he's really working with Hart, he'd have another phone at the very least. He might even be rotating them, buying a new burner cell every week.'

Harvey felt a complete idiot: such obvious points and he'd missed them both. 'Good point. Well, that complicates things, to say the least.'

Small smiled knowingly. 'Want to know how to find his other phone number, assuming he has one?'

Harvey nodded, and Small smiled as he reached into a drawer, pulling out a box the size of a cigarette packet.

'I finished this a few days ago,' he said. 'It scans the area and logs every IMSI—or International Mobile Subscriber Identity number—in range. The screen will display them in a list, and clicking one will give you details such as provider and phone number. Think of it as a mobile phone mast with a large electronic footprint: devices connect to it automatically based on signal strength.'

'How close would I have to be to detect his phones?'

'You should get fifty yards with clear line-of-sight, maybe thirty if he's in a building.'

'How accurate is it? I mean, if two people were standing side by side and you had two signals, could you tell which phone belonged to which person?'

'No, but I can get it down to a two-metre area. If you can isolate him, it'll give you the details of any devices he's carrying.'

That was good enough for Harvey. 'I'll arrange a meeting for four this afternoon,' he said. 'Bring that along.'

Before Small could object, Harvey left the office and went back to his desk to call Gray.

When his phone chirped, Tom Gray checked the caller ID and saw that it was Harvey. He excused himself and walked into the garden before answering it.

'Hi, Andrew.'

'I need the mobile number of that detective, Frank Wallace.'

Gray pulled out the detective's card and read off the digits. 'Did you find anything?'

'Yes, but I need your help with this.'

Gray agreed to do what he could, but was disappointed with the response.

'Your job is to avoid contact with Wallace at all costs.'

'Avoid him? Why?'

'Because Wallace might be dirty.'

'Dirty?' Gray asked. 'How so?'

'He might be in bed with Hart.'

The conversation paused as Gray digested the news.

'I'm serious,' Andrew said. 'Don't call him or do anything that could tip our hand. We're setting up a sting operation to catch him in the act, so please, just leave it to us.'

Anger boiled inside Gray, a raging heat that consumed his whole body. Now he saw it: Wallace had played him, good and proper. *Drop the charges, Mr Gray, and let us build our case.* And all the while, he was taking backhanders to keep Hart and his family out of trouble.

That's what you get for doing the right thing.

Gray's mind filled with visions of Hart squealing in pain as a blowtorch played over his body, but Harvey cut short the fantasy.

'Please, Tom, for Melissa. Let me handle this.'

Melissa.

Would she be lying in her bouncy chair, gurgling and smiling, if he'd demanded the Hart boys be charged? Had his decision cost his daughter her future and his wife her life?

'Okay,' he said, as convincingly as possible under the circumstances, 'you deal with it.'

Gray hit the button to end the call and put the phone back in his pocket. He stood for some time, staring at the swing set he'd bought for Melissa, but his focus was disturbed when Len and Sonny came out to join him.

'We're heading home, Tom,' Smart said. 'You gonna be okay?'

Gray considered the simple question. 'Not really.' He brought them up to speed on developments, and the two men exchanged glances.

'What are you planning to do?' Sonny asked, warily.

'I honestly don't know,' Gray admitted. 'I know what I'd *like* to do, but as Andrew said, I have to think of Melissa now.'

'When are you going to visit her?' Len asked.

'In about an hour.'

'Any change in her condition?'

'No, but they'll be waking her up on Monday, so I'll finally get to hold her again.'

'That's settled then,' Sonny said, grabbing Gray's arm. 'You're coming with us.'

'Where are we going?'

'To the hospital, followed by a visit to the arse-end of a bottle of scotch.'

<hr />

Harvey ended the call and found Gerald Small standing beside his desk.

'Here you go,' Small said, handing over a mobile phone. 'Use that to call Wallace.'

Harvey studied the phone but saw nothing special. 'What does it do?'

'It makes phone calls,' Small smiled, 'but the number is untraceable and it changes your voice. Watch this.'

Small dialled Harvey's number and nodded for him to answer it.

'Hello, this is your early morning wake-up call,' Small said into the handset, but through Harvey's mobile it sounded as though the specialist had a New York accent.

'You have a menu to choose from,' Small said, handing the phone over. 'Fancy being Scottish, or Irish?'

Harvey smiled, impressed. 'I'll come and get you in a few minutes. I just need to arrange a meeting place and decide how to entice him in.'

Small left Harvey to it, and the section lead sat back, concocting a story likely to lure Wallace into the open. He eventually decided to keep it simple and succinct, while ensuring compliance.

'DI Wallace,' he heard when the call connected.

'William Hart's going to take out his favourite copper,' Harvey said, his modified voice carrying a thick Belfast accent.

'Who is this?' Wallace asked.

'Meet me in an hour, and come alone.'

Harvey read out an address and hung up, hoping the concise message would be enough to convince Wallace to turn up.

He went to Small's office to collect the specialist, who was waiting at his desk with a laptop bag in hand.

'This might come in handy,' Small said as he rose to go, but didn't elaborate.

Harvey drove them to an MI5 safe-house just south of the river: a nondescript terraced house that was one of dozens the service used for various purposes, such as hiding defectors. They were also ideal for sting operations like the one Harvey was setting up.

He parked in the next street and walked back to the building, which was always occupied. The landlady, herself an operative, recognised Harvey from previous visits.

'Hello, gorgeous,' the woman greeted him. 'Long time, no see.'

'Hi, Dee,' Harvey smiled. 'Sorry it's been so long; they never let me out to play these days.'

He gave the fifty-year-old blonde a peck on the cheek and introduced Small before walking through to the living room, which had a good view of the street. He peered through the net curtains and could see the red postbox he'd instructed Wallace to wait next to. After consulting Small and confirming that the target would be within range, they settled down to wait.

Dee made tea for the pair, and while she was gone, Harvey handed Small a slip of paper.

'This is Wallace's mobile number. Once it appears on your screen, we'll know he's here.'

'I'll keep it turned off until we have a suspect,' Small said. 'The battery doesn't last long and I didn't have a chance to give it a decent charge before we left.'

When Dee returned they caught up on the latest news, letting Small keep an eye out for the detective.

Wallace turned up five minutes early, wearing a long coat over his crumpled suit, and immediately checked his watch. He scanned the area, looking comfortable as he cast his gaze over the surroundings.

Small called Harvey over to the window while he powered up the device. Twelve numbers appeared, and Small wiped two of them off to the side of the screen.

'That's yours and mine,' he said. 'Dee, you got any mobiles here?'

The landlady gave him two numbers, and Small removed them along with Wallace's, leaving just seven entries on the display.

'What now?'

'Can you narrow it down a little?' Harvey asked. 'We must be getting hits from the surrounding houses.'

Small recalibrated the handset to reduce the range to twenty yards, roughly the distance to Wallace, who was still standing at the rendezvous point, checking his watch intermittently.

'Okay, down to four.'

Harvey selected a Scottish accent from the menu and handed Small's voice-altering phone to Dee, asking her to call each of the numbers in turn. She put the phone on speaker when the first one answered.

'Hello, this is Evelyn from the surgery. Can I speak to Mrs Alowemba, please?'

There was silence in the room as the recipient explained that she had a wrong number, then Dee apologised and hung up. She dialled the next number on the list, while Harvey kept an eye on Wallace. He was rewarded by seeing the policeman reach into his pocket.

Dee repeated the performance, and Wallace gave a terse 'wrong number' before hanging up halfway through her apology.

'Looks like we got him,' Harvey said to Small. 'Call the number in and get a trace started.'

While Small was on the phone, Harvey wondered how long it would be before Wallace and Hart had their next conversation. He hoped it was sooner rather than later, because Gray was unlikely to sit around waiting for the investigation to run its course. If they spoke only once a month, or even less frequently, it could be weeks before he had a phone call to work with. As things stood, they had a policeman who carried a spare mobile, which wasn't the crime of the century by any means.

It suddenly struck Harvey that he might even be wrong about Wallace. It could be that the policeman was simply humouring Gray by promising to investigate the anonymously written letter, in which case the fact that he had two mobiles meant nothing. Perhaps one was his work number, the other his personal phone.

'The trace is set up,' Small said, interrupting Harvey's thoughts.

'We need to get them talking,' Harvey said absently. Silence followed as they all tried to think of ways to force Hart and Wallace to communicate with each other.

'Tell Hart that Wallace is about to roll on him?' Small suggested at last.

'He's more likely to kill Wallace than have a cosy chat with him,' Harvey said, shaking his head.

'You could let Hart know that he's going to be raided in the morning,' Dee offered, 'though a call at this moment might seem too much of a coincidence. You might want to leave it a couple of hours.'

Harvey considered her advice, but he wanted to be eyes-on if and when Wallace answered the phone.

'Noted,' he said, 'but I'd rather do it before Wallace gets suspicious, and that's what's going to happen when no-one turns up to meet him.'

He called the office and asked Hamad Farsi to find a known contact number for William Hart. He got an answer thirty seconds later.

Small began unpacking his laptop. 'This acts as a middle-man radio tower,' he explained. 'If Hart calls Wallace, we'll be able to intercept their conversation.'

A minute later he declared them good to go, and Harvey switched to a different accent before dialling Hart's number.

'Hart.'

'The coppers are gonna be raiding you in the morning,' Harvey said, waiting for a response.

None came.

The phone went dead in his hand, and Harvey wondered if he'd miscalculated.

'Here we go,' Small said as the laptop played a ringing tone, followed by a now-familiar voice.

'Wallace.'

'What the fuck is going on, Frank? I just got a call saying I was going to be raided in the morning!'

'Who was it from?'

'No idea,' Hart said. 'Some Geordie. Are you planning on hitting my place or what?'

Silence ensued, before Wallace's voice came back on the line. 'I'll get back to you.'

The call ended abruptly, and from his vantage point by the window Harvey could see Wallace was agitated. After looking round, studying the area, the policeman walked back to his car and sped away.

'Looks like you nailed it,' Small said to Harvey, but the section leader wasn't convinced.

Neither was Dee, who had several years in the field to fall back on.

'Judging by his reaction, I'd say you just tipped your hand,' she said, without a hint of I-told-you-so.

Something in the pit of Harvey's stomach agreed with her.

Frank Wallace almost wiped out a pedestrian as he shot through a red light, his mind preoccupied with the mysterious Irishman. He forced himself to concentrate on the road, but couldn't shake the feeling that something bad loomed on the horizon. Someone knew about his relationship with Hart.

The question was: who?

He made it back to the station in record time and went straight to his deputy's office.

'Anything new on the boards?' he asked.

'Nothing, boss,' the detective sergeant said. 'Interpol flagged up a Dutch team planning a visit next month, but apart from that we're business as usual.'

'What about Hart?' Wallace pressed. 'Anything planned for that scumbag?'

'Not that I'm aware of.'

Wallace asked for details of the Interpol notice to be sent to his inbox and headed for his own office. He hung his coat on the back of the door, which he closed and locked, wanting a few minutes of quiet time to digest the events of the last hour.

He sat behind his desk and began putting the pieces together. Now that he didn't have the distraction of driving, he mentally jotted down the facts.

Someone had wanted him at that location this morning, and it couldn't have been a coincidence that Hart had called him while he was there. The only reason he could think of for being lured out into the open was to record his phone calls.

So who was it?

MI5 was the obvious answer, but it made no sense. Hart was his investigation, and certainly wasn't big enough to attract the attention of the security services. Besides which, he'd done nothing in recent months that was out of character and would warrant a closer inspection, and the only time Hart had come to the team's attention was the incident with Tom Gray.

Gray.

Could he be behind the calls? Wallace remembered the furore surrounding Gray's fifteen minutes of fame. Senior officers—himself included—had been tasked with sifting through the subsequent debris in search of lessons to be learnt. The technology Gray had employed at the time had been impressive, so it wouldn't be a huge leap to be able to intercept mobile phone calls. Tabloid hacks had managed it, so it shouldn't be too difficult for someone in the security industry.

If Gray *was* recording his phone calls, it meant he was building evidence, which suggested he was unlikely to go hunting for Hart.

So much for that plan.

Wallace realised he faced trouble from both directions, and he needed to decide which one had to go first.

Hart was growing increasingly erratic with every passing day, but he was still controllable, if barely.

Gray, however, was an unknown quantity. It was impossible to know what he was planning, and that made him the most dangerous in the short term.

Fortunately, Hart and Gray weren't exactly bosom buddies. He would use that to get them at each other's throats and pick up the pieces afterwards.

Grabbing his coat, he left his office and told his deputy that he was leaving for the day.

'If anything comes in, call me.'

Once in his car, Wallace headed for the local supermarket, purchasing a couple of cheap pay-as-you-go phones. He declined the offer of registering them and drove to an industrial estate, where he parked up outside a body workshop. It was one of many front operations Hart used to launder funds, and the ideal place to get in touch with him, especially as he'd managed to keep it off the force's radar. Because Hart wasn't registered as a director with Companies House, the convoluted series of holding companies meant it unlikely he'd ever be associated with a majority of his legitimate interests.

Wallace walked into the body-shop office and slapped his badge down on the counter.

'I need you to get William Hart down here, right now.'

'Never heard of him,' the surly, oil-stained mechanic said.

'Don't fuck about,' Wallace warned him. 'If Bill finds out that I wanted a meet and you didn't tell him, he'll rip your balls off.'

The mechanic suddenly seemed to remember who Hart was, though he was torn between his dislike for the police and incurring Hart's wrath. Eventually he picked up the phone and started dialling.

'Who shall I say wants him?'

'Just tell him we have Tom Gray in common,' Wallace said.

The mechanic passed on the message, though without Wallace's eloquence.

'It's Don at the garage. The filth's here an' 'e wants to see you. Something about a guy called Tom Gray.'

He listened to the response and then put the phone down. 'He'll be half an hour.'

Wallace returned to his car and took out the phones, charging one with the in-car kit while he set the other one up. After fifteen minutes he switched them over and made sure each had the other's number in the contact directory.

Hart turned up five minutes late, and with barely more than a glance in Wallace's direction he walked straight inside the workshop. The detective followed and joined Hart in the office.

'I thought we weren't supposed to meet,' Hart said after Wallace closed the door.

'We're not,' the detective said, 'but we've got a problem.'

He explained his thoughts behind the phone calls, and Hart seemed to be taking it calmly.

'Are you sure it's him?'

'Almost certain,' Wallace said. 'It's too much of a coincidence.'

'Sort it out then,' Hart said.

It wasn't the response Wallace was expecting. 'And just what do you expect me to do? Arrest him?'

'Why not?'

Wallace was at a loss for words. The only reason Gray was on their case was Hart's inability to swallow his pride, yet here he was, passing the buck.

'Have you actually heard of Tom Gray?' Wallace asked, incredulous. 'He held the whole country to ransom for over three days! He managed to keep the police, SAS and security services at arm's length, so don't you think he'd have the foresight to make a few copies of any evidence he has?' He began pacing the small office, hands in his pockets. 'The moment I pull him in, one of his buddies will go to the papers and then we're royally fucked.'

Hart lit a cigarette, ignoring the 'No Smoking' sign that legislation dictated be displayed on the wall. 'I'll send the boys round to sort him out.'

Wallace threw his hands in the air. 'Brilliant! Another beating! That'll stop him! Christ, Bill, why did you have to torch his family? Why couldn't you just let it go?'

Hart leapt from his chair and grabbed Wallace around the throat. 'Because I don't let things go!' he snarled, spittle landing on the policeman's face. 'You let one little thing slide and everyone thinks you're a pussy. Do I look like a pussy to you?'

Wallace trembled involuntarily, aware of what Hart could do when enraged. He managed to shake his head and utter a squeak that Hart took as a *No*. Hart pushed him back into a chair and stood over him.

'When I send the boys round, it's never just another beating.'

The detective rubbed his throat as the natural colour returned to his face. 'You'll need to know where all of his copies are, and I'm not sure your boys can get that out of him. He's ex-SAS. Do you know what that means? They go through intensive interrogation training. By the time your people get him to admit his name and number, his friends will know something's up.'

'Then I'll do it myself,' Hart said, stubbing the cigarette out on the wall. He went out into the garage and came back a few minutes later with a toolbox, which he emptied out onto the counter. He repacked the power drill, angle grinder, hammer and pliers, then went back into the service area, returning with a portable blowtorch.

Wallace rubbed his forehead. 'Why don't you let me do some more checking first? If it isn't Gray, you could be digging us an even bigger hole.'

Hart slammed the lid of the toolbox. 'Do you want this done or not?'

'Just give me a few days,' Wallace said, handing over one of the phones. 'Use that when you need to talk to me. He shouldn't be able to get anything more on us, and what he has is flaky at best. Let me look into this and make sure we're on the right track.'

Wallace knew that if Gray wasn't behind the phone calls, having him killed would put Hart and himself squarely in the frame. For the umpteenth time, he cursed his situation. He was also pissed at Gray for not reacting as expected to his letter. He'd been convinced Gray would take Hart out, but something must have held him back.

More's the pity, Wallace thought. If Gray had dealt with Hart, none of this would be happening. He'd be staring at a comfortable retirement rather than a prison cell, and the thug would have brought it all upon himself.

Perhaps it was time to use the German passport after all.

⌣

Tom Gray was on his third beer, but it was doing nothing to dull the pain he felt inside. After making his excuses to Vick's family, he'd taken Sonny and Len up on their offer and found himself at Sonny's bachelor pad. Conversation had been steered towards better times, the men swapping war stories they'd all heard a dozen times before.

When his mobile rang, Gray checked the screen before answering.

'Hi, Andrew. What's up?'

'It looks like Wallace was working with Hart all along,' Harvey told him, going on to explain the evidence they'd gathered earlier in the day.

Gray put the phone on speaker so that his friends could listen in. 'When are you going to bring them in?'

'Not so fast, I'm afraid. All we've got so far is a brief conversation. We need to build on that if we're going to make a case against them.'

That seemed reasonable to Gray, but he wasn't thrilled with the answer when he asked about timeframe.

'It could be months,' Harvey said. 'Wallace seemed spooked by the calls, and if he's smart, he's got new phones and is working on damage limitation as we speak.'

The combination of beer and bad news was too much for Gray. 'Well that's tremendous,' he said. 'So you're telling me you can't do a thing until they trip themselves up?'

'I know it doesn't sound good, but—'

'Damn right, it doesn't. It sounds like bullshit to me.'

'And what would you do, Tom? Pop round for a quick chat? Just you, Hart and a meat cleaver?'

'Don't tempt me.'

Len Smart took the phone off Gray in an effort to defuse the situation.

'Tom, pull your neck in,' he said, looking at Gray. Then he spoke into the speakerphone: 'And Andrew, stop giving him ideas. Sonny and I will make sure he doesn't go after Hart or Wallace, but I suggest you shift your arse and get something on these guys, sharpish.'

Smart hung up the phone and tossed it to Gray. 'So now what?'

'You heard him,' Gray said. 'I sit here with my thumb up my arse while Hart and Wallace live it up.'

'Will the real Tom Gray please step forward?' Sonny smiled, popping another beer. 'Who is this imposter?'

Smart took a pull from his bottle. 'What our young friend means is, what do you want to do now, Tom?'

Gray wondered if it was the alcohol he'd consumed that left him so confused. 'Are you saying we go after Hart? Because you told Harvey—'

'Exactly what he wanted to hear,' Sonny finished, putting an arm around Gray's shoulder. 'We loved Vick, too, and we know what you're going through. Len here promised that you won't go after Hart, and you won't.'

Gray shook his head. 'You've lost me.'

'You don't have to go after him,' Smart said, 'but that doesn't mean we can't.'

'No,' Gray said. 'I can't ask you to do that. I won't ask you.'

'You don't need to,' Sonny said. 'We're already in. We just need a plan.'

Gray stood and faced the seated pair. 'Enough!' he shouted. 'You have no idea how much I want to look into Hart's eyes as I stick a knife through his heart, but Melissa needs me. If you touch Hart, it'll come back on me, and I can't afford that now.'

He grabbed his coat from the back of a chair and threw it on, leaving them with a final warning.

'Forget about Hart.'

Gray walked out into a crisp evening, the first sign of rain splattering the pavement. He was tempted to walk the four miles home, despite the onset of a heavy downpour, but he couldn't afford to catch cold and miss Melissa's reawakening the following day, so he waited at a taxi rank until a battered Nissan pulled up.

On the journey home, he tried to focus on the things Melissa would need once she left the hospital, but all he saw was his daughter lying in the Perspex sarcophagus, helpless and alone.

To the taxi driver looking in his rear-view mirror, the sight of a grown man crying in the back seat of his cab was all part of a days' work.

Chapter Thirty

Monday 21 October 2013

Tom Gray was halfway through the new nursery rhyme book he'd bought for Melissa when Dr Duckitt arrived, closely followed by a couple of nurses, one blonde, the other a brunette who was pushing a trolley loaded with sharps and a selection of phials.

'Hello, Mr Gray,' the doctor said, taking Gray to one side so that the nurses could get on with their preparations. 'In a few moments we're going to turn off the Propofol feed that's keeping her under. It will be a few hours before she's fully awake, but at this point Melissa's particularly vulnerable to infection. We'll need to get you into some scrubs before you can hold her.'

Gray nodded, glad that the moment he'd been waiting for would soon arrive.

From where he stood, he couldn't see any movement in the crib, though the cardiac monitor was indicating a very slight increase in activity. Duckitt, scanning two other machines for vital signs, gave Gray a smile to indicate that everything was going well.

The doctor gave the nurses some instructions before leaving Melissa in their hands, and Gray went for a coffee while they monitored and recorded her vitals.

As he sat stirring the drink, he said a silent prayer in the hope that someone was listening. No child should have to go through this nightmare, much less any parent. Unfortunately, this line of thinking once again reminded him of Hart.

The man was living the high life, and only his own stupidity would see him come to justice, but Gray wasn't holding his breath. Anyone who had managed to build an empire based on fear and violence would almost certainly be clever enough to keep his head down for a while. No prosecution would take place without concrete evidence, and lots of it. Hart was sure to know this, and would no doubt have a solicitor capable of explaining away anything untoward.

His coffee cup shuddered as a mother carrying her child bumped into his table. After assuring her no damage was done, he turned his thoughts back to his own daughter.

Would she ever get to dance like a normal child? To chase butterflies in the park, or scale the climbing frame in the school yard? He knew he'd have to wait and see, but whatever the outcome, Melissa was going to get all the love he could give.

Gray finished his drink and returned to the room, where the blonde nurse intercepted him and led him to a changing room.

'You'll find a gown, hat and gloves in there,' she said. 'Strip down to your underwear and put your own clothes in one of the lockers. You can keep your socks on, but put the baggies on your feet.'

Gray changed quickly and hurried back to Melissa's room, where the plastic cover had been removed from the crib. His daughter was now swaddled in a blanket, though the wires monitoring her condition remained in place.

'How is she?'

'Doing fine,' the brunette said, as she straightened his paper hat. 'Go over and see her.'

Gray walked to the cot and gently stroked his daughter's forehead, careful not to dislodge any of the sensors.

'Daddy's here, darling.'

He stood there for twenty minutes, whispering to Melissa and waiting for a response. When it came, he was shocked by its ferocity. Melissa began shaking, convulsing, and the cardiac monitor increased in tone and frequency as her heart began pumping harder.

'What's wrong?' Gray asked the nurses.

'It's perfectly normal,' the brunette replied. 'Her pulse is at 135, which is well within the range for a girl of her age. As she comes around, brain activity picks up, which is why you saw her trembling. Limbs that haven't been used for a while are suddenly getting signals again.'

'Are you sure?'

While one nurse convinced Gray that everything was going as planned, the other called for the doctor. Duckitt arrived a couple of minutes later, and after being brought up to speed he removed the tube feeding oxygen to Melissa's lungs.

A few minutes later, Melissa briefly opened her eyes and immediately began crying.

'She's photophobic,' Duckitt explained. 'She hasn't used her eyes for some time, and it'll take time to adjust to the light.'

One of the nurses used a dimmer to reduce the intensity, but Melissa continued to cry.

'I think she wants her daddy,' Duckitt said with a smile, and Gray scooped her into his arms, mindful of the electrodes still attached to her. He made soothing noises and his daughter gradually settled down, her reserves of strength yet to be replenished. For once Gray didn't mind the noise: it meant his daughter was alive, and that was all that mattered.

The brunette held out her hands and Gray handed his daughter over. Melissa was placed back into the cot and Duckitt began performing neuromuscular tests, ensuring her limbs worked normally.

'Physically, Melissa's fine,' the doctor said, but Gray could feel he was holding something back.

'But . . . ?'

'The area we've always been most concerned about is her brain. At this point, there's no telling what damage has been done. She may well recover fully, but we won't know until Melissa's ready to start talking. There were signs of swelling to the Broca's area of the brain, which can affect speech and language, so communication may be a problem as she grows.'

His joy of a few moments earlier fizzled out, but Gray was determined not to become too disconsolate. He still had his daughter, and whatever problems she faced, he would be there to help her.

'When can I take her home?' he asked.

'It will be a couple of days, at least. We need to monitor her for a while, but as things stand, Melissa should be ready to leave on Wednesday.'

Duckitt left to continue his rounds, and the brunette disappeared for a few minutes, returning with some baby formula.

'All yours, Daddy,' she said, handing Gray the bottle. He pulled a chair over to the side of the cot and lifted his daughter out, caressing her cheek with his finger while he gave Melissa her first proper meal in over a week.

Chapter Thirty-One

Tuesday 22 October 2013

·

When his burner phone rang, Frank Wallace knew there could only be one person on the other end of the line. Still, after recent events, he wasn't taking anything for granted.

'Hello?'

'What's the latest?' Hart's unmistakeable voice boomed.

'It looks like I was right,' Wallace told him. 'This has Gray written all over it.'

'That little cocksucker. He's a dead man. Him and that fucking girl of his.'

'Don't be hasty,' Wallace warned. 'We need to get him isolated, otherwise you may not have enough time for what you need to do. I'll meet you in a couple of days, after I've come up with some options.'

Hart mumbled something unintelligible before hanging up, and Wallace afforded himself a little smile.

Whoever was behind the phone calls, it certainly wasn't Tom Gray. One simple check had confirmed that he'd been visiting his daughter at the hospital when the calls had come in, and he was unlikely to have mounted a surveillance from the intensive care unit.

That meant it was either the IPCC or MI5.

The Independent Police Complaints Commission was unlikely to go to such lengths, he knew, which meant the security services were most likely on his case. That revelation had hastened his decision, and he was in the final stages of his preparations.

He would still send Hart after Gray, despite the ex-soldier not being involved. The hope was that Gray would take Hart down permanently, his odds shortened by the letter Wallace had posted earlier that morning. Gray would receive it sometime the following day and would be prepared for an attack, and history told him that Tom Gray prepared very well indeed.

With Hart out of the way, the possibility of building a case against Wallace shrank immeasurably, but he knew there was still the chance of Hart's original blackmail recording turning up.

That was why Frank Wallace had to die.

He'd already scoped out the spot on the beach where he'd park his car with the suicide note on the dashboard and walk into the water. Footprints would lead in, but not out again, as he would traverse the beach until he came to a rocky outcrop. From there it was a short stroll to the other car he'd recently purchased in the name of Herman Ulrich, and then off to sunnier climes.

Not the most original idea, he conceded, but with only a few days to plan his escape, it would have to do. By the time anyone became suspicious, he'd be in Brazil, and from there the world would be his oyster. A little plastic surgery, a change of hair, perhaps a beard, and he'd be able to enjoy the money Hart had been throwing at him over the years.

———

'Andrew, we've got incoming.'

Harvey took the phone off Hamad Farsi and listened to the report from the field team camped near Frank Wallace's flat.

He gave instructions for the men to send the recording to his station and remain in place.

'Told you we'd get something within a week,' Harvey said, holding out his hand.

Farsi dutifully handed over a five-pound note. 'You got lucky this time.'

Harvey's computer beeped to signal the incoming message and he played the audio file it contained.

'I think we should warn Gray,' Farsi said, once the recording had finished.

'Definitely,' Harvey agreed, 'but we might be able to turn this to our advantage.'

'What do you have in mind?'

Harvey outlined his idea, and they batted it back and forth until they were happy that they had something workable.

'All we need to do now,' said Farsi, 'is convince Gray to go along with it.'

Gray was just finishing the washing-up when his phone rang, and he quickly dried his hands before answering.

'Hi, Tom.'

'Andrew. Have you got any good news for me?'

'I think we have. We overheard a conversation between Wallace and Hart. It looks like they're coming for you.'

'And that's good news?' Gray said.

'Hear me out, Tom. It won't be for a couple of days, and we'll be ready for them. The plan is for us to have armed officers surrounding the area. As soon as Hart and his men show up, we take them down. Game over.'

'That's it? Doesn't sound like much of a plan to me. Why don't you just go and arrest them now?'

'At the moment, all we have is a conversation. That can be explained away by any half-competent lawyer. We need to catch them in the act.'

'What did they say?' Gray asked.

'Just that they were going to pay a visit in the next few days.'

Gray detected a hint of hesitance in Harvey's voice. 'I want to hear the recording.'

The line went silent for a while, and Gray used that time to hit the 'Record' button on his phone. Up until now, the free app he'd downloaded had been used mainly to record conversations with clients, but Gray felt this was something he'd want to hear again.

'Okay, here it goes.'

Harvey played the brief discussion, and Gray gripped the phone with white knuckles when he heard that Melissa was also on Hart's agenda. He tried to control his breathing, but Hart's words had ignited something deep inside, and his heart rate hit the one-fifties. His mind swirled as he tried to comprehend how someone, even a thug like Hart, could target his little girl.

Not once, but twice.

'Tell me what you want me to do,' Gray said, his voice betraying his anger.

'We want you to meet with Wallace and tell him you're going away for a few weeks. Give him the address of a safe-house we've got lined up, and then we just wait for Hart to show up.'

Gray considered the proposal, but there was one thing troubling him.

'I want Melissa out of the way before we do this,' he said. 'She can't be there.'

'Of course, Tom. There's no way we'd involve your daughter in this.'

It was Gray's turn to go silent, his mind working overtime as he considered the plan. Less than a minute later, he agreed to go ahead with it, though he threw in a few caveats.

'I want Ken and Mina rehoused while this is going on, just in case Hart decides to hit me at home.'

'No problem,' Harvey said.

'Also, I can't bear to be separated from Melissa. Do I actually have to be in the safe-house? Can't you get someone with a similar build to parade in front of the curtains?'

'I guess that would work,' Harvey conceded.

'Then that's settled,' Gray said. 'I'll give Wallace the address, then take off with Melissa until it's all over.'

'Okay. I'll arrange for somewhere safe for you and—'

'No. I'll arrange it myself. Hart's got a senior police officer in his pocket, which means he could have others. At the moment I don't really feel like trusting too many people with my daughter's life.'

'Fair enough. I understand.'

Harvey rattled off the address to give to Wallace, and once Gray had read it back, he hung up, promising to be in touch once everything was in place.

Gray toyed with the slip of paper, and knew it was time to make plans of his own. He called Sonny and told him to be at the office within the hour, then threw on a jacket and made his way there.

Chapter Thirty-Two

Wednesday 23 October 2013

Gray read the note one more time before stuffing it back into the envelope it had arrived in that morning. Like the first one, he had no idea who'd sent it, but it fit nicely into his plan.

He zipped his jacket and got out of the car, running the fifty yards to the front door of the police station while a gale blew the rain horizontally. Despite being exposed for mere seconds, his jeans were soaked and his hair was plastered to his scalp.

'Nice weather we're having,' the duty sergeant said, clearly thrilled at being desk-bound for the day. 'What can I do for you?'

Gray gave his name and asked after Wallace, and then took a seat while the officer made the call to one of the upstairs rooms. The detective inspector arrived a few minutes later and showed him into an empty interview room.

'What can I do for you, Tom?'

'I was wondering if you had any new developments,' Gray said, but Wallace shook his head.

'Sorry, but I wouldn't want to get your hopes up. I think we've done all we can right now.'

Gray pulled the envelope from his pocket and handed it over, studying Wallace's face as he absorbed the brief missive.

Hart is coming for you in the next few days.

Wallace handed it back with a shrug. 'I'm sorry, but I'm not sure what I can do with this.'

'Can't you at least run it through forensics?'

'If we did, we'd have to interview and eliminate a dozen people from Royal Mail, not to mention the people who work in the stationery factory. That takes up a lot of time and resources and I can't justify that if a crime hasn't been committed.'

Gray let his frustration show, thrusting the letter back into his pocket. 'Then what about protection? Can't you have a couple of armed officers outside my place for a couple of weeks?'

'Have you read the news recently?' Wallace asked. 'We've had our funding cut so much, we can't even put bobbies on the beat anymore.'

Gray pulled out a piece of paper and handed it to the policeman.

'I didn't think so. That's why I'm taking my daughter away for a few days,' he said, 'just in case this isn't all bullshit, which is what you seem to think. If anything comes up, you can find me here. I lost my mobile phone a couple of days ago and won't know the landline number until I get there, but if you need to contact me, just send someone round with a message.'

'I'm sure I won't need to, but I'll hang on to this, just in case.'

Gray turned to leave, his disgust obvious, but Wallace stopped him.

'I really am sorry, Mr Gray, but you have to understand the constraints we're working under these days.' Almost as an afterthought, he said, 'This Hart guy is resourceful. If the threat turns out to be real, you might want to be prepared.'

Gray nodded, and Wallace followed him into the lobby, ensuring Gray had left the building before pulling out his alternate phone.

'It's me,' he whispered, when Hart picked up. 'Meet me at the same garage. One hour.'

He hung up before the gangster could reply and went to get his coat.

William Hart was already sitting in the smoke-filled office when Wallace arrived at the body workshop five minutes early. The big man wore brightly patterned clothes that looked garish on his large fighter's frame.

'What's so urgent, Frank? I'm supposed to be playing golf.'

The thought of Hart playing golf—in the rain, no less—almost made Wallace smile. 'I thought you hated golf.'

'I do. Waste of fucking time, if you ask me, but my playing partners are respectable businessmen, and it doesn't hurt to move in their circles. One of them's in finance and is helping me shift some of my loot offshore.'

Wallace feigned interest, but couldn't care less what Hart got up to anymore.

'Gray is taking a few days away,' he said, handing over a piece of paper. 'He'll be there tomorrow night, but I don't know how long he'll be staying, so you'd better hit him quick.'

Hart looked at the address. 'Anyone with him?'

'Just him and his daughter,' Wallace said.

That drew a rare smile from Hart. 'I'll take a few of the lads round. Should be a fun evening.'

It should indeed, Wallace thought. What he wouldn't have given to be a fly on the wall as Hart finally got his comeuppance, but he had his own affairs to deal with.

'Don't forget your alibi,' Wallace said, as he rose and made for the door.

'Never a problem,' Hart called after him in a jaunty voice. Clearly he was looking forward to an evening of real sport.

Once in his car, Wallace headed back to the station, the final part of his plan in place. The getaway car was safely parked near the beach, the ticket for the short hop to Orly Airport in Paris was booked, and then it was just twelve hours to Rio de Janeiro.

Wallace looked at himself in the rear-view mirror and managed a smile.

'I'm gonna miss you, Frank.'

As Tom Gray drove through the rain, something didn't add up.

If Wallace wants me dead, why did he warn me to prepare for Hart?

He thought about it as he drove to the hospital, but couldn't understand why the policeman would want him to be ready for Hart's arrival. He checked the clock on the dashboard and saw that he still had three hours before Melissa was due to be discharged, so he pointed the car towards the office.

When he arrived twenty minutes later he found Len Smart sitting at his desk and taking a phone call. Smart held up a finger, so Gray used the time to call Sonny Baines.

'How soon can you get to the office?'

Sonny promised to be there within fifteen minutes, and Gray made the same request of Campbell and Levine.

Smart hung up the phone and explained that he'd managed to convince one of the major clients to stick to the contract.

'Now that you're no longer running the show, they seem a lot happier to hang around.'

'Oh, well, I'm glad it's nothing personal,' Gray said. 'That reporter's got a lot to answer for.'

'Forget Boyd,' Smart said. 'We're doing fine despite the son-of-a-bitch. So what brings you here?'

Gray said he'd rather wait for the others to arrive, so they grabbed a coffee from the kitchen and discussed the plan for Melissa.

The trio arrived within five minutes of each other, and Gray waited until they got their drinks before convening the session. He brought Campbell and Levine up to speed on the last couple of days, then recounted his meeting with Wallace at the station.

'So let me get this straight,' Campbell said. 'Wallace and Hart are working together and they want you dead, but the copper is warning you to watch your back?'

'That about sums it up,' Gray said. 'Only question is, why?'

'Looks like he doesn't want Hart to succeed,' Sonny suggested.

'I agree,' Levine said. 'Maybe he wants you to take Hart out for him.'

Carl's words brought the moment of clarity Gray had been seeking.

'Wallace sent me those notes,' he said.

Now it all made sense. Wallace wanted Hart out of the picture, and who better to take him down than a man with a history of taking the law into his own hands?

'Why doesn't Wallace just arrest him?' Campbell asked. 'He must have so much information about Hart's operations, it should be an open and shut case.'

'Maybe Hart has something on him,' Sonny said. 'Photos, recordings, or perhaps he's just scared of what Hart might reveal during a trial.'

The others nodded, seeing it as the only logical explanation.

'Okay, so we're agreed that Wallace wants me to take Hart down,' Gray said. 'Now we just need to figure out why.'

'And what to do about it,' Sonny added.

For the benefit of Campbell and Levine, Gray explained what Andrew Harvey had planned for Hart.

'Then that's it sorted,' Levine said. 'They arrest Hart at the scene and bring Wallace in later. I'd say that was job done.'

'Really?' Sonny asked. 'You think Hart's just going to take life in prison on the chin?'

Campbell nodded. 'He'll come after Tom again, even if he's behind bars. That type have friends on the outside, and Tom's never going to be safe.'

'And you agreed to Harvey's plan, Tom?' Levine asked.

'I did indeed.' Gray stood and asked Smart to fill the boys in, before heading for the door.

'Wallace must have a backup plan, just in case Hart manages to get to me. We need to figure out what it is.'

Everyone nodded, and Gray checked his watch.

'I'm going to pick Melissa up. I'll see you guys later.'

Chapter Thirty-Three

Thursday 24 October 2013

'We've got a car approaching. Looks like four up.'

'Understood.'

Harvey looked at his watch for the hundredth time that evening and wondered if this was false alarm number fifty-three. It was just before midnight and for the main part, the street was quiet. The exception was the house two doors along, where the occupants had decided to hold an impromptu party after the pubs had kicked out the last customers. Harvey could feel the beat of the music that had started thirty minutes earlier, and cursed his decision not to nip it in the bud. That would have meant officers out in the open, and he couldn't risk scaring Hart off.

As it turned out, there'd been no sign of the gangster, and he knew he would have to put up with the drum and bass until the operation was over.

He peered through the window of the top floor bedroom as the target vehicle cruised slowly past the building, then continued on to the end of the street.

The car turned the corner, and Harvey sat back in his chair, wondering where Hart was. His men had seen Hart being picked up from his house three hours earlier, only to lose the car in traffic. That meant Hart and his people had had ample opportunity to change vehicles, collect others, and do God-only-knew what else.

He hated when missions started off with a balls-up, but that was often the nature of the game.

⁓

'Go round again,' Hart said. 'I want to make sure no-one's expecting us.'

The driver did as ordered, and the occupants of the car scanned the area for suspicious vehicles.

'It looks clear,' Aiden said.

His brother Sean agreed. 'There's fuck all out there.'

'Okay,' Hart said. 'Go back to the house and pull over.'

The driver cruised along quietly, not wanting to alert anyone by roaring down the road.

'You got my bag there, son?'

'Got it,' Sean said, holding it up so that his father could see it in the rear-view mirror.

'Good lad. Now listen, when we get in there, you leave that fucker to me. I don't want you shooting him before I've had a chance to work on him.'

The boys agreed, knowing full well what the consequences of upsetting their father were. Both had taken enough beatings from the man, and though neither was a genius, that was one lesson they'd learned pretty early in life.

The car came to a stop and the driver asked if he should come along.

'No,' Hart said. 'You wait here and keep an eye out for plod. If we need you, we'll shout.'

The doors opened and the Hart family headed towards their evening's excitement.

⁓

'Heads up, that same car is coming round again.'

Harvey was immediately alert, and he watched the car once more turn into the street and park up a few yards from the house.

'Wait for my signal,' Harvey said, as he watched the doors open. The rain lashing against the window made it difficult to make out the faces, but when he saw one of the rear passengers emerge with a dark holdall, he knew something was about to go down.

'Go, go, go!'

He'd barely finished barking the command into the radio when the first of the armed response units sped into the street, disgorging firearms officers who yelled for the occupants of the car to get down on the ground.

The men appeared shell shocked, standing in the middle of the road, the rain soaking them to the skin.

'Armed police! Down on the floor, now!'

The severity of the situation began to dawn, and they complied with the commands, lying face down with their arms spread-eagled. The officers approached in numbers, two for every suspect. Each of the prostrate figures had an MP5 trained at them while another officer cuffed them before performing a comprehensive body search.

Harvey ran out into the street as the men were being read their rights.

'Any weapons?' he asked the squad leader.

'Nothing so far.'

Harvey spotted the holdall and asked a gloved officer to open it, not wanting to contaminate any potential evidence.

The man slung his rifle and knelt down, carefully opening the zip before letting out a long whistle.

'Man, these guys know how to party.'

He pulled out a bottle of Glenlivet and held it up for Harvey to see.

'That's it?

'Nope. They've also got a bottle of vodka and a dozen beers. Oh, and a rugby strip that needs a good wash.'

Harvey went over to the first of the suspects and indicated for the officer to get him to his feet.

'What are you doing here?' Harvey asked.

'We were invited to a party,' the man said, nodding towards the booming house. 'Go and ask Sue. She lives there and rang us fifteen minutes ago.'

Harvey wiped the rain from his face, the weather matching his current mood.

'Get 'em out of here!'

The armed officers removed the men's cuffs and the protestations began immediately.

'Hey, I'm fucking soaking here. What the fuck was that all about?'

One of the suspects walked over to Harvey and spun him round.

'I'm sorry,' Harvey said flatly. 'The officers will take your details and we'll be round to make a full apology in the next few days.'

'Fuck the apology, I want to make a formal complaint. What's your name?'

Even though the man towered a foot above him, Harvey wasn't in the mood for histrionics.

'Look, son, you just fucked up a highly sensitive police operation, and I've a good mind to have you arrested for obstruction. I could have you all searched for drugs and tear the car apart looking for evidence.'

The man was speechless, the drug remark having obviously struck a chord. He was considering a comeback when Harvey's earpiece burst into life.

'Another car just indicated into the street, then changed its mind. There were three up.'

Great, Harvey thought. Any chance they had of catching Hart in the act was probably blown, and with a number of people braving the rain to see what was going on, there was no way things were going to return to normal in the next few hours.

'Okay, wrap it up,' he said into his collar microphone. 'Teams one and two, stay at the flat, alternate shifts. Let me know if he shows up. The rest of you, stand down. I repeat, stand down.'

The tall suspect decided that wet clothes were preferable to losing his stash, and he picked up the holdall before heading towards the party, leaving Harvey the unenviable task of explaining the mess to Ellis.

———

The Harts walked the hundred and fifty yards to the cottage, sticking to the bushes that ran along the side of the country road. They were soaked by the time they reached the wooden gate that led to the thatched building, but their minds were on other matters.

One of the upper floor rooms was illuminated, and they could see Gray standing by the window, holding a bundle in his arms.

Sean started towards the door, but his father grabbed his coat.

'We stay here until he's asleep,' Hart said, leading them behind a large rhododendron bush.

As if on cue, the light went out and the garden was bathed in darkness, the late autumn clouds blotting out the faint glow from the third-quarter moon.

'How long?' Aiden asked.

'At least half an hour,' Hart said, though he didn't particularly relish the thought of waiting. The alternative, though, was to take on a wide-awake ex-soldier who, by his own accounts, had killed more than his fair share of men.

Hart was by no means a coward, but he knew when to play it safe.

The minutes dragged, but with every passing moment, Hart felt more confident. The plan was for Sean to break in through a rear window and open the back door, then Hart would climb the stairs and subdue Gray with the Taser he was carrying in his pocket.

Once he was tied up, they would extract the information they'd come for, perhaps using the girl to demonstrate their resolve.

'It's been half an hour,' Aiden said, and Hart nodded.

'Follow me,' he whispered, and led the boys to the rear of the house.

'In there,' Hart said, pointing to the kitchen window.

Sean pulled a knife from his pocket and went to work on the wood until the window gave silently. Within seconds he was inside and he unlocked the door for the other men.

Hart took the lead, motioning for the boys to stay close as he climbed the stairs to the first floor landing. After getting his bearings, Hart knew that one of the two doors on his right was the front-facing bedroom where they'd seen Gray. The first door they came to was open, and inside they found a toilet and bath.

This one, Hart mouthed, and on the count of three, they burst into the second room.

Hart went in first and spotted the mound under the blanket that covered the double bed. His Taser sent two barbed electrodes towards the dark outline, and as he kept his finger on the trigger, fifty thousand volts ran through the wires.

After five seconds, Hart released the trigger and the boys pulled back the covers.

'What the fuck is this?'

Three pillows lay end to end on the bed, but there was no sign of Gray.

Sean went over to the crib in the corner of the room and removed the bundle they'd seen Gray carrying earlier. It was heavy, and when he removed the blanket he found himself holding a fire extinguisher. Hart saw a note taped to the bottom, and he snatched at it.

I thought you might need this.

At that moment, Hart knew he'd been set up. With thoughts of self-preservation overriding any paternal instincts he may have had, he ran from the room, already at the top of the stairs before he shouted a warning to his sons.

'Get out! It's a trap!'

He almost jumped down the entire flight of stairs, knowing that an inferno would erupt at any moment, but he managed to reach the back door without being grilled alive. He swung the door open and ran out into the rain, only to find a shadowy figure waiting for him.

Tom Gray stood ten yards away, holding a six-inch blade in his right hand.

Sean and Aiden followed their father out into the rain, and Hart spun when he heard the air forced out of their lungs. The boys were being held in headlocks with knives to their throats by two large figures, who had obviously been waiting on either side of the door.

'You stole something from me,' Gray shouted through the storm. 'Something I loved very much.'

'Fuck you, Gray!' Hart reached inside his jacket, but when a round whizzed past his face he froze like a statue.

'Pull the gun out, nice and slow, or the next shot won't be a warning.'

Hart obeyed, tossing the gun to his left. Carl Levine and Sonny Baines walked out of the darkness, Levine collecting the weapon and frisking him while Sonny kept the silenced 9 mm aimed at his head.

Satisfied that he was clean, the two men stepped away.

'Why, Hart? Why did you kill my wife?'

'I don't know what you're talking about.'

'Oh, I think you do,' Gray said. 'Why else would you run screaming at the sight of a fire extinguisher? You thought I was going to burn you to death, didn't you? And why would you come down here tooled up?'

'I had nothing to do with it,' Hart persisted, trying to think his way out of trouble.

'Wallace told me,' Gray pressed, and saw that he'd scored with that remark. 'It doesn't really matter,' he continued. 'Whatever you tell me will be lies, and I've had enough of those lately.'

Gray pointed his knife towards Smart and Campbell, who had the boys subdued.

'Do it.'

They simultaneously pushed the Hart boys to arms' length and shoved the knives into their chests.

'NO!' Hart cried.

'You know, there really isn't that much guilt when you ask someone else to do your killing for you,' Gray said. He closed in on the father, who'd collapsed to his knees in tears.

'I bet it was much the same when you sent Robert Harman round to kill my wife.'

Hart looked up at him, rainwater dripping down his face, his eyes shining with hatred. Exactly the reaction Gray had hoped for. He dropped his knife at Hart's knees and walked away.

The boys had already bled out, leaving only the sound of the rain, but that wasn't enough to drown out the sound of Hart's ungainly footsteps as he ran towards Gray, who spun and deflected the clumsy lunge.

'They say revenge is a dish best served cold,' Gray said, 'but you're running awfully hot.'

Hart tried again, stepping in and slashing with the knife, but Gray easily skipped out of reach and delivered a hammer blow with his fist that caught Hart on the temple.

The older man fell to the grass, and Gray knelt on his chest while he groped for the knife that had fallen to the ground. He found the blade and held it to Hart's throat.

'Fortunately, I'm decidedly frosty.'

The answer he got was a face full of spittle, which he wiped away with his sleeve.

'You can have that one,' Gray said, pressing his nose to Hart's. 'This, however, is for Vick.'

Gray turned the blade up and pressed it to the underside of Hart's fleshy mouth. As Hart's eyes widened, he plunged the knife upwards, through Hart's tongue and into his brain, all the time looking into the gangster's eyes. It took several moments for them to cloud over. Once it was done, Gray climbed off him and walked away without a backward glance.

His four friends surrounded him, concern etched in their faces. Before they could say anything, Gray pointed his knife at Smart and Campbell. 'Can't you guys at least roll around in the mud a little? Maybe make it look like we had a fair fight?'

'But this jacket cost me a fortune,' Campbell complained.

Gray pointed to the ground. 'Get down and give me five, soldiers.'

While Campbell and Smart covered themselves in everything but glory, Gray called Sonny and Levine over and went through the checklist.

'Carl, get rid of everything in the bedroom.'

Levine disappeared into the house, while Gray made sure Sonny had the guns covered.

'I stripped and cleaned my weapon wearing gloves, so no prints inside or out.'

'Same go for the mag and ammo?'

Sonny nodded.

'Okay, empty it out and make sure you get Hart's prints all over it. Every nook, every round.'

As Sonny dashed off to complete his part of the ruse, Gray told Smart and Campbell to get to their feet.

'Get their prints on the knives,' he said, pointing to the corpses. 'I don't know if they were left or right handed, so do both.'

Five minutes later, the men were once again assembled before him.

'What about the driver?' Gray asked.

'On the way back from our midnight walk, we came across his car,' Sonny said, in his best courtroom voice. 'He got out and pulled a gun on us. A fight ensued and it went off.'

'Really? Where's the shell casing with Hart's fingerprints all over it?'

Sonny held one up for inspection. 'Ta da.'

'Serial number filed off the weapon?'

'Clean as a whistle.'

'Good man. Go get the driver's prints on the 9 mm and drop it next to him, then put Hart's gun in the bag they brought.'

Sonny disappeared again, and once more Gray was grateful to the driver for having gotten out to take a leak, thereby enabling Gray's men to dispatch him in what would appear to have been a fair fight.

When all four men were finished, he gathered them round. 'What are we missing?' He looked from man to man. 'Come on, guys, there's always something.'

They all thought hard but came up empty, so Gray had them all go through their stories one more time.

Satisfied that all bases were covered, Gray pulled out his phone and dialled the number.

Chapter Thirty-Four

Thursday 24 October 2013

For Joe Brandt, there was nothing like the night shift to make some progress on his latest book. A long-time fan of sci-fi, Brandt had been writing his own stuff for several years, and constantly dreamt of the day an agent would give him the thumbs up. Despite over two hundred query letters and barely half a dozen responses, his enthusiasm hadn't waned, and he attacked the next chapter with gusto.

He was just about to orchestrate a deadly battle between the Vxlen and the Gords when his headphones signalled noise inside Wallace's apartment. He put the tablet aside and fired up the infrared camera.

Sure enough, Wallace's blurry figure could be seen heading for the bathroom. Brandt assumed he was simply going for a midnight pee, but when the detective finished and turned on the shower, he marked the time in the journal.

3:15 AM.

'Can't sleep, eh?'

Brandt woke his companion, John Orwell, and told him about the new development.

'Any coffee left?' Orwell asked, rubbing the sleep from his eyes. Unlike Brandt, he didn't find night duty to his taste.

'Finished hours ago,' Brandt said.

'Great. So what's he doing up so early?'

'Dunno,' Brandt shrugged. 'Maybe he's just got an early start today.'

'Well, it's your turn to follow him. And remember, don't get too close. Let the tracker do the work.'

Brandt checked the camera and saw that Wallace had yet to finish his ablutions, so he grabbed his tablet and quietly opened the back door of the van and closed it behind him. The company car was parked around the corner, and when he reached it he was glad to see it still had all of its wheels.

'All set here,' Brandt said into his throat mic. 'Let me know when he sets off.'

He climbed in and started the car, cranking the heater up to full before reconvening the intergalactic war.

An hour later, Orwell informed him that Wallace was on the move.

'He's carrying a bundle of clothes. Looks like he's just going to the laundrette.'

'I doubt it,' Brandt replied, turning on the tracking device. 'He's got a washer-dryer in his flat.'

He waited until the dot on the screen began to move and counted twenty seconds before pulling out and following. The device attached to the underside of Wallace's Ford had a two-mile range, so Brandt was able to sit far enough back that he wasn't visible in the detective's mirrors.

After half an hour, Brandt found himself on the M23, and he called in his position.

'Looks like we're heading to the south coast.' The dot on the screen showed Wallace just over a mile ahead, and a signpost declared him thirty-two miles from Brighton, and seven from the airport.

'We're coming up on Gatwick,' Brandt said. 'He'll be there in five minutes. If he takes the turn off, call it in and see if there are any flights booked in his name.'

Wallace continued on past the airport and towards the south coast, before turning east five miles from Brighton. Brandt continued to report in, and eventually the target car came to a stop near a secluded beach.

'Looks like we're here,' Brandt said, giving his current location. He stopped the car half a mile away and made his way on foot, jogging at a comfortable pace until he had the detective's Ford in sight.

Wallace appeared to be walking towards the water. Some ten yards from the shore he dropped the bundle of clothes and removed his shoes and socks. After rolling his trousers up, he continued on into the water, carrying only his footwear and a towel.

Bit nippy to go paddling, Brandt thought.

He watched Wallace traverse the beach until he came to a rocky outcrop, then climb up and dry his feet as best he could in the driving rain. With his socks and shoes back on, Wallace headed towards a small hamlet, where he climbed into a ten-year-old Fiat.

Brandt raced back to his car and used the satnav to identify possible routes out of the area. He was thankful that there was only one, and set off in pursuit. He called in his findings and asked someone to check out the abandoned Ford, then gave his current heading.

Wallace led him through the countryside until they once again hit the A27, this time westbound. Brandt held back, letting the Fiat guide him with its taillights, until they reached the outskirts of Shoreham-by-Sea.

'He's taken the exit towards the airport,' Brandt said into his mic. 'Do I stop him?'

Orwell told him to wait until he got orders from the office. 'For now, just hang back and see what he does.'

With no other choice, Brandt continued the pursuit until Wallace slowed and took the turning towards the airport car park.

'It looks like he's booked on a flight,' Brandt said, as Wallace exited the car carrying a suitcase and hand luggage.

'I'm still waiting to hear from HQ,' Orwell said. 'Do nothing until I get back to you.'

'You'd better hurry. These planes don't exactly hang around all night.'

Brandt sat in the car, desperate for a response, but when the Piper Cherokee began to taxi away from the hangar, he knew the chance was gone.

'Wallace just reached the end of the runway,' he said, disconsolate. 'Tell the boss we lost him.'

His job dictated he be thorough, though, so Brandt braved the wind and rain to run to the small passenger terminal.

'I need to know who just left on that plane,' he said to the balding man behind the counter.

'I'm sorry,' the man smiled, 'but we can't give out that information.'

Brandt placed his ID on the counter. 'In that case, I'll speak to your boss.'

———⏑———

When Andrew Harvey reached the cottage just after five in the morning, he found half a dozen police cars already on the scene.

After showing his badge, he was allowed through the outer cordon and found Gray standing next to a police car, a uniformed officer taking his statement. Harvey once again made his introduction and asked for a moment alone with Gray.

'Tom, please tell me why the hell I'm standing in the Welsh countryside looking at you and a pile of bodies.'

'What can I say? Somehow Hart found out where I was staying and he came after me. I had to defend myself.'

Harvey looked round and saw a few more familiar faces.

'So Sonny, Len, Carl and Jeff just happened to be passing, did they?'

'No, I decided to use my time wisely and asked the team to join me. We were going over new deployment tactics for the sentinels. We came back from a night exercise and found these guys waiting for us.'

Harvey leaned in closer. 'That's bullshit, and you know it.'

'Maybe, but if it walks like a duck, and quacks like a duck, maybe its name's Donald. We've given our side of the story, and we're sticking to it.'

Harvey was exasperated. 'I thought you were going to let it go. For Melissa.'

'Exactly right, Andrew. For Melissa. Whether Hart was behind bars or free to go about his business, she would never have been safe. Now she is.'

'So you gave Wallace this address instead of the one for the safe-house, knowing he would send Hart after you.'

'You know, I *did* have two addresses in my pocket. I must have given him the wrong one. By mistake, obviously.'

Harvey looked around the scene. The forensic tents were already in place, with technicians inside working on the bodies. An ambulance sat silent, too late for the dead and not needed for the survivors. A normal scene, but he felt something was missing.

'Where's Melissa?'

'Len's wife is looking after her,' Gray said. 'I thought about bringing her here, but just in case she relapsed, I wanted her near the hospital.'

Harvey suddenly felt weary. He was severely pissed off with Gray, yet at the same time glad he was okay. The fact remained that he knew Hart had been set up, and would have to report it to his boss. What Veronica Ellis made of it would be anyone's guess.

'I'm too tired to think right now,' he said to Gray. 'Call me when they're done with you.'

Harvey walked back to his car and climbed in, not relishing the three-hour drive back to London.

Although, he reflected, the drive would be bliss compared to his next meeting with Ellis.

⌣

After the drive from Orly Airport to Paris Charles de Gaulle, Frank Wallace was ready for a drink. He hit the bar and swallowed a double whisky before setting off for the departure gate. The clock on the wall told him he had fifty minutes to wait, so he dug into his bag and found the book he'd brought along for the journey.

After turning to the dog-eared page, his mind began to wander. The next step was to reach Brazil, but after that, he had no firm plans. He decided to find a decent hotel, and from there he would research the countries of the world to see which ones had no extradition treaty with the UK. He knew that Suriname, to the north of Brazil, was one such haven, and he could hang out there until he found another country to settle in. He suspected that his options would be limited to the African continent and Southeast Asia, but what the hell. He was sure he could manage a few years on a Thai beach with young locals to provide his entertainment on the lonely evenings.

'*Entschuldigen Sie, bitte. Kann ich Ihren Pass sehen?*'

Wallace stared at the stranger, a man wearing jeans, a leather jacket, and a quizzical look.

'*Entschuldigen Sie. Kann ich Ihren Pass sehen?*' the man repeated the question, pointing to his own wrist.

'Ah,' Wallace exclaimed, and held out his hand so that the man could see his watch. The stranger grabbed his wrist and Wallace heard the familiar click as the handcuffs were applied.

'Really,' the man said, the English tinged with a heavy French accent. 'If you're going to use a German passport, Mr Wallace, you should at least learn a few rudimentary phrases.'

'What's going on?' the detective shouted, drawing stares from his fellow passengers.

The leather-clad man held out his warrant card. '*Direction Générale de la Sécurité Extérieure.* It seems you left a few unanswered questions back in London, Mr Wallace, and our counterparts there are rather keen to speak with you.'

Another agent from the DGSE arrived, and indicated the exit. 'Shall we?'

Epilogue

Tuesday 29 October 2013

Tom Gray was in the middle of mixing Melissa's dinner when the gate buzzer sounded, and through the CCTV he could the familiar face.

'Come on up, Andrew.'

He hit the gate release and turned back to the formula, ensuring it was exactly the right temperature before opening the front door.

'Hi,' he smiled.

Harvey wasn't so cheerful, which immediately had Gray on edge.

'What's the problem?'

'I just came from a meeting with Ellis,' Harvey said, standing over Melissa's bouncy chair. The little girl looked none the worse for her recent ordeal, gurgling away, eyes transfixed by the set of multi-coloured keys in her hand.

'Melissa seems to be doing well,' he remarked, helping the girl jiggle the plastic toy.

'She's a Gray,' Tom said. 'We're fighters.'

'I noticed.'

'So what did Ellis say?'

'Well, she was rather less than chuffed that you left a pile of bodies at a Welsh holiday cottage. That was somewhat tempered by the fact that we caught Wallace just as he was about to disappear.'

'You're kidding.'

'Nope. Faked his own death, had a new life planned out, everything. We got lucky when one of our operatives refused to give up the chase.'

'But what about Harman?'

'He'll be pulled in, don't you worry. Wallace knows that cooperation is his best chance at a lighter sentence.'

'Sounds like it all worked out for the best,' Gray smiled.

'You think? I told Ellis about your little *faux pas* with the addresses, and she thinks that might come back to bite you on the arse. Did you mention that to the police when they interviewed you?'

'No,' Gray admitted. 'I told them about the sting you'd arranged, and that I decided to stay well clear of it. When they asked how Hart knew where to find me, I just shrugged.'

'Then I suggest you stick to your original story,' Harvey said. 'Ellis spoke to her bosses, and the last thing they need is a court case where you stand trial under these circumstances. Christ, the media will have a field day, and the government can't face that again. You've embarrassed them twice, and they aren't looking forward to round three.'

'Is that why they dropped our bail this morning?'

Harvey nodded. 'Someone in power spoke to the CPS and they agreed it wasn't in the public interest to prosecute you.'

Gray smiled, but Harvey wiped it from his face.

'That doesn't mean you're untouchable, Tom. Your national hero status won't mean shit if you fuck up again.'

'Andrew, please, not in front of Melissa.'

Harvey apologised and actually appeared stricken, clearly unaware that infants would be unaffected by things like swearing at such an early age.

'I have to feed her now,' Gray said, and Harvey nodded, heading for the door.

'Take care. I'll see you around.'

'Have a good one, Andrew.'

Gray went back to the living room and lifted Melissa out of her chair, cuddling her close as he took her to the dining room and manoeuvred her into her highchair. Once settled in his own seat, he smiled down at his daughter as she gulped her food down.

'Just ignore what that man said,' he cooed.

'We *are* untouchable.'

THE END

If you enjoyed this series and want to know when Alan McDermott releases his next book, just send an email to alanmac@ntlworld.com with 'Next Book' in the subject line.

Acknowledgements

I'd like to thank Dr. Roger Wellesley Duckitt, consultant physician in acute medicine at Western Sussex Hospitals NHS Foundation Trust, and Andrew Matthews from the West Sussex County Council Fire and Rescue Service for their help in researching this book. I'd also like to thank everybody who read the other books in the series and gave me the encouragement to carry on.

About the Author

Alan McDermott is a husband, father to beautiful twin girls and a software developer from the south of England.

Born in West Germany of Scottish parents, Alan spent his early years moving from town to town as his father was posted to different Army units around the United Kingdom. Alan had a number of jobs after leaving school, including working on a cruise ship in Hong Kong and Singapore, where he met his wife. Since 2005 he has been working as a software developer and currently creates clinical applications for the National Health Service.

Alan's writing career began in 2011 and the action thriller *Gray Justice* was his first full-length novel.